a
Very
Important
Teapot

STEVE
SHEPPARD

CLARET PRESS

Copyright © Steve Sheppard 2019
The moral right of the author has been asserted.

ISBN paperback: 978-1-910461-40-2
ISBN ebook: 978-1-910461-41-9

All rights reserved. No part of this publication may be reproduced, stored in or introduced into a retrieval system, transmitted, in any form, or by any means (electronic, mechanical, photocopying, recording or otherwise) without the prior written consent of the publisher. Any person who does any unauthorised act in relation to this publication may be liable to criminal prosecution and civil claims for damages.

A CIP catalogue record for this book is available from the British Library.

This paperback can be ordered from all bookstores as well as from Amazon, and the ebook is available on online platforms such as Amazon and iBooks.

Cover and Interior Design by Petya Tsankova

www.claretpress.com

For Anabel

Without whom Dawson would still be sitting
in The Cricketers

Acknowledgements

There are a number of people I need to thank. Firstly, my wife, Anabel, son, Jack, and cat, Poppy, for not appearing to be too overly disturbed by my constant tip-tapping on the keyboard (I am a very heavy typist) for the best part of two years. Also, Rob Sheppard and Anna Pitt for their encouragement, support and advice. Peter Smith and Trudy Patterson for introducing me to the esoteric delights of the Yackandandah Folk Festival, out of which a germ of an idea was born. And finally, Katie Isbester and all at Claret Press (including but not exclusively, Isobelle and Josh) for believing in Teapot and in me and striving to help me improve my first rambling manuscript.

Dawson wasn't expecting the police car. Clearly he wasn't or he wouldn't have stayed for the extra couple in the Duke of Marlborough.

There was a brief flash of a blue light in his rear-view mirror. Dawson cursed his luck and pulled over, hard up against the verge. Open countryside stretched all around and there was no traffic other than the police car, which came to a stop twenty metres behind. He wound his window down and waited for the policeman's sniff, trying to think of a way he could hold an acceptable conversation while staring into the footwell. The copper sauntered up the road towards him. Policemen always saunter in these circumstances. 'Possibly not if I'd hared off into the countryside though,' thought Dawson.

It was a chilly night in September, and he was on his way home from his latest entry into the Grayfold acting fray, an audition for *Ali Baba and the Forty Thieves*, the upcoming Christmas pantomime. There had been several established Grayfold faces there, and there had also been Rachel Whyte, whom Dawson hadn't seen for two years, since *Jack and the Beanstalk*.

Now, it's true to say that he hadn't really paid much attention to Rachel two years ago. His mind had been on other things and other people, and she'd been just another new Grayfold chorus girl. Tonight though, Dawson couldn't for the life of him understand why – his awareness of her after just one evening had hit him like the proverbial train. He couldn't really understand quite which switch Rachel had flicked. It wasn't as if she was beautiful, although he couldn't remember her being quite as tall, or her hair as – what was that colour? It wasn't red, was it auburn? Dawson wasn't sure that he'd ever known what colour auburn was. And there'd been something about the way she moved (at this point he'd felt a song coming on but had quickly suppressed the urge), a sort of glide that carried her around the room much more quickly than it appeared to.

Those random, jolty thoughts had been distracting Dawson to such an extent that his speed had crept up, as had the cop car in response.

For a moment, he failed to see the policeman in his mirrors. But suddenly, there he was again, breathing heavily.

'In a hurry, are we, sir?' He wasn't going to die of originality.

'Sorry, officer, lost a bit of concentration,' Dawson murmured towards the pedals. He considered trying the old one about the Nissan Micra's inability to break speed limits but decided that two cliches in ten seconds was one too many.

'Hmm,' the policeman said, belief not exactly chiselled into his expression. 'Also,' and he paused... for such a long time Dawson had the feeling he was about to be evicted from a game show. Finally, 'You've one rear light missing.'

'Really? I didn't know.'

'One would hope not, sir. Get it fixed first thing tomorrow.'

'I will, of course I will. Thank you, officer.'

'Not at all, sir. Good night. Drive safely.' And he was gone. Mind you, the going took a while, what with the sauntering. Dawson drove home very slowly, and that night his dreams were filled with images of tall, red-headed girls sauntering around, closely followed by gliding policemen.

Not once did it occur to him to wonder where the policeman, on his short journey from one car to the other, had disappeared to, albeit only for a few seconds, or what he might have been doing during those seconds. Nothing clicked the next morning either when he discovered that he did in fact have two working rear lights.

And neither Dawson nor the policeman had noticed the medium-sized black car with dimmed lights that had drifted quietly and unobtrusively to a stop two hundred metres behind them, and which had just as unobtrusively pulled gently away again afterwards.

___ In which Dawson opens an
     encouraging email, and goes to
     the pub to celebrate

The email was in his spam folder, hidden away amongst polite requests for his bank details and inside-leg measurement from respectable Nigerian businessmen. Not to mention insistent offers of marriage from stunning blonde Ukrainian teenagers with extended families. The word PRIZE was mentioned loudly in several places, so Dawson read it three times in case the PRIZE was likely to be heading in his direction. Being currently unemployed, any possible additions to his prosperity levels needed thorough examination before being consigned to the trash.

Eventually, he concluded that he had been "selected to receive" the oft-mentioned PRIZE and that if he replied to the email or rang the number provided, he would be enlightened further. He rang the number, and a voice contriving to be both impersonal and feminine told him that he would have to come in person to collect his PRIZE, or in her words FANTASTIC PRIZE – she had a slightly worrying ability to talk in capital letters. As Dawson had nothing much arranged for the rest of his life, he agreed to visit the voice the following Thursday week at an address near Oxford Circus.

Further investigation of the email revealed that he had possibly won a brand new Ford Focus, which he decided was definitely worth pursuing, having sold his Micra a couple of months ago; or an iPod; or a forty-two inch Plasma telly; or a twelve-piece porcelain tea service. Dawson had absolutely no use for most of those things, including and especially the porcelain tea service, but the prospect of walking off with a new Ford Focus was irresistible.

Deciding that all this definitely qualified for the tag "possible good fortune pending further information", he resolved to celebrate liquidly in the pub up the road.

—

The pub up the road was a small-to-middling red brick building hidden amidst a row of building societies, estate agents and charity shops. It called itself The Cricketers although, having lived down the road for six years, Dawson knew for a fact that the nearest cricket pitch was at least two miles away.

One of the clientele was waving at him. The waver's mouth was opening and shutting in Dawson's direction, but the pub was so noisy he couldn't hear what it was trying to say. Having ruminated on this for a few seconds, he decided the easiest solution was to go over and find out. So he did, and discovered that the mouth was asking him to buy it a drink.

'Ah, Dawson,' it was saying. 'Just the person. Mine's a large one.'

'That's not what I've heard,' Dawson answered with familiar ease. He smiled at a passing barmaid, who decided to serve him ahead of a trio of local estate agents trying to celebrate the morning's latest gazumping and who, judging by their reactions, had been waiting for some time already.

'Hello, Laura,' he smiled. 'Two small scotches, please.'

'Who are they for?' asked the mouth, which sat in the middle of the plumpish, reddish face of Alan Flannery, Dawson's closest friend for all the six years he'd lived in the town, although neither of them had ever visited the other's home.

'Me and you. You and me,' Dawson replied.

'That's four people. You'll need to get a couple of straws. Very tight-fisted.'

'We great, unwashed unemployed can afford only to be tight-fisted, and sometimes more tight than that. Now, next Thursday week you might find me in more generous mood, but until then one small scotch is all you're getting.' He took out the copy of his PRIZE email that he'd printed off, and passed it across. Alan perused it closely.

'If I didn't know better, I'd say this was the work of dreaded timesharers,' he said at length. 'Don't sign anything.'

'Oh, is that what they are? I thought they'd all bitten the dust in the 90s.'

'Clearly not. Old scams are the best scams, so they say.'

'Anyway, for a free Ford Focus, I'm even willing to undergo inquisition by timeshare salesmen. Although they've got another think coming if they reckon I'm a buyer. I haven't got two pesetas to rub together at the moment. Their market research is atrocious.'

It does seem rather a waste of their time,' agreed Alan. 'Especially as you have to be earning £20,000 to qualify. I didn't know the dole was so generous these days. It's enough to make an honest worker like myself give up his job.'

'£20,000? Where does it say that?'

'Here, old bean, page two, "Details of Eligibility". Detail number three.' Dawson read where he indicated.

'Oh, bugger. I thought it was too good to be true. Don't drink that whisky, I can't afford it any more.'

'Don't worry, Dawson, it doesn't seem a very serious obstacle. You've got nearly two weeks to find a job paying twenty grand. No problem.'

'Except that I've been looking for twelve weeks already. Not to mention the fact that I'd willingly settle for less than 20,000. Well, not willingly, but you know what I mean.'

'Hmm,' said Alan considering this, and emptying his glass at the same time. 'I know, you can work for me. Laura dear, two more whiskies if you please, one large, one small.'

'Work for you? Doing what?' Dawson asked, frowning at the small scotch his friend had bought him. After six years as drinking companions, he was still none too sure what exactly Alan did for a living. Something to do with pest control, or drains possibly, but he'd never given it much thought. Mind you, Alan certainly gave the appearance of being very much his own boss, and he was undeniably never short either of funds or time to spend propping up the bar of The Cricketers. Whatever it was, he didn't look too bad on it, apart from the waistline that was perhaps a little too spherical for a man in his late forties. 'Pray tell me, Mr Flannery, why, if you are in a position to offer me worthwhile employment, you've kept your trap shut on the subject for the last three months?'

'I'm not, I never have been and I wouldn't employ a friend if he were the last person left on the planet. Especially you. You drink too much.'

'Not as much as you.'

'I'll let that pass. I'm not about to offer you a job, but if it will help you acquire a valuable twelve-piece porcelain tea service, then you may certainly give my name as an employer. I can say you sell things for me if they ask, which they won't, and all I want in exchange is another large scotch. Pardon me, you haven't yet bought me a large scotch. Two large scotches, please.'

_ In which Dawson tries to take
a bath, and attempts a little
light acting while ill

It was late in the afternoon on the Sunday following the exciting arrival of the email from the timesharers. Dawson had just returned home after spending most of the day set building at Stallford Borough Hall, where the Christmas panto of *Ali Baba* was due to take place in a few days. Working with his hands was not his forte, and he invariably spent most of his time holding up bits of wood while more gifted carpenters and painters miraculously turned them into moderately-convincing scenery. He was always the one who volunteered to make the coffee, or who rushed up to B&Q for more paint or nails when they ran out. This being so, he was never quite sure why it was he always came home covered in dust and paint, with cut hands and an aching back. So many things in life were a puzzle.

He ran a bath and was preparing to step in armed with half a tumbler of scotch and the sports section of *The Sunday Times*, when his mobile rang from the living room.

'Bugger,' he thought. He had never had any compunction about letting the phone go unanswered while he was actually in the bath, but on this occasion, seeing that he was not yet irrevocably committed to the water, he put down the scotch and returned to the living room.

'This is not a good time to be ringing, whoever you are. Both the hot bath and cold scotch – that are currently growing respectively colder and hotter – are more important than anything you might have to tell me.'

'I'll ring off then,' answered Alan Flannery, 'and you'll never know what my exciting news is. All through the long, dark watches of the night you'll lie awake wondering.'

'I very much doubt that, but since you never phone, I

assume it must be fairly important. What is it? Don't tell me I've been sacked already?'

'Sacked from what? You can't be sacked from a job you ain't got. Still, as it happens, this mythical employment we talked about the other day does have a bearing on what I've got to say. When can I meet you?'

'Any lunchtime in The Cricketers, bar Tuesday when I have to go and grovel at JobCentrePlus so they can graciously pay me a few pence dole money.'

'Hmm,' said Alan. 'Actually, lunchtimes aren't good for me this week. What about one evening?'

'No can do, I'm afraid. You may recall that for the past two months I've been bending your ear about coming to see this pantomime wot I'm appearing in, and you've been quickly changing the subject. Well, this is the week, chum. All my evenings are accounted for by forgetting my lines and wearing fetching tights and make-up.'

'Okay then. Let's kill two birds – when's the show on?'

'Wednesday to Saturday, 8 o'clock pip, mat on Sat.'

'I'll come on Wednesday night, laugh myself silly at you in tights, and we'll have a pint and a natter after.'

'I'll leave a ticket on the door for you. Just the one?'

'Just the one.'

'It'll be fun.' Dawson rang off.

——

Dawson was not feeling at all well.

He was lying on his back on a hardboard rostrum in the wings of a large stage that dominated one end of Stallford Borough Hall. The action of the pantomime in which he was – just – appearing was going on within a few feet of his head. His head ached abominably.

Dawson was due on stage. He stood up, waited for his cue and, when it came, parted the tabs, walked into the light and promptly fell over. He was supposed to fall over: it was after all a pantomime and he was playing the part of a comic magician. The audience, mostly children, howled with laughter. He tried a trick, attempting to conjure a rabbit from a fez, but the only thing that appeared was a dried-up cheese sandwich. Again, the audience howled. Dawson was an undoubted success in the part, but still he felt extremely ill.

After five minutes, he was able to make an exit, and gratefully moved back to his rostrum, lay down and closed his eyes. On and off stage the action continued around him. Then there was a prolonged burst of applause and the lights in the wings went up. It was the interval.

Dawson had not appeared on stage before his moving to Stallford from his parents' house in Ealing, and had initially joined the Grayfold Operatic and Dramatic Society – overweeningly referred to as GODS – by accident. A Sunday lunchtime drinking session at the rugby club had mysteriously evolved into an afternoon spent in a dingy church hall, where a rehearsal for *Under Milk Wood* was taking place. His drinking companion had turned out to be the producer of this minor epic who, being of a somewhat vitriolic nature, especially after lunchtime drinking sessions at the rugby club, had found that several members of his cast had had enough of being insulted and had walked out. Although he could never subsequently recall the exact moment in the conversation when this had taken place, Dawson had apparently agreed to help the group out in its hour of need, had taken on two small roles in the play involving fish and clocks, and had found, much to his surprise, that not only had he enjoyed himself immensely, but that he actually possessed a little acting ability.

An almost indecently rapid and rather torrid affair with the make-up girl had merely cemented his membership of GODS.

In the wings, his head pounding, Dawson screwed his eyes further shut and groaned quietly. Even the interval applause hurt.

'Are you all right?' asked a female voice. Dawson knew the voice. It was of course Rachel Whyte. Rachel had unaccountably become infatuated with a fat solicitor named Pat since late last year but, despite that, Dawson was beginning to see signs that his persistent advances towards her were perhaps not completely hopeless. Certainly the level of flirting on both sides had recently taken a distinct turn upwards.

Rachel was dressed in a long blue and gold gown that wrapped itself voluminously around her and billowed when she walked. She was playing the part of the friend and confidante of the beauteous princess. She would have preferred to be playing the beauteous princess herself but was not really beauteous enough. This she accepted placidly, secure in the knowledge that she had something that made men (and Prat-the-Solicitors) look at her.

Dawson looked at her. 'Hello,' he said.

'Hello. Wouldn't you be better off in the dressing room?' She sounded concerned. Dawson was pleased she sounded concerned, so he groaned a bit, hoping her concern would increase. 'You should be at home,' she added with a touch of asperity.

He tried a wry grin, but it didn't quite come off. 'The show must go on, surely?'

'Not if it's going to kill you. You're not a professional, you're supposed to be doing it for fun.'

'And who says I'm not enjoying myself?'

'Oh, you're impossible. You men just won't look after yourselves.' She turned to walk away.

'Wait,' he called. 'Stay and talk to me.'

'All right. What do you want me to talk to you about?'

'Let's go to the after-show party together.'

'Together? Like a date?'

'Exactly like that, yes.'

'You're ill.'

'It's not until Saturday.'

'Looking at you, you might not last 'til tomorrow, let alone Saturday.'

'If I don't, I'll let you off.'

She looked at him steadily. 'I'm sorry, Dawson, but Pat's taking me.'

'Prat? He's not invited, it's cast and backstage only.'

'Pat, not Prat, and family are invited too.'

'When did he become family? I don't remember getting an invite to the wedding.'

'Ha ha. And I doubt if you will get one.'

'I didn't think the groom needed an invitation.'

'Again, ha ha.' There was a pause. Dawson suddenly felt very tired, as well as very ill. 'What's the matter?' she said finally. 'You're not lost for words, surely. You must be ill.'

'Can't you put him off?' He could feel the note of disappointment in his voice, and hated himself for it.

'Why should I?'

'Because you'd have more fun with me.'

'You don't look much like a bundle of excitement. You look as if you're dying.'

'Grant a dying man a last wish?' Without answering, she touched him gently on the shoulder and left, billowing quietly.

___ In which Alan Flannery remembers
     he doesn't care for the theatre,
     and learns of the unexpected
     sale of a car

Alan Flannery was in the audience wishing he wasn't. He was not a theatre person. He considered Shakespeare to be almost totally indecipherable and vastly overrated, and on the few occasions he had been persuaded to visit a theatre, he almost always found himself nodding off after half an hour or so.

He wouldn't be nodding off during this. It was the first pantomime he had ever been to, and he promised himself it would be the last. He hated every minute but couldn't for the life of him get to sleep. He seemed to be adrift in a sea of small children, every one of whom was eating crisps very loudly from a never-ending supply.

He felt his mind wandering from the action in front of him and refocused rapidly, especially since Dawson was making an entrance. Dawson, his programme notes informed him, was playing the part of Abu, the court magician, and the tricks he was attempting certainly looked convincing enough, even if the results were not always as expected. Tommy Cooper he wasn't, but at this level, Alan reflected, Dawson was not at all a bad performer.

That might prove to be a useful quality when it came to the job Alan had in mind for him. He had been looking for somebody for a while, time was moving on and his options were beginning to look a tad limited. If he didn't find someone pretty damn quick, he might have to do it himself, which would not be a good idea. Not a good idea for Alan anyway, which was his primary concern. One way or another, all roads were beginning to lead Dawsonwards.

The pantomime was drawing to a close. Some of the younger children in the audience had by now dozed off, and the crisps had finally been eaten. At last the curtains swept shut, opened again briefly for a rather disorganised curtain call, and shut again amid a few desultory calls of "encore!" from friends and relatives in the audience.

Alan rose and joined the miniature tsunami of people edging towards the exit. In the lobby he waited, scanning the mug shots of the cast pinned to a felt board on one wall. After ten minutes or so there was a tap on his shoulder and he turned to see Dawson, who did not look too good.

'You don't look too good, old son,' said Alan. 'I thought you were a bit pale when you were on stage, but you look even worse close up. Aren't you well?'

'It feels like flu.'

'My advice is to go and put your make-up back on before you start frightening children. Are you well enough for this drink you promised me?'

'Strange, I thought it was you who'd done the promising.'

'Whatever,' shrugged Alan. 'Although I would have thought that buying me a drink was the least you could do in exchange for paid employment.'

'Hang about,' said Dawson, frowning. 'Now I'm confused. Are you offering me a job after all? I seem to recall phrases like "last man on Earth" and "mythical" being bandied about.'

'Come on,' said Alan. 'The pubs shut in twenty minutes. What's that one round the corner? Is it any good?'

'The Three Pigs? It sells alcohol. It's good enough.'

'Fine, then thither us thence and all will be made clear.'

The Three Pigeons was full of GODS and their friends, but having fought to buy two pints of Old Butcher's Hook real ale, they managed to secure a relatively quiet corner near the Ladies.

'Well?' Dawson asked, wedging himself uncomfortably into a niche in a wall liberally festooned with cases of elderly stuffed wildfowl. 'What did you think?'

'I'm sorry?' said Alan, meaning pardon.

'The pantomime?' prompted Dawson. 'Crossdressing? Two people in a camel suit? Brilliant magicians? Ring any bells? Don't say you slept through it.'

'Sleep? I should have loved to sleep through it, but I could hardly hear myself think. You were all right though.'

'You hated it then. I knew you would. Okay, subtle change of subject. Job. What, where and when? Not to mention how much?'

'Um,' prevaricated Alan, looking thoughtful. 'Tell you what. When are you going to see these timeshare charlatans to pick up your priceless tea service?'

'Ford Focus,' Dawson corrected him. 'Next Thursday morning. Why?'

'What time?'

'10.30, I think.'

'Come and see me first,' said Alan, fishing out his wallet and extracting a blue and cream business card, which he passed across. 'This address. Your people are where? Oxford Circus somewhere?'

'Yeah, I think so.' Dawson was a bit puzzled.

'Well, we're only just round the corner, so you can do both in one morning. Look how good I am to you.'

'What the hell is Aardvark Amalgamations?' Dawson asked, reading from the card. 'How come I've never heard those words pass your lips in all the time I've known you.'

'You must have,' murmured Alan, sounding a little vague. But Dawson knew he hadn't. He'd have remembered the Aardvark bit for certain.

'I thought the whole point of your suffering the slings and arrows of unfortunate panto tonight was so we could thrash this whole job thing out here and now. There is still a job, isn't there?'

'Oh, yes, there's a job all right. I just haven't got all the details on me.' He peered closely at Dawson. 'Anyway, you really don't look very well, mate. Let's leave the business to another day, shall we?'

It was true enough. Dawson's legs were like jelly, and he could feel himself sweating. He didn't even want the second half of his Old Butcher's Hook, which was definitely a bad sign.

'Come on,' said Alan, straightening. 'I'll drive you home. We can collect your old wreck in the morning.' They got up and left the pub.

'I no longer have an old wreck. And it wasn't an old wreck. It was extremely reliable, if a little noisy.'

Alan caught his breath. 'Are you talking about the Micra? Have you got rid of it?'

'Ages ago. Do keep up. Why do you think I'm so keen on acquiring a new Ford Focus? Anyway, yes, the Micra. I've sold it.'

'Sold it? You mean someone gave you money for it? What idiot would do that? And anyway, you never told me it was for sale.'

'Well, first off, I didn't think you were a potential buyer, given that you have this German monstrosity.' They had arrived at Alan's absurdly oversized BMW. 'And, secondly, it wasn't for sale. Somebody offered me 500 quid for it, and 500 quid held a certain attraction at the time. Still does, in fact.'

'So, let me get this straight,' said Alan, trying hard not to sound too concerned. 'Completely out of the blue, some man – man, yes?' Dawson nodded. 'Some fella turns up, knocks on your door, says, "here's 500 smackers, I really love your grotty old Micra", gives you the money and drives off. When was this?'

'Yep, that's about the size of it. And, er, November, I think. You seem awfully bothered. I'll pay you for the petrol if it's a problem. I've still got a few of the 500 ferreted away.'

Alan took a deep breath. 'Don't be daft, I just hadn't heard, that's all.' They stopped outside Dawson's flat. He got out of the BMW, but turned round and stuck his head back in.

'Thanks for the lift,' he said. 'And he was Australian, by the way. Nasty scar, worse manners and missing half an ear.'

'All that and you didn't get a name?'

'Can't remember. It was ages ago. But he was definitely an Aussie.'

Alan drove slowly home. So Dawson had sold the Micra, possibly as much as three months ago. How had he not known that? And how had he not considered the possibility? An Australian with a missing ear and no manners, and clearly with a strong smell of rat about him, had driven off with the car. Together with the small item that Alan had got Arthur Jobson to stick securely to the underside of the rear bumper back in September. For safekeeping. Well, if that wasn't just the biggest buggering fuck-up of all time.

__ In which Dawson finds a girl at a
    party, and then loses her again

On Saturday, sufficiently recovered to be able to walk more or less upright without seeing a facsimile of the Aurora Borealis flashing before his eyes, Dawson went to the after-show party. He went alone. Rachel had rejected his advances and despite Dawson invoking Section 3 of Clause 2 of Paragraph 8 of the GODS "After Show Party Rules Directive", which he'd written himself that afternoon, she had gone with Prat-the-Solicitor. Dawson felt undeniably jealous, watching through the serving hatch as the two of them danced closely together. At least he didn't feel like death any more – not his own death anyway. He decided this was a good sign, and moved off in search of alternative company.

Standing in front of the fireplace in the long through-lounge of their host's several-times-extended semi, picking at a plate of chicken and mixed rice with a plastic fork, was a small, pretty blonde girl with a pony-tail and just a hint of freckles who Dawson did not recognise. This was unusual for an after-show party, because only members of the cast and crew, immediate families and (clearly) Prat-the-Solicitors were invited. Dawson had not been so ill during the four days of the panto's run, or indeed the three months of rehearsals preceding that, that he would not have recognised anyone involved with the production, especially anyone who had the good fortune to look like the blonde girl. Dawson felt that his luck had been unfairly buffeted during the last few days, but he was willing to give it another go, and in any case the blonde seemed quite definitely to be alone. Maybe she was a Polish au pair, he thought, probably without a word of English.

'Hello,' he said. It seemed as good a way as any to start.

'Hi,' she replied. Dawson considered for a moment whether or not this was the Polish equivalent of "fuck off", and decided the evidence was inconclusive. He pressed on.

'Why are you alone?' he ventured.

'I don't know,' she said. Definitely English, he concluded. Or at least, not Polish.

'Are you at the right party?'

'Look,' said the girl. 'Have you got a form I could fill in later or something? I'm eating my supper, and if you've got many more questions, it'll get cold.'

'I'm sorry. It's just that I don't know you, and at shindigs like this, everyone knows everyone. Usually.'

'There's a first time for everything.' Then she grinned and looked up at him. 'Actually,' she said, 'I live here. Your revered producer sired me many years ago, before he lost interest in sex and took up The Stage instead.'

'I see. And you're not interested, I take it.'

'In what?' She frowned. 'Sex or The Stage?'

'I was thinking about The Stage. I doubt if I've known you long enough to think about the other.'

'I'm going to carry on with my supper. I'm not sure you're nice to know.'

'Perhaps we should start again. I'm Dawson.'

'Just Dawson? Are you too important to have a first name? Or have you forgotten it?'

'Neither. I don't like it, so I tend not to use it.'

'Ooh, what is it? No, don't tell me. Is it Endeavour? Like Morse?'

'Nothing that exciting. It's Saul.'

'I know.'

'You know. So why ask?'

'Because hiding it is a bit bloody pretentious. Like Sting or I don't know, Bono or someone. There's nothing wrong with Saul.'

'It's dreadful.'

'Granted, it's a bit different, but that's good, surely? Makes you stand out from the crowd.'

'Can't say I've ever noticed it having that effe

'That's because you don't use it. Ta da! Anyway
like it, you could use your second name. What is it

'Jeremy.'

'Hmm. Okay, scrub that. Stick to Saul.'

'Or Dawson. Which is where we came in. Anywa,, ..uw aid
you know that was my name?'

'I came to the show tonight. I bought a programme. Mystery
solved.' She paused. 'You haven't asked me my name yet.'

'A thousand pardons,' he said. 'It would certainly be nice to
know who I'm arguing with.'

'Lucy,' said the girl.

'Where?' he asked, looking around.

'Oh, God, a comedian,' groaned Lucy. 'I'd never have guessed
by your performance tonight.'

'Fair enough,' he smiled. 'Although I read in some magazine
that it's the job of the man in these situations to entertain the
lady.'

'Blimey, where did you read that? *Manners and Etiquette for
the Victorian and Edwardian Withdrawing Room*?'

'Oh, you subscribe too, do you?'

Lucy laughed. 'I think this is one of the silliest conversations
I've ever had.'

'Really? You don't talk to people much then?'

'Not if I can help it. I'm always a bit afraid I'll end up talking
to a lunatic. I was right.'

'Are we getting on really well, or are you standing there
thinking "What a dick!"?'

'Come and dance,' said Lucy.

'Good answer,' he replied, smiling.

—

Two hours later, the party had livened up a bit. Like most
people, Dawson had had a few drinks and at some point in the

.our he'd lost touch with Lucy. However, he couldn't quite .member when, or indeed how. Had he gone to get drinks and not made it back to her? (This seemed unlikely.) Or had it been the other way round? (More likely.) Or was there a trip to the toilet involved somewhere? Anyway, whatever the case, he couldn't see her now, although it was quite a big house and she did, after all, live there so had probably gone to bed. Dawson consulted his watch. It was getting on for half past 2, so yes, bed seemed the most likely answer. Still, he knew where she lived, after all.

After a while, he found himself in the same group of people as John, the show's producer, owner of the house in which they stood and father of his new-found future girlfriend.

'I didn't know you had a daughter,' said Dawson.

'And I didn't know you had a mole on your bottom, young Daws.'

'I don't.'

'Neither do I.'

'Why are we talking about moles?'

'I thought we were playing a game of unlikeliest hypothetical interjections, and that's not easy to say after six glasses of single malt.'

'We were talking about your daughter?' suggested Dawson, hoping to steer the conversation back in the right direction.

'As I say, I don't.'

'Don't what?' Dawson was getting more and more confused.

'I don't have a daughter. I have a son, Tom, away at uni. Daughter? No. Unless my wife's been keeping something from me.'

'But she was here.'

'Jane? Of course she's here. She lives here.'

'Jane?'

'My wife, Jane.'

'No, your daughter, Lucy.' There was a pause while they looked at each other. Then, slowly, Dawson said, 'You don't have a daughter, do you?'

'Got there at last, congratulations. I think you either need a lot more to drink, or to stop drinking entirely for the rest of your life. Your choice, but if it's the former, please lay off my single malt, I need a bit more myself and I suspect the cellar's running dry.'

It had been ridiculously easy to sneak into the party – in fact sneaking hardly came into it. I'd simply strolled right in after following a couple of carloads of pantomimers from the Borough Hall. I was only planning to be there as long as it took, and it took less than half an hour. Only two people had approached me before Saul did, and it was Day One Induction stuff to pull the wool over their eyes. I'd been counting on Saul wandering over sooner rather than later, the single lovelorn male being apt to head in my direction. I'd like to say I can't think why, but of course I can. I'm not that naïve.

I was well aware that Napoleon hadn't been sure about giving me the job, but really, what choice did he have? We're not exactly bursting at the seams with staff, especially young, reasonably attractive women. Napoleon isn't his real name, of course. Touch of the James Bonds I suppose, although I think it comes from Animal Farm, not that I've noticed a Snowball lurking about the office.

I'd only been working for Napoleon for about six months and, until now, hadn't been much more than a sort of glorified secretary with a modicum of minor investigative work thrown in. It hadn't been why I'd joined so I was glad to get out from behind a desk. However, the job was still several times more interesting than my four-year stint with an insurance broker after I came down from Cambridge. I've always enjoyed surprises, so I'd been sending off more and more job applications to more and more obscure and arcane advertisements for three months before Napoleon (or Mr Joyce as he'd been on the phone) called me out of the blue at 11 o'clock one night on my landline, a number I'd not put on my CV. These two facts alone were enough to make me jump excitedly towards the interview he'd suggested for 8 o'clock the next morning, and when he offered me the job two hours later while inviting me to sign the Official Secrets Act at the same time, as long as I could start that minute, I'd said yes before he'd finished talking. I'd phoned the insurance brokers immediately to say I wouldn't be in again and could they possibly put my belongings in a bag for me, and they'd told me they already knew I'd left and my belongings were currently in a box in reception awaiting immediate collection or I would risk losing them for ever. I'd mentioned this to Napoleon, as he had by now become, who'd merely shrugged as if to imply what could I expect?

Until the last few days, this auspiciously intriguing start to my life with Aardvark Amalgamations (I know, me too) had become something rather more mundane, but now at last things were looking up and I couldn't have been happier. Well, not much happier. For instance, he's a bit stuck in the past, Napoleon. I mean, timeshares? Do they even exist any more? Surely nobody could fall for a ruse like that? But they had, of course. Or rather, Saul had. I'd just shaken my head when Napoleon had given me the "I told you so" look. I mean, what could I say? One born every minute. And he'd not just fallen either. Saul had rung within half an hour of the email being sent, and I'd had to put on my best Call Centre voice to take the call.

___ In which Dawson catches a train, and has a slight accident

It was the following Thursday morning, 7:30, and it was raining, although that was a rather inadequate description for the deluge of water that had been assaulting Stallford for the past hour. Dawson was standing on Stallford Railway Station waiting for a train that had been due to arrive six minutes ago, but which had been held up, a lugubrious, slightly muffled voice over the antediluvian Tannoy had informed them, by a renegade leaf or two. Dawson had previously imagined that leaf fall was something that happened in the autumn, not in late January, but doubtless Southern Railways knew better.

Eventually the train arrived. It was thirteen minutes late, and it was full. Or at least the coach that drew to a halt opposite Dawson was full, and he was faced with an apparently impenetrable wall of backs when the door nearest to him opened. However, he was nothing if not game, and having two important appointments in London, he did not fancy waiting a further forty-five minutes for the next train. By dint of a good deal of undignified pushing and shoving, and even cursing, not all from his own mouth, he eventually managed to gain a toe-hold on the train, and the hour-long journey thereafter into the capital was made with his buttocks flattened by the door. He prayed the door would not fly open of its own accord, and mercifully it didn't.

Dawson knew the geography of central London less well than might have been presupposed from his years of living in Ealing. When he arrived at Victoria Station and was spewed forth onto the main concourse at the same time as about a thousand others, he stopped and stood irresolutely for a moment while getting his bearings. This immediately endeared him to absolutely nobody at all. Commuters travelling by rail into London require at least two attributes: the ability to remain silent at all times under often intense provocation such as small children and mobile telephones (although a small discreet tut-tutting may be allowed on occasion); and the art of giving the impression of knowing exactly where one is going at all times, even if one doesn't. Put simply, this means that no one is permitted to stop suddenly on a London railway terminus.

Dawson stopped suddenly just beyond the end of the platform and within five or six seconds the following events occurred as a direct result of this flagrant breach of the rules. First, an intensely serious young lady wearing horn-rimmed spectacles with her hair in an unfashionable bun, who was striding purposefully along behind Dawson at a distance of approximately one millimetre while conducting an important phone conversation with the staff at Costa Coffee, collided with him. Since she had been travelling slightly faster than an Olympic thirty-kilometre-walk gold medallist, this collision propelled Dawson solidly forward. Off balance, he thrust out a hand to stop himself falling, and caught hold of the sleeve of another champion six-kilometres-per-hour walker (male). Without so much as a sideways glance or a break in step, the subject of Dawson's involuntary assault deftly swung the metal briefcase he was carrying in his other hand in a wide parabola and at ever increasing speed until it struck Dawson firmly on the side of the head. The speed and force of the blow had all the sixteen stone weight of the gentleman in question behind it, so Dawson only caught the first word or two of the 'Bloody beggars! Out of my way, you scum!' that was directed his way before unconsciousness overtook him. As he fell, he collided with a passing porter who happened to be driving a motorised, articulated luggage trolley. The porter fell off and his vehicle, now unnavigated, motored away in haphazard fashion in the general direction of a concourse Burger Bar. This flurry of activity caught the attention of everyone within a fifty-foot radius of Dawson's prone form. Everyone, that is, except the manager of the Burger Bar, who had his back turned to the world and who was fervently engaged in grilling a rack of burgers. About 100 interested onlookers remained totally silent as the runaway luggage trolley trundled on to its doom. When the final, awful collision came, it was spectacularly cataclysmic. The serving counter of the Burger Bar, being of modern construction, was unable to offer more than token resistance to a half ton of trolley with attendant luggage, and the whole bar collapsed inwardly with a loud thwump as cases and boxes and, shortly after, burgers, tomato ketchup, various other delicious fillings and the bar manager flew in all directions. The trolley overturned slowly and expired amidst the debris.

Dawson, meanwhile, was sleeping peacefully with a large bump, expanding by the second, on the side of his head.

For a while he was completely ignored, the much greater devastation of the Burger Bar understandably gaining the lion's share of attention from the crowd. Not that the crowd, as a whole, seemed to be especially interested in doing anything to help. As diverse representatives of the emergency services began to appear on the scene, once again, the remains of the Burger Bar and its unfortunate manager were the focus of their attention. Dawson remained lying where he was for quite a while until a young police constable, hurrying sedately across the concourse, almost tripped over him.

Being reasonably intelligent, he didn't immediately assume that Dawson was a homeless person choosing to sleep in the wrong place at the wrong time, and so stopped for a closer look. A delicate prod with a size twelve boot elicited no response from the recumbent Dawson, and an even closer look revealed the truth to the officer, that Dawson was in fact in need of some assistance. A quick call across to the smouldering remains of the Burger Bar brought a paramedic running and Dawson was bundled on to a stretcher and packed away in the back of an ambulance, together with the manager of the

Burger Bar. The latter, although conscious, had a leg broken in two places and an alarming amount of what appeared at first glance to be blood on his face, but which turned out on further inspection to be ketchup. The ambulance rolled gently off towards St Thomas' Hospital, and left the police in charge of the accident scene.

Napoleon wasn't happy. 'So where is he?' he rasped in my direction as I entered the room. He was sitting on the windowsill with his legs crossed. On a scale from one to ten of unhappiness, he was probably at about five or six. He wasn't pacing about and he didn't have a glass in his hand, which were encouraging signs. I'd certainly seen worse, even in my brief time working there, but I also knew I might be about to see the scale rise closer to nine or ten. I had no choice but to break the bad news and hope for the best.

'He had an accident at Victoria, and they whisked him off in an ambulance.'

He didn't ask how Saul was or even what the accident was. 'And you couldn't stop them doing that? Any of you?'

I felt I had to defend myself. 'There were only two of us, sir, as you know. And we couldn't get there before the police. The opportunity to intervene really didn't present itself.'

'The opportunity to intervene... for God's sake, speak English, woman!' Then, after a pause, 'I'm sorry, that was uncalled-for. And I shouldn't call you "woman".'

'Well, I am one, sir.'

'Yes, well. Okay, tell me what happened.' So I did, and I could see his mind whirring while I spoke. 'God forgive us, this could only happen to Dawson. What was I thinking of? Let's move on, got no choice really.'

'I understand he's only got concussion, so I guess he'll be out tomorrow. Look, why don't you visit him? He'll be expecting you to, I imagine. And I certainly can't.'

'Not sure what it will achieve.'

'I was thinking reassurance.'

'Yes, you're probably right. I don't think we've got time

to faff about any more. Let's pile the manure towards the
fan. And Lucy?'

    'Yes, sir?'

    'Thanks.'

    'No thanks needed. This is why I joined.'

__ In which Dawson converses
with a nurse, and receives an
invitation to visit Australia

When Dawson woke up, he immediately spotted he was in hospital. Something about the nurses and the smell of antiseptic and cabbage gave it away. He assumed he was in London, but had no idea exactly where. There was, as they say, only one way to find out.

'Nurse!'

A small, round, middle-aged woman with crinkled elbows and a stern face wandered over. 'You're awake.'

'I've been known to cry out in my sleep.'

'Possibly, but I'm a professional and I know my stuff. You're awake. How are you?'

'I doubt if I'm as well as I was this morning or I wouldn't be in hospital. I've got a headache, but apart from that, not too bad.'

'Do you remember what happened?'

'Some bastard hit me with a briefcase.'

'Language, Timothy.'

'Oh my God, is my name Timothy? I may be more ill than I'd thought.'

'The reference is before your time, Mr Dawson. You've got a touch of concussion. The doctor will be around to run the rule over you in a bit.'

'Not a long bit, I hope. I'm missing a job interview and the acquisition of a new car.'

'I'm sorry about that, but this is the NHS, time means nothing to us. If it did, I'd have gone home half an hour ago.' She moved off down the ward.

Halfway down she passed a man walking in the opposite direction. Alan Flannery had a concerned look on his face. He'd practised it in front of a mirror before setting out.

'I told you you were unreliable,' he said, stopping next to Dawson's bed.

'When did you say that?'

'Many times, I'm sure, and if I didn't, I meant to. Keeping appointments means very little to you, I see.'

'How are you, Dawson?' said Dawson. 'Not great, if I'm honest, Alan, but thanks for asking. Oh, you didn't.'

'You've made the papers, you know,' remarked Alan, waving a copy of the *Evening Standard*. 'Rather wish you hadn't, actually. You probably do too, given that a couple of million people now know your first name.'

Dawson took the paper and scanned it briefly. 'Hardly mentions me,' he said. 'Doesn't mention the tosser who hit me at all. I'd quite like to know his name. I could sue. Should sue. I could do with the money and that's a fact.'

'Doubt if you've got time for all that. I want you on a plane to Aus as soon as possible. You've got a passport, I presume.'

'Whoa!' said Dawson, in an alarmed voice. 'What are you talking about? Oz? Yellow brick roads, scarecrows and witches? That Oz?'

Alan looked at him with a blank expression. 'God, I really hope you're joking.'

'I've had a serious crack on the noggin. Not sure what I'm saying to be honest. You mean Australia, don't you?'

'Australia. Sydney. To start with anyway. Hopefully within forty-eight hours.'

'Why?'

'You work for me, remember? And I'm telling you to go to Sydney.'

'I need more than that, mate. And anyway, I don't work for you. I never turned up for the interview.'

'This is the interview. If Muhammad won't come to the mountain...'

'But...'

'Yes, I know, stuff to sort, people to see, dole people to

tell. You'll be out of here tomorrow. There's a weekly Qatar Air flight that leaves 9am Sunday. That gives you Saturday to sort out whatever you need to sort out. I'm being generous, you've got 'til then.'

'Are you planning to tell me what I'm going to do in Sydney?'

'Await further instructions.'

'I can do that, I suppose. How long am I going to be there?'

'How long's a time that's longer than a short time?'

'Don't know.'

'Neither do I.'

'All right then, why not? Oh, and yes.'

'Yes what?'

'I do have a passport.'

'Wouldn't have mattered if you didn't, as it happens, but it makes it easier. Your ticket will be on your computer by this time tomorrow. Oh, and you'll need this,' and he handed over a phone.

'I've already got one of those,' said Dawson, waving his iPhone in the air.

'It's a company phone, take it. You don't want to be paying all those roaming charges, so it's got an Australian SIM. I'd be extremely grateful if you'd keep it switched on and powered up. As I say, you're going to be awaiting further instructions, and I don't want to have to send a carrier pigeon.'

'Of course,' said Dawson, slightly affronted. 'Why wouldn't I?'

'I could say experience, which tells me you can be frustratingly difficult to get hold of.'

'As are you.'

'Maybe so, but I've never really considered your calls important.'

'Thanks for the vote of confidence. Couple of questions.'

'If you must.'

'Where do I stay when I get there, while I'm "awaiting instructions"?'

'Close to the airport, I should think. Your flight doesn't get in 'til 10 o'clock at night.'

'Are you booking me a hotel?'

'What are you, eight years old? Book it yourself. Do it tomorrow, if you like.'

'What's the number?'

'Number?'

'Of the phone.'

'No idea. Why do you need to know that? You won't be calling yourself, will you?'

Dawson was indeed allowed to go home the next day. Not so much allowed as told. He still felt a bit dizzy but the stern, dumpy nurse was adamant. 'You're taking up a bed. We need it for someone genuinely ill. Do you have anyone to look after you at home?'

'No.'

'Oh, never mind, you'll probably cope.'

'My taxes pay your wages, you know.'

'Hmm, it says here you're out of work. Not paying enough, I'd say. Home you go, young man.'

So that was that. He rang his mum, hoping for a lift, but got her voicemail telling him that she and his dad were hiking in Ireland, so he was forced to catch another train. Taking no chances, he planned his route across the concourse at Victoria extremely carefully before taking a step, and managed to negotiate his way safely on to the Stallford train.

Arriving at his flat, he was met outside by his neighbour, Mabel. Mabel was not as old as her name suggested, and while she was indubitably a busy-body of the first water, it is also true that the block of six flats could not have functioned anywhere near as well without her tireless efforts in undertaking all the gardening duties in the shared grounds, frightening off the local cat population and clearing up all the rubbish left by the bin men.

'Hello, Mabel,' said Dawson. She was carrying a large square package wrapped in brown paper.

'This arrived for you,' she replied. 'Yesterday. You weren't here,' she added with a somewhat accusatory tone to her voice.

'No,' said Dawson. 'Sorry.' What on Earth was he apologising for? 'Thanks.' Mabel handed the parcel over. It was bulky and fairly heavy.

'Who's it from?' asked Mabel, not going anywhere.

Rude Dawson struggled with Polite Dawson before replying. Polite Dawson won the battle – just.

'I'm really not sure,' he said. He studied the package but there were no sender's details anywhere, just half a dozen stamps above his own name and address. 'I'm not expecting anything.'

'Aren't you going to open it?'

'I imagine so, but probably not out here. Thanks for taking it in for me.'

'The man who delivered it was quite insistent.'

'Insistent? What about?'

'Getting me to take it in and give it to you. I mean, it could be anything, a bomb for example. Frankly, I'd rather he'd taken it to the sorting office.'

'So he was a postman?'

'Oh no, not a postman. He was in a white van.' Dawson decided the conversation really wasn't going anywhere, so he thanked Mabel again and took the parcel into his flat.

He put it on the table and looked at it. Perhaps it was a bomb after all. The worldwide spate of terrorist attacks had not yet landed in Stallford, but there had to be a first time. No, he was being ridiculous. The likelihood of a fundamentalist picking him at random was laughably small. So he laughed and then went to boil the kettle for a cup of tea.

Returning with the tea and a pair of scissors, he cut open the brown paper. A plain white cardboard box, securely taped, was revealed. And inside the box was... Dawson could hardly believe his eyes. Sitting in front of him was a twelve-piece porcelain tea service. Not a Ford Focus. Four cups, four saucers, a milk jug, sugar bowl and teapot (with lid), all in a hideous shade of pale blue with pink roses.

'What the fuck?' he said out loud.

There was nothing else apart from the tea service and quite a lot of bubble wrap. No card, no note, nothing. Clearly, it had to be to do with his aborted trip to the timesharers. Dawson wasn't entirely stupid, and adding two and two and coming up with an answer not far from four, the name Alan Flannery popped into his head. This surely had to be connected to Alan, the trip to Australia with no reason thus far provided, and Alan's whole strange, devious behaviour ever since their conversation in The Cricketers.

Dawson decided to call Alan to get to the bottom of things and, remembering that he had just acquired a brand new phone, thought that he might as well try it out. But of course it needed charging first, as did his old phone. Plugging them both in, he made another cup of tea to replace the one he hadn't drunk. Just what was going on? If he actually did have a job, he certainly didn't have a contract, and nor had a salary been mentioned. Why was he going to Australia? And what was he going to do when he got there? And how did the tea service come into things?

Starting up his computer, he saw that he had, as promised, received an e-ticket for a Qatar Air flight to Sydney on Sunday morning. There was nothing about a return flight.

When the phones had charged, he tried calling Alan but just got his voicemail. He left a message but had no very great expectation of receiving a call back. He was therefore quite surprised when his old phone rang five minutes later. But it wasn't Alan. It was, unexpectedly, Rachel's name that came up on his screen. However, when he answered she wasn't there. Dawson phoned her back, and she picked up.

I buttonholed Napoleon. 'Remind me again, why are we sending Dawson to Australia? What's the place called? Yackandandah? Why there?'

'It's just something needs collecting,' Napoleon replied in that irritatingly smooth tone he used sometimes. 'Easy job. He just goes there, picks it up when we tell him and comes home again.' But his eyes were looking past me as he spoke, and if it was the easy job he suggested, why all the subterfuge?

I persisted. 'Assuming we had to send someone, why not one of us?'

He looked around the room. There were only two of us there. 'Who did you have in mind?'

'Who's that guy in Sydney? Laurie, is it?'

'Laurie doesn't work for us, we're just allowed to borrow him occasionally.'

'What about Arthur Jobson?'

'Are you planning to run through the entire staff list?'

'I think I just have.'

'Apart from darling Juliet, you're right. No, not Arthur. Arthur's good for walk-on roles – he especially likes playing coppers – but nothing much more.'

'I could have gone,' and I meant it too. As previously mentioned, I hadn't joined Aardvark to sit behind a desk.

'Yes, actually you could, but it had to be someone unknown.'

I felt quite chuffed. I was known? By whom? My role in life's great game suddenly took on a greater significance. 'Who knows me?' I asked. 'Should I be concerned?'

'Of course you should be concerned. You should always be concerned. And wary. And vigilant, and everything else that goes with signing the Official Secrets Act and working for a British Intelligence Agency, even a little one like this. Anyway, you're going too, to keep an eye on him. From a discreet distance,' he added.

'So, back to Saul. He's supposed to be a friend of yours, isn't he? Generally speaking, people don't put their friends in danger.'

'He's not in danger. And as I say, you'll be there to watch over him. Think of yourself as a guardian angel. Look, we needed someone urgently, Dawson needed a job – he's always moaned about not doing enough travelling – so everything stacked up. And there's more to young Dawson than meets the untrained, or in your case, partly trained eye. Trust me, he's got something about him.'

'I don't think a ready wit is enough.'

'Actually, humour usually helps defuse most uncomfortable situations. No, he'll be fine. You'll both be fine.'

'Back to the top of the conversation,' I persevered. 'What exactly is happening in Yackandandah?'

'I understand they put on quite a well-regarded folk festival. Quite soon too. There'll be crowds of people. Crowds are good. All in all, Yackandandah is a place that may be about to acquire significance over and above its normal station in life. Or not. There are few certainties in this world, after all. We believe there may be an item of utmost importance there, or not far away, and we are certainly not the only people with an interest in acquiring it. Hence my enthusiasm in sending someone to take possession of that possible item if, for example, hell should break loose while everyone else is engaged with the, how shall I put it? meeting and greeting. Clear?'

'As mud. None of that seems to agree with your previous comment about a lack of danger. It also sounds like it's not really our show.'

'It's always good to be involved in interesting things,

especially if they might have a bearing on the continuation of our funding from HMG. But yes, you're right, I got a call from certain pals, and I use that word with extreme caution, to ask if we could help, and as you know, I always try to be helpful.'

I knew nothing of the sort. 'These pals asked for our help? With our resources? Sorry, I mean, total absence of resources.'

'Yes, well, their own resources in Australia are basically non-existent so, seeing as we will shortly have two people on the ground there, we're positively flush by comparison.'

__ In which Rachel ponders a
proposal, and phones the wrong
person

Rachel Whyte had been harbouring doubts. She had already been regretting taking Pat to the party and now, obviously emboldened by being allowed into her inner circle, he had only gone and asked her to marry him. And obviously, she'd had to say yes as he had chosen to pop the question last night during dinner at her house with both her parents in eager attendance, and she had felt it was only polite not to upset them all. Her mother couldn't have been more eager had she been a gun dog. Rachel was pretty sure her mother had been in cahoots with Pat for months as he was exactly the sort of son-in-law she had always wanted.

But was he the sort of husband Rachel wanted? She wasn't sure. On the plus side, he was reasonably good-looking, well off and, importantly, taller than her. Rachel was a tall girl herself, five foot eleven in her stocking feet, so considerably over six foot in high heels, and she hated looking down on her man. Pat was six foot three, so a definite plus on that score, especially when she compared him to, for example, Dawson (a name that popped into her head entirely at random), who was more or less the same height as her and not inclined to wear high heels, at least not in her company. She was well aware that Pat was also smug, pompous and with a tendency to smell of expensive after shave, or possibly hair gel, she wasn't sure which. He was also conniving, as the choice of a dinner party with her parents as a suitable venue for asking the marriage question proved. And he was inquisitive. Yes, of course he wanted to know about her, that was only to be expected, and she had asked him questions about his earlier life too. Obviously. It's what people in a serious relationship did. But he'd also asked her lots of questions about her other friends and, it seemed to her, particularly Dawson. Admittedly Dawson was often around, he was a bit like a loveable but slightly annoying lapdog in that respect, and she'd always put Pat's regular interrogation about him down to jealousy. Unwarranted jealousy.

On the other hand, she had to get married quite soon and she was fairly confident that whomever she eventually decided to marry, whether Pat or someone else, she would be able to eradicate all his faults and enhance all his good qualities.

She needed to talk to someone before things got too far advanced, although how far advanced they could get when no ring had yet been forthcoming, was something else she wasn't sure about. And why was there no ring? Rachel was starting to get confused, and needed to untangle her mind, preferably over a drink with a friend. And the only friend she had who would listen, understand and not burst out laughing was Dani, her colleague at the travel agency. Rachel dialled her number.

Dawson answered.

Rachel hung up and went bright red, even though she was alone.

Her phone rang. It was Dawson. She looked at the phone for a few seconds, then answered. 'Hi,' she said, with a sort of brittle, artificial brightness, which Dawson failed to notice.

'We got cut off,' he said.

'Yes.' There was a pause.

'Did you want something?'

'Um, yes, I suppose I must have. Do you want a drink?' What was she doing? Rachel grimaced. Why had she said that? She couldn't talk to Dawson about Pat's proposal; he'd either laugh like a hyena or threaten to top himself. Still, a drink wouldn't do any harm.

'A drink? Are you sure? Is Prat abroad or something? Or ill?'

'No, neither. Can't friends have a drink?'

'When did you have in mind?'

'I don't know. Saturday?' She felt herself panicking slightly for no reason whatsoever.

'We never see each other on a Saturday. There's usually a large, tubby solicitor about.'

'Imagine I'm feeling brave enough to see you not on a school night.'

Dawson found himself with mixed emotions. This could have been a breakthrough. However... 'It'll have to be tonight, I'm afraid, Rachel,' he said with a sigh.

'That was a sigh. You've been angling for a Saturday date – and I use the term in no sense that you can put unwarranted meaning to – for months, and now, when I graciously give in to your very – if I may say so – forward demands, you have the temerity to sigh?'

'I do. I can't believe I'm saying this, but I can't make tomorrow night. I'm booked on a plane to Australia early Sunday morning and I'll need my beauty sleep.'

'Australia? You do know where Australia is, do you? You get travel sick driving to Littlehampton.'

'It was only the once, but thanks for reminding me. And yes, I do know where Australia is, I didn't fail A-level Geography by much.'

'Well, I'm buggered. We'd better have that drink after all. I'll pick you up at 7 o'clock tonight.'

____ In which Dawson finds a hotel, and
reflects on a conversation and an
instruction_

Dawson was in the nearest, cheapest hotel room he could find around Sydney Airport. The plane had arrived in Australia after a flight that had been trouble-free, apart from his nearly getting lost in Doha Airport trying to find his way from one end of the vast terminal building to the other while having the strangest feeling that somebody was following him. Unable to actually spot anyone, he decided that the current series of odd life events was simply making him slightly paranoid.

It was now the next morning and the sun outside his window shone out of a cloudless blue sky onto a gently steaming car park. His phone told him that the temperature was 30° and likely to go much higher. He felt overdressed – despite being naked – sitting on his bed with the air con turned up high.

He pondered on the helpfulness of the taxi driver. Having chosen one at random, he had been surprised to find, as it drove off, an envelope in his jacket pocket that had not been there before. He couldn't be certain that the taxi driver had put it there but who else had had the opportunity? Opening it, he'd found it stuffed with Australian dollars, a thousand of them. There'd been a note as well, which ran to all of two sentences. The first read, "You'll need this, I imagine". It was right; he did, as he had less than £100 in his bank account. The second sentence said, "Go to Yackandandah tomorrow."

Where, or what the hell, was Yackandandah? Was it even real?

He Googled it, and discovered that it was a town halfway between Wooragee and Kergunyah, which wasn't particularly helpful. Looking deeper, he found that it was in northern Victoria, 586 kilometres by road from Sydney, which was about

364 miles in English. He was going to need transport. He looked up the Wikipedia entry, which was brief. Yackandandah, understandably often shortened to Yack, was a former gold mining centre known for its alluvial wet mining techniques. It boasted a population of 950 and its post office opened on 13 June 1857. Somehow, Dawson felt he might have need of the post office, if it was still open after 160 years. Later in the month, the town would be hosting its annual folk festival, so he sincerely hoped that whatever it was Alan Flannery wanted him to do there, he would be able to get it done by then. He couldn't think of anything worse than a folk festival. Apart from a jazz festival.

He lay back on his bed and reflected on his evening with Rachel. She'd been offhand and distracted for the first hour and, as she was doing the driving, he hadn't even been able to ply her with drink to loosen her up a bit. Clearly, she'd had something on her mind but she'd insisted on quizzing him about his sudden departure for Australia and he had failed to move the conversation from that to whatever it was she was hiding. It is true to say that she was doubtful about his trip in a sort of "What the hell do you think you're doing?" sort of way. She'd never liked Alan Flannery, (she'd met him once), and wouldn't trust him as far as she could kick him, she said. Dawson had had to admit that although he liked Alan's company as a drinking companion, he also didn't entirely trust him and really didn't know much about him.

'You don't know where he lives?' Rachel had asked, disbelief etched into her expression. 'How long have you been friends?'

'Six years.'

'And you don't know where he lives.'

'You're repeating yourself. No, I don't, well not exactly, one of the villages I think, East Meaning, possibly. Round there anyway. It's never come up.'

'Why do men not want to know this sort of thing? I couldn't

know someone for six years, or six months even, without knowing where they live.' She was warming to her theme. 'And I certainly wouldn't trust them. Why is he sending you to Australia? And what's he paying you?'

'I don't know and I don't know. But I've never been there and frankly I'm not doing much here. It actually sounds quite exciting in a slightly nefarious way. You've always said I'm not exciting enough.'

'I have never, ever said you're not exciting. I mean, obviously you're not, but who is, for God's sake? I'm certainly not. Neither is Pat, for that matter.'

'Oh, I don't know, there's a sort of grim excitement in wondering if he'll eventually end up eating and drinking so much that he actually explodes. "Just a wafer-thin mint".'

'Stop comparing my fian... boyfriend with Mr Creosote.'

'Well, he does get through a lot of giant lunches. You've said so yourself.'

He paused, suddenly struck by something. 'Wait a minute, what did you just call him?'

'Who?'

'What do you mean, who? Prat the Fat Solicitor, of course. You were about to say "fiance", weren't you?'

'No,' but Rachel was looking into her drink as she spoke.

Dawson stared at her for a long time. She stared at her drink for a long time. Finally, he said, 'So you're marrying him, then.'

She looked up at last. 'Yes, I mean no, I mean, I don't know. He hasn't given me a ring. Why hasn't he given me a ring?'

'I couldn't care less whether he's given you a ring. Either you're marrying him or you're not, and the fact we're sitting here at short notice and you've been shifty all evening tells me you are. However, I do appreciate the fact that you feel you have to tell me. Not that you really did.'

'It's why I asked you out. I sort of wanted your opinion.'

Dawson severely doubted that. It didn't sound like the kind

of thing she would seek his opinion about. 'Anyway, even if I wanted to, I couldn't marry you. You're about to go to Australia where you'll be stung on the bum by a funnel-web spider and die.'

'Now you're just trying to cheer me up.' But somehow the evening descended into silence after that and both of them were relieved to finish their drinks and call it a night. Rachel dropped him back at his flat with a quick peck on the cheek and a mumbled, 'Look after yourself. See you soon,' before driving off.

I'd never flown business class before and it was brilliant, especially on a twenty-one hour flight, although I'd spent most of the twenty-one hours plus a two hour stopover in Doha worried that Saul would spot me through the dark glasses and darker wig of my hastily put-together disguise. The stopover had especially concerned me as Doha Airport turned out to be huge and not particularly well-populated and it was hard, even for us posh passengers, to keep away from the riff-raff in steerage. So I'd spent most of it in the ladies' with a travel guide to Australia. I'd mentioned to Napoleon that it might have been safer to book me on a separate flight, but he'd just given me a disdainful look and mumbled something about resourcefulness. Apparently, I needed to keep Saul in sight at all times, which was going to be hard to do from inside the female toilet but I didn't think that Napoleon had really thought this through.

Anyway, the journey had gone well enough and doing it business-class enabled me to relax and not think about the problems that the next few days or weeks were likely to throw up. On arrival at Sydney I'd rushed ahead, wig over my face, collar up, dark glasses firmly on my nose, and had succeeded in handing the envelope to Laurie, the completely fake taxi driver, without being spotted. Laurie had had a much harder job making sure that Saul got into his taxi rather than any of the dozens of others, but he had also succeeded, as I ascertained by hiding behind a nearby pillar. Perhaps I was getting better at all this Spooks stuff.

Twenty minutes later, Laurie had returned with a grin and given me not only the name of Saul's hotel (Airport Hotel, quite easy to remember that, I was trying not to *write too much down), but also his room number and, if I should need it, the name of the member of staff whose job it was to clean his room (Maria). An example, I guess, of the sort of resourcefulness that Napoleon expects of me. Laurie and I decided it was safe for me to stay in the same hotel. In fact, he'd already booked me a room, immediately above Saul's. I think he thought I could bug the room through the ceiling but unfortunately I had neither the wherewithal nor the competence to do so. And I couldn't quite see why that would be useful, although maybe that said more about my inexperience than anything else. I imagined that, if he felt anything like I did and frankly, as he'd been in economy, he probably felt much worse, Saul would go pretty much straight to bed for eight to ten hours, so I decided I was safe to give myself at least six before donning the wig and glasses again and hovering incognito in the lobby.*

___ In which Dawson has an idea, and
   Martin Evans is embarrassed by a
   gate

Something had been worrying Dawson ever since he'd arrived in Australia, but he hadn't been able to put his finger on it. Things just didn't add up. Was Alan Flannery a spy, and if so, whom did he work for? MI5? MI6? Spectre? Could be anybody, really. And what was he, Dawson, doing in Australia if he didn't trust Alan? And what was the significance of the tea service? It had something to do with this; the coincidence was too great for it to be otherwise. But what was "this"?

And then he'd got it. One of his favourite films was *Charade* with Cary Grant and Audrey Hepburn. The twist in that film was that the "money" that all the protagonists were chasing had been in the form of a small collection of very valuable stamps on an envelope. Hidden in plain sight as it were. Stamps! The tea service had arrived with Dawson's name and address on it and a few stamps, nothing else. But Mabel had said that it had been delivered by a man in "a white van", not a postman. So why the stamps? There must be something important about them. He had to find out what. Unfortunately, he was in Australia, currently on his way to Yackandandah, still 220 kilometres ahead, and the wrapping was in the recycling bin back in Stallford. He needed to follow up on the stamps as soon as possible and phone someone. But who? Not Rachel, although he wasn't sure why. Martin Evans. Of course, he'd phone Martin. He worked for the local paper, so investigating stuff was what he was good at.

—

Martin Evans had moved to Stallford from the Rhondda the previous February, having been offered an unexpected career progression to become editor of the *Stallford Sentinel*. He had felt quite chuffed to be headhunted as he hadn't realised that his erstwhile sub-editorial post on *The View from the Valleys* free rag had given him that sort of profile. Putting some distance between himself and a still-nagging ex-wife had also been a major consideration. Consequently, he had accepted the job without undertaking much in the way of due diligence and had wasted little time in upping sticks and moving to the Home Counties.

Martin was a short, smiley man with curly black hair, an innate sociability and a liking for real ale. He made friends easily, and one of the friends he'd made had been Dawson. They had both been propping up the bar of the pub one evening soon after Martin's arrival, and had struck up a conversation. Dawson had talked about the GODS and Martin had been vaguely interested in the arcane world of am-dram as, being from The Valleys, he had something of a voice on him and had occasionally been known to sing in public. However, he wasn't sure he could act, so had limited himself to writing reviews of the group's shows for the *Sentinel*.

He was sitting at the corner of the bar in The Cricketers, wondering why neither Dawson nor Alan were in their usual places on a Tuesday evening when his phone vibrated in his pocket. He always left his phone on silent as he felt it gave him an excuse not to answer it. He saw a strange number come up on the screen, a bit longer than normal, which began with the digits 0061. Martin had something of a photographic memory for phone numbers, so he immediately thought: Australia, that's unusual. He decided to answer it.

If he was surprised to receive a call from Australia, he was astonished when he discovered it was Dawson calling him.

'Martin?' said a breathless-sounding Dawson. 'Thank God, mate, I need you to do something for me.'

'And hello to you too, Daws,' replied Martin. 'I take it this means you're not about to walk through the door and buy me a drink.'

'What? Sorry, er, no, no I'm not. I'm in Australia.'

'I know.'

'How do you know?'

'It's not rocket science. The number's come up and it starts 0061.'

'Oh, I see, yes. Sorry, pardon, what's 0061?'

'Oh God,' sighed Martin. 'International dialling code for Australia. Hence, my magnificently tuned journalistic brain immediately jumped to the seaworthy conclusion that you might be calling from... wait for it, Australia! Clear now?'

'Yes, clear, sorry.'

'Stop saying sorry.'

'Sorry, yes, look, are you able to do something for me?'

'Being a very helpful Welshman, probably. Now?'

'Well, a few days ago would have been better, but yes, now please.'

'I'm intrigued, well, a bit intrigued. What do you want me to do?'

'You know my flat?'

'I'm your local newspaper editor, remember? I know where everyone lives.'

'Yes. Quite. Can you hop across to the flat as quick as poss? Round the back there's some recycle bins. In one of them you'll find a large cardboard box and some bubble wrap. And the brown paper it came in. Addressed to me. Bit squashed now, but easy to spot. Pick it up and put it somewhere safe until I get back.'

'Okay, not too difficult. Begs a few questions though.'

'Please, later. I can't talk over the phone.'

'You're doing a pretty good job so far,' began Martin, then realising there was something a little hysterical about Dawson's voice, he changed tack. 'Right, two swigs of beer and I'm out of here, boyo. Do you need me to call when I've got it?'

'If you wouldn't mind.'

'On my way, Daws. Nothing to fear, Evans is here.' So he rang off, finished his Mugwitch and trotted off up the road to Dawson's flat.

A small problem materialised on his arrival, shortly followed by a larger one. The small problem was that the back gate was locked and, having discovered there was no other means of gaining access to the yard where the bins were kept, he decided he was just about agile enough to shimmy over the gate. He was halfway across when the larger problem appeared in the shape of Mabel. Martin had never met Mabel and, although Mabel had never met Martin, she knew exactly who he was as she was an avid reader of the *Stallford Sentinel*, if only because he had his picture attached to the weekly editorial column, a column that Mabel never missed reading but usually disagreed with. So she wasn't very enthusiastic about Martin at the best of times, and much less so when she was catching him with his legs astride the locked gate that she herself had only recently painted.

'Can I help you, Mr Evans?'

'Ah, good evening, madam,' replied Martin, in his best Welsh lilt and with what he hoped was an ingratiating smile. 'I was just calling on my friend, Mr Dawson.'

'You seem to have missed the front door. And Mr Dawson is away.'

'Oh dear. I thought I'd try to spot him through the kitchen window. He wasn't answering the door.'

'You haven't tried the door.'

'How do you...? I meant, he wasn't answering his phone but...' thinking quickly, 'I could hear it ringing inside the flat and Dawson was supposed to be meeting me in the pub, and I was, well, er, worried, so I, er, thought I'd try the, er, back door?' He tailed off with another failed attempt at an ingratiating smile.

'I see. Well, why didn't you say so? Come down off there. I have a key. Let's go and see if he's all right. I mean, he told me he was going away, but young people today cannot always be relied upon to... Anyway, come along, quickly now, *EastEnders* is on pause.'

Martin clambered uncomfortably down from the gate and followed the scary woman round to the front door and through it into the ground floor hallway. Dawson's flat was on the left and opposite it another door was open. 'I'm sorry,' said Martin, beginning to recover. 'You appear to have me at a disadvantage, Miss, er...'

'Scutt,' said Mabel. 'I'm Mr Dawson's neighbour. Wait here, I'll fetch a key.' She was back almost before she'd left. 'Here it is. Stand back.'

Martin wasn't too sure why he needed to stand back, it was almost as if Ms Scutt was expecting the door to explode when she turned the key. It didn't.

'Right, follow me,' she said, and they went in. Martin had been in Dawson's flat a few times and it had never been anything but untidy, but this evening it was truly chaotic. The furniture looked as if it had been scattered by a tornado, there were masses of pieces of paper and household objects lying around and when he poked his head into the kitchen he saw that all the drawers had been emptied on to the floor. Mabel Scutt, however, didn't seem to find anything amiss.

'He's been burgled,' said Martin. 'I'll call the police.'

'What? Are you sure? He's very messy, you know.'

'This isn't messy, this is a ransacking.'

Two hours later, the police constable had been and gone. Martin had been forced to reveal that he had received a call from Dawson in Australia earlier in the evening, at which Mabel's eyebrows had disappeared into her hairline as she reminded him that he had told her that he'd called on Dawson, expecting him to be at home. They had tried to phone Dawson, but neither he nor anybody else answered.

Eventually, they'd all left the flat, and Martin had wandered a little distance away as the police car drove off. Mabel, with an icy good night, had shut her door behind her to continue watching *EastEnders*. Martin still had not got hold of the packaging and he realised that what had at first seemed an easy, if weird, favour for a friend, had now taken an altogether more sinister turn. Dawson was in Australia. And Dawson had been burgled. Both of those facts needed more investigation. And he was pretty sure that the investigation needed to start with the packaging. So he hopped back over the gate with no difficulty whatsoever, found the correct recycling bin at the first attempt, retrieved the box, brown paper and bubble wrap, and took it home as quickly as he could.

Without much expectation of getting a reply, he tried Dawson again, but the ringing tone went on and on until finishing with a female voice only fractionally less icy than Mabel's declaring, 'The person you have called is not obtainable'.

Martin decided there was something fishier than a school of salmon going on, and he needed to find out exactly what.

_ In which Dawson has a late lunch,
   and goes for an unexpected ride

In the end, Dawson had delayed leaving Sydney until Tuesday morning, suffering from what he could only suppose was jet lag. He stopped at Gundagai and after a lengthy lunch, repaired to an armchair in the lounge to do some more thinking and soon found his head nodding again. When he woke up, it was actually getting on for dusk but, refreshed by the sleep, he decided to push on into the evening to Yackandandah, which was only about another two hours up the road.

He was concentrating on trying to remember where he'd left his hire car when two large men, one black, one a rather disconcerting shade of red, appeared out of a shadowy doorway and grabbed him by the arms. The car they pushed him into was not his and, unlike that one, it didn't lack for acceleration.

Dawson found himself pinned firmly in the middle of the back seat, both by the violent take-off and by the red man and the black man, neither of whom spoke. Dawson himself was too confused and scared to say anything for at least half a minute.

Finally, he croaked, 'I didn't order a taxi, guys', but silence came the stern reply and then suddenly that silence was broken by the sound of a phone ringing. Dawson momentarily wondered whose phone it was before a slight vibration in his breast pocket showed it to be his own. Red man, on his left, reached over and plucked the phone out of Dawson's shirt and pocketed it. It carried on ringing for a few more seconds before stopping.

Dawson decided that cowardice was the better part of anything that might be construed as valour and hunched back down to make himself as comfortable as possible. He didn't quite know what to think. Here he was, an ordinary bloke, suddenly pitched into the Australian outback for no yet apparent reason. He was aware that a number of things didn't quite add up but he hadn't had the slightest prior expectation of being kidnapped by two unfriendly men and driven off in silence to who knew what fate. He was sort of hoping that it might all turn out to be a joke, although try as he might, and he was, he couldn't quite see the funny side. Perhaps he'd be met at some cosy hotel by Alan Flannery, who'd roar with laughter and the four of them would drink whisky and carouse until the early hours, with red man and black man swearing undying fealty to Dawson for as long as they all should live.

As long as they all should live, at this exact moment, seemed likely to be a lot longer for his two giant bodyguards than it did for Dawson himself.

_ In which Dawson meets a tall man,
   and makes reacquaintance with
   someone unlikely

After about ten minutes, the noise of the car engine stopped beating quite so forcefully into Dawson's brain. He wasn't sure if the driver, a shadowy, equally silent presence up front, had ever heard of fourth or fifth gear, so it was a blessed relief when they slowed down. Relief was replaced by fear as they turned sharp right, bumped briefly along what could have been a dried up river bed but was more probably just a badly maintained drive, and pulled up outside a large, dark house.

The driver pressed twice on the horn and the door of the house swung inwards to reveal a tall, thin, bald man of indeterminate age, lit from behind. The man nodded towards the car, turned on his heel and walked back inside. The red man opened the door and heaved himself out of the vehicle. Dawson received an ungentle shove in the back and stumbled out after him. On straightening up, he found that he was still being squeezed by his two hefty, untalkative companions and was forced to hobble through the front door into an entrance hall illuminated by a single overhead lamp. Hearing a sound from behind, Dawson turned his head and glimpsed another man, whom he took to be the driver, shut the front door from the outside. Something about him seemed oddly familiar, but it was too dark to be sure, and in any case Dawson had more important things to worry about, namely red man and black man who were busy pressing him towards a door in the corner.

The room they all entered was surprisingly spacious and even more surprisingly well-appointed, with soft-focus lighting, tasteful wallpaper, some very expensive-looking Australian-themed pictures on the walls, two deep sofas on either side and in front of him a large, black leather swivel chair inadequately filled by the cadaverous-looking man who had appeared at the front door on their arrival.

On the inside, Dawson was scared, of course he was, but on the outside, he was as incapable as he had ever been of taking things seriously. It was just the way he was. It wasn't bravado; if anything it was nervousness. He'd always had the need to try to make people like him, and that need somehow seemed quite important now.

'Thanks for bringing me to the hotel, guys,' he started with a faint smile. 'But I'd decided not to stay around here, so if you could just take me back to my car...' His voice trailed off. Red man and black man, now standing a merciful step or two behind him, continued to say nothing. The thin man sitting in front of him was wearing heavily ironed beige trousers and a crisp, white, long-sleeved shirt, although Dawson was unsure why the man's sartorial splendour seemed so noteworthy when there were clearly other things he should be more concerned about.

The thin man spoke in a low, pleasant voice, or at least in as pleasant a voice as an Australian voice can be, particularly when it is directed at a rather frightened Englishman a long way from home. 'I don't think you quite appreciate the gravity of your situation, sir.'

'Yeah, gravity,' grunted red man from behind him.

'Don't mind Rambo,' said the thin man. 'He's a bit of a bogan. Thinking's not his strong point.'

'Rambo?' asked Dawson. 'Seriously? And what is his strong point?'

'He's strong, that's his strong point. We call him Rambo because it suits him better than Sebastian. Also, he can't pronounce Sebastian.'

Red man grunted again. 'Rambo.'

'Okay,' said Dawson. 'So now we're introducing ourselves, I don't think I'm who you think I am.'

'Oh, I rather think that you are who I think you are, Mr

Dawson.'

Dawson worked that sentence backwards to its start and found himself coming to the inescapable conclusion that no mistake had been made. At least not by thin man, red man and black man. Definitely by Dawson and almost certainly by Alan Flannery though. Still, he kept trying – he didn't really have many other options. 'I was rather hoping you wouldn't say that,' he said. 'Perhaps you could at least let me know who I have the honour of being kidnapped by?'

'Kidnapped?' smiled the thin man. 'Oh, no, not kidnapped. That would somehow imply we wanted something in exchange for your safe return.'

Dawson didn't like the sound of that. He now felt very scared, very tired and, oddly, quite hungry again. 'So you don't want anything?'

'Oh, I'm sorry. You may have misunderstood me. Of course I want something, and you are definitely going to give it to me. It's the safe return bit that isn't finalised yet.'

Dawson felt his knees starting to sag. 'Can I sit down?' he asked, more in hope than expectation.

'Of course you can, where are my manners?' The thin man waved an immaculate hand towards the sofa to Dawson's left.

Dawson sat down gratefully, but the gratitude fell a long way short of the scaredness. 'You were about to tell me who you are.'

'I wasn't, as it happens but, once again, rudeness isn't really my thing.' He smiled. 'You can call me Mr Big.'

Dawson looked at him for a few seconds. This man was a joker. You couldn't be a joker and a cold-blooded killer too, could you? Could you? 'Oh, come off it. You're kidding me. What is this, some sort of trashy spy novel?'

'You tell me.'

'I am telling you. No, it's not. What's your first name? I'm not calling you Mr Big.'

'Really.'

'You're telling me that your name's Really Big? Did your mum have a sense of humour? All right then,' pointing at black man, 'what's his name? Go on, surprise me.'

'You can call him Chuckles,' said Mr Big, leaning back in his black leather chair. The smile suddenly disappeared. 'And I don't care what you call me as long as you stop fucking me about and tell me where it is.'

'This is ridiculous,' said Dawson, who was beginning to find his anger overtaking his fright, which quite surprised him. 'I don't know what you're talking about.'

At that moment, Dawson's phone started ringing again from inside Rambo's side pocket. Everyone in the room jumped slightly at the ringtone, even Mr Big, and Rambo himself looked confused, apparently unable to work out where the noise was coming from. However, before anyone could say anything, all the lights went out and the room was plunged into darkness. Then there was a small creak and Dawson found himself being pulled up the back of the sofa.

Dawson hadn't the faintest idea what was happening, but he didn't like it, although he also realised that leaving the company of Mr Big, Rambo and Chuckles could have long-term beneficial consequences. He imagined that this was what an out-of-body experience would feel like as he was transported apparently without any effort through a door behind the sofa that he hadn't noticed before. In fact, the darkness was so complete that he was only aware that it was a door he was being carried through when he heard it shut softly behind him and the sounds of confusion from Rambo and Chuckles became suddenly muffled. Just as the door closed, a shot rang out. Dawson had never heard a gun fired outside a television or cinema screen but it was fairly unmistakeable. However, it didn't seem to come anywhere near the door he'd been lifted through, and it wasn't followed by a second shot as the thin man yelled, 'Don't fire, you galahs, you'll hit each other! Or, worse, me! Get outside and block the exits. Get that bloody driver to help you. Now! Go!'

'Yeah, well, good luck with finding the driver,' murmured a soft voice in Dawson's ear. Dawson was abruptly certain that he knew that voice and it forced him to turn his attention to where he'd arrived rather than where he'd come from. His eyes were starting to get used to the darkness by now and he could just make out the faint outline of the person he was with and who had at least put Dawson back on his feet. It was quite a large outline, and now Dawson was catching a faint whiff of something that also seemed oddly familiar.

It couldn't be, could it? Both the voice and the smell of nasty hair gel were saying the same thing to him: Prat-the-Solicitor they were saying, but that was impossible.

'Pat?' Dawson remembered to keep his voice to a whisper and, crucially, bearing in mind he was addressing his saviour, not to call him "Prat".

'Yes, shut up. Let me think. We need to get out of here sharpish before Chuckles and Co manage to work out where we are.' Dawson heard a window open and then Pat whispered, 'Okay, follow me, mind the sill, I'm not carrying you again, you're heavier than you look.'

Outside, it was marginally lighter than inside, and after managing to extricate himself from a small bush into which he'd fallen, Dawson made out the sizeable shape of Pat. There was a line of thin trees a dozen metres away and Pat scuttled towards them, motioning Dawson to follow. They reached them just as the lights in the house went back on again, together with what was clearly a security light over the front door to their right. Pat bent even lower and edged further back into the tree line, and Dawson followed suit, although it was clear they were not very well shielded from sight should anyone be looking their way. However, nobody was, although Rambo and Chuckles had by now started communicating in what sounded like a series of grunts from their stations outside the front and rear doors. They could see Chuckles at the front, but he was fidgety and kept wandering around, in and out of eyeshot.

Dawson realised that asking Pat for an explanation as to his sudden, totally unexpected appearance in this dangerous backwater of New South Wales could probably wait until they had reached some sort of safety. How that safety was going to be achieved was a whole other ball game. The big Mercedes that he had been brought in was still sitting in the drive but Dawson couldn't see how they were going to reach it without being seen, and even if they did, how they were going to drive off without a key. That did seem to be Pat's plan though, and suddenly Dawson had a revelation. Pat must have been the driver. There was no one else to be seen, and hadn't the man who'd shut the front door earlier seemed familiar? Apparently reading his thoughts, Pat turned to him, held up an unmistakeable set of car keys, pointed at the Merc and, rather melodramatically, put his finger to his lips. Pat seemed to be waiting for something and then, completely unexpectedly, if not to Pat, then definitely to Dawson and even more so to Chuckles and Rambo, there was a loud crash from the far side of the building. Chuckles started at the noise and broke into a run out of sight round the side of the house, obviously keen to investigate, not least because of Mr Big's immediate shout of 'What the fuck was that?' Chuckles had clearly decided it was his job to find out what the fuck it was.

Dawson suddenly realised he was alone and a momentary panic set in before he saw Pat, crouching low and sprinting as quickly as his not inconsiderable bulk allowed towards the car. Dawson hurtled after him, somewhat more quickly, so that they reached the vehicle at the same time. Pat wrenched open the driver's door and had already got the car moving as Dawson piled in on the other side. Pat gunned the car in reverse down the rutted drive, undertook a niftily impressive handbrake turn, and they were on the road before the first shots rang out.

Pat had turned the Mercedes to the right on the road, away

from Gundagai and civilisation, but at least they were clear and out of immediate danger. Dawson imagined there would be a second car somewhere around and it would only be a matter of time before they were followed, but Pat was keeping up a steady 120 kph and no headlights appeared on the road behind, so after a few minutes Dawson began to relax.

Before he could open his mouth Pat said, without turning his head, 'Not just now,' and as he was concentrating on breaking the speed limit and his tone of voice brooked no argument, Dawson remained silent. Twenty minutes later, the car turned right on to another main road. Dawson glimpsed a sign, which indicated they were now headed towards Wagga Wagga. He'd heard of Wagga Wagga, and somehow that comforted him a bit. Not much else did. He stayed quiet, immersed in his own muddled thoughts, as the big car roared on into the night.

Fuck, fuck, fuck, fuck, fuck! I really didn't think Napoleon had thought this through. 'Don't let him out of your sight,' he'd said. 'Do not, under any circumstances, let him see you,' he'd said. Do five impossible things before breakfast, he might just as well have said.

Australia is a very, very big place and Saul Dawson took up an infinitesimal portion of it. It was currently not a portion I was looking at. I'd lost him. It wasn't my fault though. I'd been doing really well up to about an hour ago, at which point my cheap, hired Holden had quietly expired by the side of a long straight road in the middle of nowhere.

Okay, I knew where he was headed, Yackandandah, so once the breakdown truck from the garage actually arrived, and assuming the Holden could be fixed, then I could probably catch up with him. I had no idea when that would be. The garage was apparently a very long way away indeed, but then let's face it, everywhere is a very long way away from everywhere else in New South Wales, not that I wished to be rude about Australia or Australians; after all, the lady at the garage had been very helpful, albeit not about the estimated, let alone actual, time of arrival. I had no alternative but to keep on waiting, getting hotter and hotter and more and more pissed off as the minutes ticked towards the hour mark.

I had Napoleon's number on my phone but I'd been reluctant to use it in case my lack of resourcefulness came up again for one-sided discussion. Eventually, I'd bitten the bullet and called him. He hadn't answered. That was forty minutes ago, so it looked like I was on my own. I'd have given my right arm for cheerful, totally resourceful Laurie to turn up out of the blue, but I had no way of contacting him.

After a further twenty minutes, I'd seen lights and heard a deep-throated rumble from the east, which very quickly showed itself to be the breakdown truck, a battered vehicle that had already seen better days at the millennium. It ground to a halt in a puff of diesel, the window was wound down, and Laurie stuck his head out and grinned at me. The bloody man was a mind reader as well as everything else.

'Wotcha, missy,' said Laurie. 'Not your day, is it? Hop in. Leave that pile of junk. You're wanted.'

__ In which Rachel Whyte mislays a
fiance, and discovers things are
not as they seem

Rachel Whyte was feeling a little uneasy and, frankly, furious at the same time – two varying emotions she was having trouble dealing with.

She had lost Pat. She realised that, on the surface, this seemed to be a hard thing to have done; Pat was, after all, quite a big unit. But he wasn't answering his phone, he wasn't at home and when she phoned his work number, something she'd never had cause to do before, there was no reply. So she'd driven to the offices of Franklin, Boasman & Bootle (Pat was Bootle) in Croydon to find out in person. When she got to the address on the card Pat had given her three months ago, there was the office, up a flight of communal stairs, and there was the shiny brass plaque next to the door saying "Franklin, Boasman & Bootle, Solicitors and Commissioners for Oaths". But the door was locked, there was no bell to ring and, when she knocked on the door, reply came there none.

She hadn't seen her boyfriend, or "fiance" (the term made her scowl), since the proposal dinner a week ago, and she hadn't managed to speak to him since then either. She'd thought at first he'd been avoiding her because of the embarrassing absence of an engagement ring, or even that he'd been spending the time buying one. Then she'd thought something must have happened to him and he was in hospital, but short of ringing every hospital in Surrey, London and Kent, she wasn't actually sure how she'd find out. And because Pat was, he'd told her, an orphan and an only child, there were no relatives of his that she could try either. She phoned her mum, what with her and Pat being as thick as thieves, but even she hadn't been able to cast any light on the problem. 'He'll turn up, love, I'm sure,' was all she'd said, showing a degree of confidence that Rachel felt unable to share.

She was sitting at home pondering all this and what she should do next, when there was a knock at her door. She opened it to see a slightly built, pretty, blonde girl standing there smiling at her in an unsure sort of way. Rachel had the feeling she'd seen the girl before but couldn't bring to mind where.

'Hi,' said the blonde girl. 'Rachel Whyte?'

'That's right,' said Rachel. 'Do I know you?'

'My name's Lucy,' said Lucy.

'Have we met?' Rachel didn't feel the conversation was going anywhere very fast but had a feeling that it might be worthwhile carrying on with it anyway.

'Well, yes, after a fashion. But we weren't really introduced properly. Or at all in fact. I was at your *Ali Baba* party for a little while.'

'Were you? Why?'

'I was with Saul. Well, sort of, and then I had to go.'

'You were, weren't you. I remember now. What can I do for you?'

'Have you lost something recently?'

Rachel was unimpressed with the question. 'What do you mean?'

'I'm sorry,' said Lucy. 'This isn't going very well. Can I come in?'

'I don't know. What's this all about?'

'It's about Patrick Bootle. Now may I come in?'

'I think you'd better,' she said and stood aside to let the smaller woman pass her into her smart but tiny new-build house, bought last year with help from Bank of Mum and Dad. Well, Bank of Dad in actual fact; her mother had never held down what could be called, with any degree of accuracy, a proper job.

Rachel was a polite girl who could normally be relied upon to offer guests, even unexpected and possibly unwelcome ones, a cup of tea or something stronger. Or at the very least a seat. Not this time.

'Okay lady, where's my boyfriend? And who the hell are you?'

'I don't know where he is, that's the point. I'd hoped you might, but then we heard you'd been looking for him too, so we thought it best if I came round here and sort of, er, pooled resources?' There was an upward inflection at the end of the sentence, which Rachel noted. She suddenly felt very tired and sat heavily down on the sofa behind her. Without being invited, Lucy took the armchair opposite.

Rachel looked across. 'My fiance has disappeared, his law firm is not answering its phone and now a complete stranger, who may or may not be a friend of my friend, Dawson, bangs on my door in the middle of the night –'

'It's only 8 o'clock,' interjected Lucy.

'– in the middle of the evening then, and seems to know a hell of a lot more than I do about it. I repeat, who are you – and who's "we" while we're about it? Are you police?'

'No, not police.'

'What then?'

'That's kind of hard to explain.'

'Try.' Rachel was getting increasingly angry, and her face was going almost as red as her hair.

'We're a sort of security agency, national security that is.'

'What? MI6? Are you telling me that you're a spy?' Rachel looked Lucy up and down. 'You're not a spy; you can't convince me you are. Do you have a badge? Any ID?'

'I know you've got a lot of questions, and I'll try to answer them,' said Lucy. 'Not MI6, no, not quite. Be nice if we were, we might get the resources to cope with something like this. And I don't have a badge or ID as such, just this.' And she fished a small cream and blue card out of her jeans pocket with Aardvark Amalgamations written above her name, Lucy Smith, and a phone number.

Rachel hardly glanced at the card before placing it on the sofa beside her.

'Okay,' she said. 'I'm listening. Start with Pat. Where is he and why are you looking for him? Is he in danger? And you've got five minutes before I call the police.'

Lucy was not certain how to start but picked up on something Rachel had just said. 'You mentioned he's your fiance. Is that right?'

Rachel seemed to deflate a bit. 'I don't know. I thought so. He asked me, I said yes, but there's no bloody ring a week down the line and now he's done a runner. I may only have said yes anyway because mum and dad were there.' Why was she telling this annoyingly pretty quasi-spy that? She didn't know, but she needed to tell someone and so far, her available options were not encouraging. And despite herself, she found she was warming to her visitor, who looked very small, very tired and maybe a little out of her depth.

'Can I ask how long you've known him?' enquired Lucy.

'I suppose that's the other thing. Not long really, months only, September, October time perhaps.'

'Aren't you sure? It doesn't sound like love's young dream. I'm sorry, I shouldn't have said that. How did you meet?'

'Is this relevant?' Rachel snapped, but she knew somehow that it really was. She thought. 'It was a pub, Epsom, a work thing, all the Surrey shops were there, you know, a social evening. Darts and pool, that sort of thing. Pat just showed up. I was getting the drinks in and he was standing next to me and offered to help carry them back to my table. We got talking. He was nice. Friendly. Interested in me. Not many people are.'

'What about Saul?'

'He doesn't count.'

'That's harsh, isn't it?'

Rachel pondered the question. 'You're right, it is, but there's a fine line between being interested and stalking, and in any case I'd only just met Dawson again after a couple of years.'

'You may hit me for saying this, but are you sure it hasn't been Pat doing the stalking? What do you actually know about him?'

'I'm guessing you're going to tell me that it's not a lot.'

But it was true. No parents, no siblings, no backstory to speak of, and then there had been the incessant questions, almost from day one. She'd met him, liked him, been made to feel wanted and secure by him, and things had developed in the sort of way she'd always imagined they would when Mr Right showed himself. He hadn't been arsey and funny like Dawson, but he'd taken her to good restaurants and even better hotels, had whisked her to Paris unexpectedly for New Year and done a dozen other things that most women generally appreciate. Dawson hadn't. Dawson in fact couldn't, not while he was jobless at any rate, but he'd never suggested he would even if he could. But Dawson made her laugh. She couldn't remember if Pat had ever made her laugh, not even unintentionally. She dragged herself back to the present.

'We know there's more to him than meets the eye,' Lucy was saying. 'And we know that Franklin, Boasman & Bootle is a front. I mean, yes, it's registered with the Law Society, although only recently, and I have to say there's a separate investigation going on to find out how that came about because Franklin and Boasman certainly don't exist. Who they really are, who Pat Bootle really is – if indeed that's his name – well, we just don't know. I'm afraid we're pretty certain they're not on the side of the angels.' She paused for breath.

'So, he's been stringing me along,' said Rachel. It still seemed highly unlikely, bordering on the impossible, but she found she wasn't quite as upset as she ought to have been. In fact, despite herself, she was beginning to feel a growing sense of excitement. 'Why? Why me?'

'We don't know yet. There's a link somewhere, but we don't know what it is. There are some items that we're looking for and it seems likely that Pat Bootle...' She stopped suddenly.

'I'm sorry, I shouldn't have said that. I just needed to talk to you, to be sure you weren't tied up in anything you shouldn't be, but...' Rachel suddenly stood up and towered over her.

'Don't stop there,' said Rachel, turning and picking up the business card from the sofa, 'Lucy Smith of Aardvark Amalgamations, whoever the fuck they are. I am tied up in this, so I need to know more than you're telling me and I'm not letting you out of here until you open up a bit. If you are some sort of spy, you're probably trained in kung fu or judo or something, but I pack a mean punch when I'm angry and I'm pretty angry now. Strangely, not with you though.'

'Don't worry, I wouldn't be a match for you, I'm not even trained in origami. I'm afraid I can't tell you any more, but I know someone who can. Whether he will is another matter entirely but look, you're a victim here. We've been watching you, and it's pretty clear you don't know where he is.'

'So, let me get this straight,' said Rachel, sitting back down again. 'You're some sort of government department, agency, spy outfit, whatever, don't bother trying to explain because I know you won't, or can't. You've been keeping tabs on Pat, and on me, for God knows how long, and now he's disappeared and you've lost him. Not very good at your job, are you?'

'You may be right, but it's more a question of manpower. And the government? They don't really know we exist, not directly, but the cuts in funding still reach us.'

'So, what now? You want to find Pat and by Christ, I want to find Pat. You'd better hope you find him first, because if it's me I'll kill the bastard.'

Lucy seemed to come to a decision, although Rachel suspected that it was probably not a decision she was entitled to come to. 'Are you offering to help?' Lucy asked.

'I rather think I am. I've certainly got a reason to.'

'In which case, there's a man I'd like you to meet.'

_____ In which Dawson gets a lesson in
received pronunciation, and Pat
rugby-tackles a foreign woman

Even at the hectic pace Pat was pursuing, it was another thirty minutes before the Mercedes entered the outskirts of Wagga Wagga, which turned out to be a much bigger place than Dawson had expected. There were a number of back streets disappearing into the dark on either side of the car and after a little while Pat turned down one of them, and then executed a number of further tight manoeuvres designed, Dawson supposed, to throw off any chasing Rambos or Chuckleses, before bringing the vehicle to a stop and extinguishing the lights and engine. He turned to Dawson. 'Now we'd better talk.'

'Here?' said Dawson. 'We're in Wagga Wagga, can't we find a pub or somewhere else a bit more comfortable? Possibly with an alcoholic drink within touching distance.'

'No, we can't. And it's pronounced Wogga Wogga.'

'They do well to keep that out of the guide books.'

Just then there was a knock on the driver's window, which made them both jump. Dawson, in particular, had had so many impossible things happen to him recently that he was beginning to feel he was in training for the Olympic high jump team. Even Pat looked momentarily disconcerted for the first time that evening but he wound the window down anyway. A handsome, middle-aged woman stood there, her face just discernible in the near-darkness.

'Can I help you?' asked Pat.

'I was about to ask you the same question,' replied the woman in a strange, lilty accent that Dawson couldn't place. Eastern European, possibly? Scandinavian? Not Aussie, anyway. 'Have you broken down, perhaps? Or are you doggers? It would not be the first time. I have had to call the police on many occasions.' Wow, thought Dawson. They have doggers in

Australia? He'd thought it was just a Home Counties thing, where frankly there wasn't much else to do of a midweek evening sometimes. The question seemed to throw Pat, who had obviously not heard the term before.

'What are you talking about? Can you see a dog?'

There was something odd about the woman, Dawson thought. Where had she come from? There were no houses around; they seemed to be in some sort of industrial park.

'Okay, let us forget that,' said the woman. Definitely Scandinavian, Norwegian perhaps. A long way from home, but then she wasn't the only one. 'I think you had better be coming with me.'

'We're quite all right. We don't need any help.'

'Oh, but I do need help. In fact, I think you can help me a lot,' said the woman, and suddenly there was a gun in her hand. Dawson was pleased that his instincts about her oddness had proved accurate but was less pleased about the gun.

'You're a bit less efficient at this escaping from the jaws of death thing than I thought, Pat,' remarked Dawson, who was by now resigned to whatever horrors were heading his way.

'You will please to shut up,' said the woman. 'Get out of the car. You are both coming with me.'

What with the appearance of the firearm, together with his latent cowardliness, Dawson was only too happy to comply with this instruction, but apparently Pat was determined to be a little more obstinate.

'Listen, lady,' he said. 'I don't know who you think you are, or who you think we are, but I've called the police, so I suggest you pack up your little pop gun and scarper smartish.'

'Ah, you English, you are so, so funny,' said the woman, not noticeably laughing. 'You have not called the police.'

'How do you know?'

'Why would you have called the police? You are a criminal. You do not want the law to appear any more than I do. Now do as I say and get out of the car.' She added, to Dawson's mind slightly unnecessarily, 'Or I will shoot you.'

Dawson got out of the passenger seat and moved around the front of the car. He was essentially quite cowardly, or at least he had always assumed he was, but then he had never before been in the sort of position he now found himself for the second time that evening. But then, as Pat opened the driver's door and started to heave himself out of the car, Dawson saw, almost subconsciously, that the woman's focus was concentrated on the elephantine figure of his companion. Equally subconsciously, he registered the darkness of the road they were in and suddenly he found himself sprinting off and half running, half leaping through some low shrubbery by the side of the road. The woman seemed to be caught unawares by this unexpected turn of events and it took her a second or two to turn and fire three quick shots in Dawson's general direction as he disappeared into what turned out to be an empty car park attached to a light industrial unit. Luckily, the direction of the shots was much more general than exact and none of them came close to hitting him. Dawson had never been hit by a bullet but he felt sure he'd know if it ever happened.

Pat was also surprised, which made three people out of three, but he was aware enough of the general sequence of events to allow him to launch his full seventeen stone at the woman in a rough facsimile of a rugby tackle. Rough or not, it had the desired effect and both of them went down in a heap, with the woman underneath. The gun went off again as the two of them landed, but the shot thwumped harmlessly into the side of the car.

Dawson heard the thwump, and also the similar but louder and thwumpier noise of the collision and landing. Then there was silence.

_ In which Lucy, Rachel and Alan
    sit in a car together, and
    Rachel drinks a cup of coffee

Lucy and Rachel got into the back seat of Alan Flannery's car. Flannery spoke without turning around. 'You seem to have started taking decisions a few notches above your pay grade, young lady.'

Rachel started. It was a dark evening and in the gloom she hadn't recognised the man in the driver's seat, but now she did. 'What the hell? You're Alan, aren't you? Dawson's drinking buddy? Alan – what's your name – Funnell, Fellows? What the fuck are you doing here?' She turned to Lucy with a questioning look, but Lucy just shrugged.

'It's a small world,' said Alan. 'It really, really is.' He turned and glared at Lucy through the half-light. 'I'll deal with you later, Miss Smith.' To Rachel he said, 'I imagine my colleague has told you that we are looking for Patrick Bootle and we thought, as he's your boyfriend, you might be able to help. God knows what else she's told you but I'm guessing she's said more than she should have. Yes, I'm Alan Flannery – not Fellows or Funnell – and yes, as you say, we share a mutual friendship with Dawson.'

'Flannery?' said Lucy. 'I never knew that. I thought you were Joyce.'

'It appears to be an evening of revelations all round. Anyway, we're straying from the point. I imagine you think that Miss Whyte can help us look for Bootle.'

'She volunteered really. I think she's as keen to find him as we are. More so.'

'Tell me who you people are,' said Rachel, 'and yes, I'll do what I can. I thought I was getting married to him, but that seems a bit unlikely now, doesn't it?'

'It's a free world,' said Alan. 'You might have to spend your marriage visiting him in prison but it's your choice. As to who we are, if you're willing to sign the Official Secrets Act I can tell you. Otherwise,' and he smiled mirthlessly, 'I'll have to kill you.' He paused. Both Rachel and Lucy sighed. 'That was a joke, by the way. We're not noted for our sense of humour.'

'You don't say,' said Rachel. 'But show me the form and I'll sign before you can say "lying bastard". Especially if you guys are licensed to kill.'

'Not really, no, we're more the desk jockeys of the intelligence community. In fact, if we get much more active, several large men in dark suits and sunglasses are likely to barge us out of the way. But for the time being at least, it's our monkey. Anyway, it's late.' He looked at his watch. 'Well, lateish, and young Lucy's just got off a plane from Australia so I'm assuming it's the jetlag that persuaded her to tell you too much. Go home, go to bed, and I'll pick you up at 9 o'clock tomorrow morning.'

'What do I tell the office?'

'Entirely up to you. Be resourceful.'

'He's very big on resourcefulness,' murmured Lucy. 'I'll see you in the morning, Rachel. And I'm sorry.'

'Don't be. I'm not.' A thought struck her, something that Alan had just said. 'Have you really just got back from Australia?'

'Yes,' said Lucy with a small smile. 'Beginning to join up the dots, aren't you?'

'Sweet Jesus,' said Rachel. 'Dawson's in Australia, and you sent him there. If you're telling me he's a spy too...' she trailed off, lost for words.

'And on that hilarious note, I'll say goodnight,' grunted Alan as he reached across and opened Rachel's door.

Rachel got out of the car and wandered back to her house. She genuinely didn't know what to think but she doubted if she'd get much sleep that night. She sat down on the sofa and glanced up at the clock. It was still not yet ten. She got up again and went to put the kettle on. A couple of mugs of strong coffee seemed like a good idea. Whisky had its attractions too, but she didn't have any and tomorrow seemed likely to be a busy day, and what wits she still possessed she'd probably have need of.

Hugging her first coffee, she pondered what she did and didn't know. If Alan Flannery and Lucy Smith were to be believed, then her so-called fiance was mixed up in something that would make even her mother think twice about offering him home-made fairy cakes ever again. Meanwhile, Dawson may or may not be a spy. An hour ago she'd thought that Lucy was the unlikeliest spy she'd ever met, but Dawson, an intelligence officer? That put a whole new meaning to the word "intelligence".

___ In which Chuckles and Rambo
decide not to shoot each other,
and Mr Big makes a telephone call

There had been a bit of a kerfuffle going on at the house outside Gundagai. Rambo was standing around, grunting incoherently and wondering what he could shoot at. He nearly shot at Chuckles as they appeared simultaneously around opposite sides of the house. Chuckles was yelling something about the car and someone he referred to as "Mutt". Only Mr Big remained calm and unflustered. He was sitting in his black swivel chair and talking quietly on the phone to someone.

After a couple of minutes, he put the phone down, stood up unhurriedly and walked out of the house. He was met at the front door by Rambo and Chuckles, the former continuing to make random grunting noises, the latter waving his arms around and still shouting about the car and Mutt.

'Be quiet, both of you,' said Mr Big. 'Go and get the other car.'

'But Mutt...' complained Chuckles. 'He's taken the Pom with him.'

'Yes,' agreed Mr Big. 'It would appear so. It seems he may not be on our side after all, a bit of a surprise I'll admit, after two years. I guess I shouldn't have sent him to England. Anyway, never mind, we'll be able to ask him in person soon. Now go and get the Range Rover.'

They did as they were told. Rambo, in particular, always did as he was told, as bitter experience had taught him on many occasions that going out on a limb without instruction was liable to end badly. Chuckles had slightly more ambition, but enjoyed the more violent aspects of his job so much that he wasn't interested in promotion up the food chain. No, he was more than happy to take orders from the tall, bald man who'd picked him up three years ago as he'd stepped out of the prison gates after five years inside.

They were back with the Range Rover within ten minutes, Chuckles driving. Rambo had never got the hang of the automatic gearbox. And he'd never passed his driving test. The boss was quite keen that they shouldn't break such a small law. They had enough to do with breaking big ones.

'Hey, boss,' said Chuckles. 'Where we going?'

'To meet my wife. I think she may have something for us. She's in Wagga Wagga, so let's be off.'

It took them less than an hour to reach Wagga Wagga and the house in Tolland that Mr Big liked to call home, although it had been someone else's home before he'd taken a liking to it. The house was in darkness, which seemed to surprise him. He nodded at Rambo. 'Check it out, Elsa should be here.' Rambo got out of the car, cradling his gun, and Mr Big punched a single digit on his phone and waited for a dialling tone that never came.

This was decidedly odd as he'd spoken to Elsa, his wife, from the house outside Gundagai and, by means of the tracking device clipped to the inside of the boot of the Mercedes, had been able to tell her exactly where Mutt and Dawson were headed. Coincidentally, it turned out to be Wagga Wagga. Like flies into a web, he'd thought. By now Elsa should have rounded up the escapees and brought them back to the house. He checked the tracker again and noted that the Merc was still stationary in the same place only a mile from where they were now. Rambo came back at this point and by a series of grunts and hand gestures managed to convey the information that the house was as empty as it appeared from outside.

There was nothing else for it. 'Rambo,' said Mr Big. 'You stay here and wait. Is your phone switched on?' Rambo grunted in affirmation; after several years, Mr Big was able to accurately translate the grunt 90% of the time. 'I'll let you know if you're needed. And if my wife turns up here, call me.'

'But boss...' said Rambo in a slightly alarmed voice.

'It's the green button. Just prod it and talk when I answer. Jesus Frederick Christ. Couldn't fart in a bottle,' he sighed. His staff recruitment had not always been spot on.

Chuckles got the Range Rover started and, following the beep from the tracker, it took them less than three minutes to arrive at where the Mercedes was. Except that the Mercedes wasn't. However, the beep was of a volume that suggested that their eyes were deceiving them. They got out of the car and looked around in confusion.

'Get a torch,' snarled Mr Big, who was beginning to lose a proportion of his renowned sangfroid. Chuckles returned with a large flashlight, and within seconds they had located the tracking device lying forlornly in the gutter. Mr Big picked it up and looked at it. He called his wife's number again but got the same lack of response, so he tried Rambo who, surprisingly, managed to answer.

'Yeah?' Rambo muttered in the sort of tone that suggested he thought the phone might explode in his hand.

'Anything?' asked Mr Big.

'What?'

'Has Elsa showed up, you moron?'

'No, boss.'

'Okay, we're coming back. Get inside the house and have another look round. A proper look. See you in five.'

'Five what, boss?' asked Rambo, but the line had gone dead.

I was absolutely shattered following the flight back from Australia, so I did as I was told like a good little girlie and went home to bed. I slept too, for about eight hours, but then woke up worried I was in the wrong country. I should still have been in Australia keeping an eye on Saul. Mr Napoleon-bloody-Flannery needed more than one "Lucy Smith" if he required me to be in both England and Australia at the same time. I'm more than confident about my resourcefulness, whatever he might say, but that was a stretch too far even for me.

When I got to the office just before 2 o'clock, it was almost empty. There was nothing unusual in that, Aardvark's manpower levels being lower than a tortoise's belly. Today, only our stalwart fifty-five-year-old Office Manager, Juliet, was there, sitting in her tiny office busy doing whatever it was she did. I didn't like to pry too closely. I actually have a theory that she is a spy sent to spy on the spies, as it were. Conspiracy theories are ten a penny in this game.

Anyway, there was no sign of either Flannery or Rachel, so I girded my loins and approached Juliet. She had a disconcerting habit of peering at people over the top of her glasses.

'Napoleon and Miss Whyte have gone to Croydon. To the offices of Franklin, Boasman & Bootle.' Well, I'm not stupid, I didn't think they'd gone shopping. 'I believe they have a warrant and presumably a small posse of police officers with them.'

'Thanks. Does he want me to join them?'

'I doubt if you have time before your plane leaves,' she replied, and suddenly, as if by magic, there was an air ticket in her hand.

'You're joking,' I said, grabbing the ticket, which clearly had the word Sydney printed on it. 'I've only just got back. Am I the only person working here?'

'One of very few, as you know. The office Christmas parties are always extremely disappointing.' That sounded like a joke, but the thought of flying back to Australia twenty-four hours after landing was not a joke. Meanwhile, Juliet was still talking. 'You'll need this too, I'm afraid,' and she picked up a passport from her desk.

'I've got one of those,' I said.

'Not with this name, Miss, er –' and she opened the passport, '– Morgan.' I took it from her. Apparently, I was now "Greta Morgan". I wondered how long that would last. "Lucy Smith" had managed to make it to about six months. Mind you, my new name had more of a ring to it than my old one, with a touch of foreign glamour thrown in. Well, the Greta was quite glamorous, the Morgan not so much. Scandi-Welsh, I thought, perhaps I could come up with an accent to match.

I looked at the ticket again and saw that I was to be in steerage, as I had been for the flight back yesterday. Yesterday! The days of milk, honey and business class were a fading memory. And, wait a minute, what was this? Gatwick? I really had better get my skates on. 'Do you know what Napoleon wants me to do when I get to Sydney?' I asked Juliet. 'And please don't say "Await further instructions."'

'I do, as a matter of fact, and frankly, Miss Morgan, I'm surprised you have to ask. Not showing much of Napoleon's much-vaunted resourcefulness, are you?' But there was a smile behind the glasses. 'Yackandandah, my dear, get thee to Yackandandah. You never know, you might make the annual folk festival.' I quite like folk festivals, as it happens; in pre-intelligence days I'd been to a few and could erect a two-man tent quicker than I could buy the beers to drink in it, and believe me, that's pretty damn quick. 'Seriously though, Mr Dawson should be there by now but we don't believe he is. You need to try to re-establish contact with him.'

'Actually or visibly?'

'Visibly to start with. Then report back to Napoleon.'

'If he bothers to answer his phone.'

'If he doesn't, I will.'

_ In which Martin Evans decides to take a holiday, and gets on a plane

Martin Evans was a journalist. Thus far in his career, he had had little opportunity to pursue his innate investigative tendencies with the vigour that he would have wished. Indeed, for most of the past five years, he'd spent his time sitting behind a desk with an exasperated expression on his open, good-natured face.

He now had a sniff of a story in his Celtic nostrils that would be more interesting than most of the stuff that the *Stallford Sentinel* usually contained within its less-than-hallowed pages. So far, he wasn't completely sure what to do about the sniff, but he thought that there was probably enough of a Local Person angle to persuade his faceless bosses in London to permit him to take time away from his desk and allow Gary, his recently appointed deputy, to take the undemanding reins for a week or two. In any case, he had holiday owing to him and had nothing booked or planned.

He phoned Head Office and arranged to take an immediate fortnight's leave of absence dependent on his producing a couple of moderately sensational articles on his return. He was able to book a flight from Gatwick for that evening although it did involve two transfers, so he rushed back to his house, threw some clothes into a suitcase and placed the teapot's cardboard box and all its packaging into a back pack.

The facts were these. Dawson had received a parcel and had then gone to Australia. Only later had the packaging suddenly acquired such a level of importance that Dawson had felt the need to phone and instruct him to go and retrieve it from the recycle bin pronto. And then Dawson had disappeared. No subsequent attempt to phone, text or message him had proved successful. Martin reflected that he had about twenty hours flying time in which to examine the packaging in more detail. He hoped that might give him some sort of clue about what to do when he arrived in Sydney. And even if it didn't, he could probably find a surfer on Bondi Beach who'd once worked in a pub in Stallford and whom he could make newsworthy.

Martin was quite pleased to get a window seat although he knew he was likely to make himself slightly unpopular with the occupants of the other two seats in the row, as his bladder wasn't his finest attribute, especially after several beers on a very long flight. For a while, however, he thought he might have struck lucky as the two seats remained unoccupied until virtually all the passengers had boarded. Then, just as he was about to lay claim to the whole row and was starting to look forward to a much better night's sleep than he'd expected, a small, very pretty blonde girl in her mid to late twenties, wearing tight jeans and a dark green hoody, came bounding down the plane and plonked herself down in the aisle seat with a brief smile in his direction. He smiled back but she was already fiddling with her seatbelt and wasn't looking at him.

___ In which Dawson emerges from the
undergrowth, and makes good use
of some jump leads

Dawson peered around the corner of the industrial unit where he was hiding to see if he could make out anything in the gloom across the car park. He couldn't. In fact, he could barely make out the line of bushes he had just scrambled through.

There was dead silence and he realised he couldn't really stay where he was all night. He faced a straight choice between trying to escape or retracing his steps to find out what was happening vis-a-vis Pat and the Scandinavian woman.

There was really no choice to be made. He edged out from behind the building and found himself actually and not metaphorically tiptoeing across the car park before realising how stupid that was and reverting to a normal, if cautious, walk. He reached the shrubbery and peered through it. He could make out the car now, and next to it there was another shape. Quite a large shape, but he couldn't work out what it was until the moon appeared from behind the cloud cover and he saw Pat, lying spread-eagled and motionless across the equally immobile form of the woman. A short distance away lay her gun, so Dawson, gaining a measure of courage, pushed his way through the bushes and picked it up. It was the first gun he had ever handled and he didn't know whether it was still cocked or not. In fact, he didn't actually know what cocked meant, or whether it was an automatic and if it was, what that meant either, so he very gingerly placed it in his pocket, expecting all the time for it to go off and ruin his trousers, or something substantially more important to his life and wellbeing.

Having the gun in his possession gave him a bit more confidence, so he prodded Pat's recumbent form with his foot. Nothing happened so he pushed a bit harder and slowly, like some sort of giant jelly, Rachel's fat solicitor boyfriend slid off the Scandinavian woman and on to his back next to her. It was immediately apparent that Pat was bleeding quite heavily from a wound on his forehead, which would probably account for his unconsciousness, Dawson realised. He turned his attention to the woman, who was flat on her back and had clearly had the wind knocked out of her by seventeen stones of chubby lawyer. Dawson suspected that this currently beneficial state of affairs was unlikely to last for long and so thought it best to tie her up as, awake, she'd shown all the signs of being quite dangerous.

That presented another problem, however, as he had nothing to hand with which to restrain her and even if he had, knots were yet another thing he knew very little about. He doubted that the method he used to tie his shoelaces would prove very effective in securing her when she came to. Dawson was starting to realise how unprepared he was for his new life of skulduggery.

He needed some rope, or at least some useful substitute for rope, and he didn't have time to go rummaging around in the dark in the rubbish bins at the back of the industrial units. Pat was a sizeable bloke and his collision with the woman had obviously been fairly cataclysmic, but even so she was probably not going to be unconscious for many more minutes and he pessimistically thought that even his current possession of her gun, bearing in mind he didn't really know how to use it, would be unlikely to tip the scales in his favour when she woke up.

He looked hurriedly around the inside of the Mercedes, but there was nothing remotely rope-like anywhere to be seen, even in the glove compartment. He found the button that popped the boot and moved round to the back of the car wondering whether there were likely to be any dead bodies in it and, if so, whether there would be room for Prat-the-Solicitor and himself as well. He took a deep breath and opened the lid, but the boot was empty. Wait a minute though, no it wasn't. Nestling in a dark rear corner was a plastic bag, and inside the bag was a set of jump leads.

They were better than nothing, so he scooped them up, ignoring the muffled clunk of something being dislodged and falling on the ground. He hurried back to where the woman was lying still asleep. With a bit of effort, he was able to roll her on to her front and he somehow managed to tie her wrists behind her with one of the jump leads. True, it was a bit too stretchy to make an ideal binding but when he'd finished, he was fairly confident that it would just about hold her for a while, so he repeated the manoeuvre with her feet and the second jump lead and stood up, feeling a little less useless.

At this point, there was a groan from the larger mound that was Pat. Dawson had no idea whether or not Pat was on his side but he was someone who had lately rescued him from the clutches of Really Big and friends and had not, yet, waved a gun in his face, so he at least had some credit in the bank. He found a large, hideous but clean handkerchief in Pat's pocket in a shade of red that would help to hide the blood and held it firmly against the larger man's forehead as he helped him into a sitting position.

'Are you all right?' He realised it was a fatuous question even as Pat's eyes blinked open and settled, glaring, on Dawson's face a few inches from his own.

'Fucking marvellous,' Pat said, slurring a bit. 'What happened?'

'Don't you remember?' The question rather worried Dawson. He hoped Pat hadn't lost his memory, as he'd quite like to ask him who he really was, what he was doing hanging out with villains in Australia and whether or not this meant the engagement to Rachel was off.

'I remember jumping on the hag with the gun. Where is she?'

'She's behind you, but don't worry, she's not going anywhere.

And I wouldn't describe her as a hag. As gun-toting bitches go, she's quite good-looking.'

Pat had discovered that turning his head to look at the woman was not the wisest manoeuvre in his condition. He breathed deeply for a few seconds and dabbed thoughtfully at the wound on his head which, Dawson was pleased to see, looked less serious than it had appeared earlier.

'Can she breathe?' Pat asked.

'Does it matter?' Dawson was beginning to feel that they should be making tracks. Perhaps they could make an anonymous 999 call, or whatever the emergency number was in Australia, before disappearing in the Mercedes.

'Course it matters,' snapped Pat. 'Who is she? Where did she come from? How did she find us?'

'Coincidence?' asked Dawson in a small voice.

'I don't believe in coincidence but you're right all the same, we need to be getting out of here.'

Dawson didn't recall saying that out loud but he was in full agreement nevertheless.

'Help me get her into the car. And where's her gun?'

'Here,' said Dawson, pulling the weapon carefully between finger and thumb from his pocket and handing it over. Pat took hold of it with rather more confidence, then bent down and, without any apparent compunction, hit the woman over the back of the head with it before slipping it casually into his own capacious side pocket.

'Why did you do that? She was already unconscious.'

'Not for much longer. Come on, you take her feet. We'll stick her in the boot.'

'You mean, we're taking her with us?'

'I'm not leaving her here. I need to ask her some questions. She can't have come far, and where she's come from I imagine she'll have some mates wondering where she's got to. I should think they were expecting us back, either dead or nicely trussed up. Properly trussed up too, unlike the attempt you've made with her. I mean, jump leads? What were you trying to do, electrocute her?'

They managed with little difficulty to hoist the woman into the deep boot of the Mercedes. The keys were still in the ignition so Pat got behind the wheel and, hardly waiting for Dawson to slip in beside him, set off up the road. Soon, they were heading west out of Wagga Wagga and passing through a series of fast-asleep little towns. After a while, just as they turned south onto the A39 at Jerilderie, there was a banging from the rear of the car.

'Ah ha,' said Pat, who, judging by the small smile playing about his lips, appeared to have fully recovered his composure. 'We've got company. Time to find a place to talk, I think.'

This was to be an even longer flight than the two I'd been on already, involving stopovers in Schiphol and Singapore. I'd already watched most of the films on offer but I'd picked up a book at random at Gatwick, so having taken off from Amsterdam after the short hop from England, I settled down to read. I wasn't tired and didn't feel there was much point putting my frazzled grey matter through hoops trying to work out what to do when I got to Yackandandah. Dawson would either be there or not. If he was, I couldn't believe that a resourceful lass like me would have much difficulty tracking him down. There were unlikely to be many places he could stay and he'd stand out like a sore thumb amongst all those leather brown sheep farmers and possums. And if he wasn't? Well, if there were any bridges in Yackandandah, I'd cross them when I arrived.

The book was of course rubbish, with an uninspiring lead protagonist, shaky support characters and the skinniest of plots. Publishers seem to churn out any old tat as holiday reading these days and this one hadn't even been written by a celebrity. However, with nothing much else to do, I decided to grit my teeth and plough on with it, terrible or not.

But if it wasn't hard enough to concentrate anyway, the man sitting in the window seat to my left was doing his best to make it harder. Like me, he wasn't asleep, but was drinking lots of beer and consequently having to visit the toilet pretty much every forty minutes. He was very polite about it but it was nevertheless incredibly irritating. 'Stop drinking fucking beer,' I thought, but didn't say.

Maybe he was reading my mind, because somewhere over the Middle East he leant across and whispered, 'I'm really sorry. Me getting up and down all the time. Must be incredibly irritating for you. I have to drink the beer for my nerves, you see, and that has a knock-on effect, as you've noticed.'

He had a pleasant Welsh lilt. Perhaps I could get some tips if I was going to try out my Scandi-Welsh accent in Australia. 'Don't worry,' I said, because I'm nice. 'I'm not too keen on flying myself, and I'm having to do far too much of it this week.'

'Oh, it's not the flying. More the crashing I'm worried about. Look, do you want to swap seats? Then I won't be disturbing you.'

'Thanks,' I said. 'I'll take you up on that.'

'I'm Martin, by the way.'

'Lucy,' I replied, without thinking. 'Oh, I mean, er, Greta, sorry.'

'Don't you know your name?'

'It's Greta,' I said, trying to inject a note of certainty into my voice. 'I was thinking of something else. Pleased to meet you.' So much for my resourcefulness, I thought as we changed seats. I returned to my book, which attempted to be some sort of spoof spy novel, complete with hapless hero, conflicting love interests and a selection of comic-book bad guys. Losing enthusiasm, I sized my fellow traveller up. He was quite small, with thick, curly, black hair, a wide, pale face with a slight smile that seemed to be in almost permanent residence, and dark, kind eyes. Probably a nice guy, I thought, but I'd been wrong about that before.

I eventually dozed off and found myself dreaming about chasing Saul across the outback. I wasn't catching him because he was riding a giant kangaroo and I was wearing clown shoes, which made it hard to work the pedals of the clown car I was driving, which in any case kept falling apart so that I had to keep stopping to put it together again.

When I woke up, the cabin lights were on, a few people were opening their window blinds onto a piercingly bright sky and the cabin staff were preparing to distribute what the airline had decided was a balanced, nutritious, or at any rate cheap and convenient, breakfast.

'What part of Wales are you from?' I asked Martin, when we'd been served.

'Rhondda Valley,' he replied with his mouth full of some sort of omelettey thing.

'So what do you do there?'

'Did. I moved away a year ago.'

'Where are you now?'

'Surrey,' he answered. 'Job move, you know. Chance to start again after a slightly uncomfortable divorce.'

'Is there any sort of divorce that isn't uncomfortable? Whereabouts in Surrey? It's my neck of the woods too.'

'Little town called Stallford.' And suddenly, a polite conversation with a stranger to kill time over breakfast on a plane, moved in a more interesting direction.

As an intelligence officer, only partly trained or not, I was well aware that coincidence is not all it's stacked up to be. However, my less-than-finely tuned senses told me that coincidence was probably what this was. Nevertheless, it wouldn't do any harm to pursue the possibility that Martin was not just jetting off to the antipodes on holiday. It was a long flight and, apart from reading the dismal book, I had nothing else to do.

'Really?' I said. 'I know it well. What do you do there?'

'I'm a reporter.' That threw me. 'Or at least, I like to think of myself as a reporter but actually I just sit behind a desk most of the time these days telling other reporters what to report on. I miss it, really, being out in the field. It's why I'm here on this plane.'

Hello! I thought. Come to momma. 'Oh,' I said with

the most wide-eyed ingénue look I could muster. I had to balance the increasingly twitchy feeling I had with a degree of nonchalance. I couldn't afford to display more than polite interest. I also had to come up with an answer to his inevitable questions about what I did to keep me busy and what I was doing flying to Australia. Alone. Not sure that "going on holiday" would cut it, but maybe he wouldn't be that interested in me. Who was I kidding?

'And you?' he asked.

'Me? Oh, er...' My eyes alighted on the terrible paperback. 'I work for a publisher. Got to go and do some stuff in the Sydney office.' I waved the book at him.

'At least you get to go to Sydney in the Aussie summer.'

Yes, twice, I thought. 'Last time I looked, it was thirty-five in the shade. Bit hot really. My freckles don't like sunburn.'

'Thirty-five? I take it you're not talking Fahrenheit. I'm Welsh, anything over fifteen's a heatwave to me.'

I took the plunge. 'Why are you going to Aus in February then? Strange choice of holiday destination if you can't stand the heat.'

'Well, it's not really a holiday. Friend of mine's out there, and I've a feeling something may have happened to him.'

What passes for my heart these days skipped a couple of beats. 'That doesn't sound good,' I said, sounding concerned (concerned, worried, elated, dumbstruck, all the above). 'What makes you think he's in trouble?'

'Oh, it's nothing, really,' said Martin, clearly backtracking. 'He's probably playing silly buggers. I'll thrash him within an inch of his worthless life if so.' He laughed in a way that sounded unconvincing even to my inexperienced ears. 'Anyway, I'll get to see some kangaroos, I imagine.' And he started eating again in a manner that suggested he didn't want to pursue the subject.

Mr Too-Much-of-a-Coincidence was now jumping up and down in front of me waving his arms about wildly. Martin's friend just had to be Saul. I had been told to get myself to Yackandandah as soon as possible after landing. Did I help point my new Welsh acquaintance in the same direction? Or did he already know more than me? Indeed, was he implicated in some way? I had no idea, but I wasn't sure how I was going to watch both Saul and Martin.

—

Martin and I managed to drift apart at Changi airport. I had a feeling that might have been deliberate on his part. I was a bit put out; I wasn't used to men moving away from me.

On the final leg of our journey to Sydney, I found I was several rows behind him. I decided to keep my eyes on him, not so much during the flight itself – he was unlikely to do a runner from an aircraft at 40,000 feet – but more after we landed.

At Sydney, Martin headed straight for the taxi rank after negotiating customs and baggage retrieval. I was travelling very light, and I was getting quite good now at surreptitiously following men through airports. Martin got into a taxi and I managed to smile winningly enough at the next man in line to jump into the cab behind. This was my chance to be a proper spy, I thought.

'Follow that taxi!' I demanded. The driver turned round and looked at me, chewing gum silently. 'Now!' I screamed. Then, 'Please?' I added.

'Okay, ladies, we following taxis, I am always wanting to do this. Holding on to your hats.' And amazingly, we were off. Even more amazingly, my obviously Greek driver proved adept at negotiating rush-hour Sydney traffic

while keeping Martin's cab in sight. We narrowly missed no more than two or three other vehicles and a couple of nuns on a crossing. It was a bit of a let-down when the other taxi pulled up outside the uninspiring exterior of the Travelodge just south of Hyde Park.

'We stopping now, ladies?' asked my driver, sounding disappointed. I looked around, but there was only me there. I sighed. 'Yes, please, stop here. What do I owe you?'

'You owing me nothings, pretty ladies. Was fun. I, Stavros, coming to get me again if you wanting more followings.' And he laughed uproariously and was gone, leaving me on the pavement, sweating slightly in the humidity.

___ In which Rachel stands around in
    an office, and finds an envelope
    under a chair

Alan and Rachel were at Franklin, Boasman & Bootle's Croydon office, although office was perhaps too strong a description for premises that appeared far too small to contain a Franklin and a Boasman, let alone a very large Bootle. There was a tiny reception area and an inner office that wasn't much more spacious, containing two desks, a few chairs, a filing cabinet and a shelf of weighty looking law books. Everything was very clean and appeared to be recently painted, as was the communal staircase leading up from the street door. Across the landing, a two-person firm of accountants occupied similarly cramped premises, while the floor above was taken up with a company that appeared to import cat and dog food, although clearly they must have had additional warehouse space somewhere else, judging by the lack of smell in the building.

Rachel and Alan were accompanied by a world-weary police sergeant, who was not inclined to take orders from "civilians". Three other officers in latex gloves were half-heartedly conducting a search, which seemed to Rachel to be taking a surprisingly long time for such a small space. On arrival, two of the officers had gone off to talk to the other occupants of the building but no one could remember having seen Franklin or Boasman. This was hardly surprising, as Aardvark had already ascertained that they did not exist. Pat Bootle, however, who was of course memorable by dint of size and whiff of hair gel, had been a relatively familiar figure during the six months since the firm had taken up occupancy. No one could recall seeing anyone else regularly coming and going, although each company in the building was fairly self-contained and nobody had really been taking too much notice.

Rachel had felt quite excited when she woke that morning, but that excitement was now turning rapidly to frustration. 'We don't seem to be getting very far,' she remarked, and Alan grunted in agreement.

The sergeant wandered across at that point. 'Well, Mr Stevens,' he said. 'We don't seem to be getting very far.' Mind-reader, thought Rachel, and also, who's Mr Stevens? 'We'll be contacting the names in the customer files, but I'm as sure as you probably are that they'll all be fictitious. Not much else we can do, frankly.' He turned in the doorway. 'Oh, and if you've got any more wild geese you need chasing, just call the superintendent and try not to mention my name.' He smiled without humour and was gone.

'You haven't actually told me what we're looking for,' Rachel remarked. 'And exactly how many names have you got? Who's Mr Stevens when he's at home?'

'I try not to take my work home with me,' replied Alan, not really answering the question.

Rachel felt suddenly deflated and flopped down on the chair next to her. She tried again. 'So, what are we looking for? It would make it easier to spot if I knew.'

'In general, anything helpful,' Alan replied unhelpfully. 'Specifically though, I can't tell you. Whatever it is or isn't or may be, I doubt we'll find it here.'

'I'm not so sure,' said Rachel. 'PC Plod and his chums didn't exactly exude enthusiasm for their task, did they? I think we need to look a bit deeper. Don't mind a bit of damage to the furniture, do you?'

'That's the spirit. You're right. It's a bit early to go down the pub, so we might as well.'

Rachel got up, picked up the chair that she'd been sitting on, turned it bodily over and there, as if by magic, was a small envelope wedged under the seat.

'Hello,' said Alan. 'What's this?' He plucked it out and Rachel put the chair down again. There was no name or address on the envelope. Alan started to slit it open using his thumbnail.

'Be careful,' said Rachel, backing away. 'It might be a bomb.'

'Thinnest bomb ever.' Alan slid his fingers inside the envelope and pulled out what looked like an ordinary memory stick.

'What does it mean?'

'Don't know, but I imagine that if we stick it in a computer, it might tell us. Of course, it may just have Bootle's shopping list or lottery numbers on it. Or it might possibly turn out to be what I believe is referred to in policing circles as "a clue". Shame the police themselves weren't bright enough to find it. You're a clever girl, aren't you?'

'Could you be any more condescending?' However, she was secretly quite pleased. She was however a little disappointed that she hadn't had the opportunity to ransack the rest of the office. Perhaps there was some latent violence in her soul that she had previously been unaware of, probably brought to the surface by Prat-the-fucking-non-solicitor. It was her turn to call him that now and she quite liked the feel of it on her tongue. 'Should we be turning over more furniture, do you think?'

'Not today. I reckon the priority is to see what's on this and if it's nothing, we can come back another day.

'There are two computers here. We could try sticking it in one of those, to use your own basic turn of phrase.'

'Probably not wise. At best, they won't be secure – we could be broadcasting the contents to all manner of ungodly individuals. At worst, it could get wiped. We'll take it to a certain tightly controlled environment to which I have access and look at it there under expert supervision.'

___ In which Dawson and Pat talk to
Mrs Bigg, and Dawson takes up
athletics

Dawson wasn't sure how, but Pat had found an empty house on the edge of Jerilderie. Entering it didn't seem to prove especially difficult for him, even encumbered by the decidedly wriggly foreign woman thrown over one shoulder. She was now very much awake but with her mouth tightly gagged with some expensive material cut from one of the seats of the Mercedes.

'How do you know the owners of this house aren't coming back?' Dawson asked.

'I don't, but I'm sure we'll work something out if they do.' Pat shrugged and in doing so, deposited the Scandinavian woman onto the sofa.

She stared at them with a degree of loathing that surpassed even that of the Grayfold make-up girl when Dawson had broken up with her. It seemed like another life.

'Here,' said Pat. 'You'd better grab hold of this gun while I take her gag off.'

'What am I supposed to do with it?'

'Well, if she starts kicking off, you could try shooting her.'

'I'm not actually sure I know how.'

'You point the straight bit with the hole in the end in her direction and pull the triggery thing underneath.'

'Surely there's more to it than that?'

Pat sighed and disengaged the safety clip before pressing the weapon into Dawson's unwilling hand.

'Look menacing but don't point it anywhere near me.' Pat turned back to the woman. 'Now, my lovely,' he said. 'I'm going to take the gag off and you're going to tell me who you are and why you decided to wave that gun at us. You're going to be calm and polite, because if you're not, my white-faced friend here is going to shoot. Admittedly, he's just as likely to hit me as you but I suggest you don't want to take that chance. And in any case, you're not going far with those jump leads round your ankles. Okay?' There was no response. 'Okay, here goes then.'

Dawson was expecting fireworks but there were none. 'You are a fool, Mutt,' the woman said calmly. 'Riley will find you, and he will kill you. And your dumb friend. You, he will kill quickly. You have betrayed him and he does not accept that. And your friend... he will get Mr Chuckles to kill very, very slowly. After he has given him what he wants, of course.'

Dawson didn't like the sound of the "very, very slowly" bit and wasn't that keen on the "kill" bit that preceded it, but it was something else she'd said that had caught his attention more.

'Who's Riley?' he asked.

'The tall skeletal chap back at the house,' said Pat.

'Riley? His name's Riley? He told me his name was Really.'

Pat laughed and a thin wisp of a smile crossed the woman's face too. 'Really?' said Pat. 'What sort of a name's that? That would make him Really Bigg. Oh, I know, it's the Aussie accent. Good one that, very funny. I'll call him "Really" next time I see him.'

'That will be very soon,' said their prisoner. 'But you will not have time to crack jokes. As you will be dead.'

'We'll see,' said Pat. 'So, putting two and two together, I'm thinking we've got ourselves Riley's Norwegian floozy. She seems to know me, at any rate, although we haven't been introduced.'

'Floozy! I am nobody's floozy. I am his wife. And I am Swedish, you moron.'

'Even better, Mrs Bigg,' smiled Pat, ignoring the geographical niceties. 'He's not going to kill me if I've got you. And he's not going to kill me if he can't find me. And Australia's a big place.'

'You are a fool, Mutt,' she repeated. 'There is a tracking

device in the car. He will be here very soon.'

'Ah, yes. About that tracking device. I'm afraid we left it lying in the road back in Wagga Wagga.'

'Did we?' asked Dawson. 'What tracking device?'

'You must have dislodged it somehow when you found the jump leads. I noticed it when we shoved Lady Muck here in the boot.' That seemed to knock some of the stuffing out of the woman, who slumped back into the corner of the sofa and shut her eyes. 'Now then, Mrs B, perhaps you can start by telling me what it is you think my clever friend here has.' But there was no reply. She was still half lying on the sofa with her eyes shut and Dawson was suddenly even more worried.

'Is she dead?' he asked.

'Not unless dead women can still breathe.' Pat was holding two fingers to the side of her windpipe. 'That's either a clever trick or she's fainted. We'll wait a while. Give us a chance to have that chat.'

'I thought we'd already had it.'

'Don't think so. I've a few questions to ask you, which you'll be happy to answer. And I imagine you've got a few to ask me, and I may answer one or two if I feel like it.'

'That sounds a bit one sided,' said Dawson, putting the gun on a table. 'So, Mutt, great name. Tell me all about it.'

Pat sighed. 'Mitchell "Mutt" Johnston,' he said. 'As you'll have noticed, our pal Riley is keen on nicknames. Except for himself of course, so he may not take kindly to "Really Big".'

'So, are you Mitchell Johnston or Pat Bootle? Or neither?'

'I'm actually Pat Bootle. Genuinely,' he added as Dawson's eyebrows headed towards his hairline. 'Well, genuinely now. It wasn't the name I was born with.'

'Of course not. What was the name you were born with?'

'Irrelevant and, for you, unpronounceable.'

'That's extremely rude. I'll have you know I've got a C in English Language.'

'Which might help if it were English. Now then, enough of

that. What the hell are you doing in Australia, and what have you got that makes our nasty pals so interested in you?'

'If I were to tell you that I don't know what I'm doing here, and as far as I know I've got nothing remotely valuable on me apart from a Crystal Palace season ticket, would you believe me?'

Pat looked at him, smiled and shook his head. 'Bugger me, you're telling the truth, aren't you? You really are a nincompoop. No wonder Rachel wouldn't touch you with a barge pole.'

'She certainly would,' said Dawson, immediately realising that being touched by Rachel with a barge pole wouldn't necessarily be a good thing. 'And nincompoop? This isn't Enid Blyton.'

'You're not what she wants, you know. She needs someone with a little more gravitas.'

'Well, if gravitas means weight, then I agree you've got about five stones more gravitas than me. Anyway, she's not going to want you back when she finds out you're a crook.'

'A crook? And you query "nincompoop"? Am I a "crook"? Is that what you think? Anyway, it doesn't matter. Now, who sent you to Australia? And what were you supposed to be doing before you decided to go making house calls with Rambo and Chuckles?'

'None of your business. Anyway, you said earlier your real name is unpronounceable. Does that make you Russian?'

'That's a huge jump to a very distant conclusion and, as I said, Pat Bootle is my real name. Now let me see, an out-of-work, penniless waste of space who can hardly afford to buy a round in the pub suddenly turns up in Australia in the middle of something very important and not very nice. You didn't do that by yourself.'

'I'm a big boy now, I decided I needed a holiday.'

'Tenerife's nice this time of year. No, somebody you know isn't who we think he is, is he? So, who are your friends? You can't have many. Nobody at the Drama Club, that's for sure, I've made it my business to sniff around that pile of old tarts.'

'You're even lovelier than I thought you were,' said Dawson who was, however, rather mortified by Pat's conclusions.

'Hang on. Who's that fat guy who hangs out at the pub you go to?'

'Is that a pot I can hear talking about black kettles?'

'I'm not fat, I'm just big. What's his name? It'll come to me.'

'You're not exactly skinny,' said Dawson, ignoring the question. 'You're being very rude to someone who saved your life.'

'I beg your pardon? I think it was me who saved yours. You remember, big house in the country, three men with guns and dubious morals?'

'I do remember that, and thanks where it's due,' conceded Dawson. 'However, I returned the compliment in Wagga Wagga, if you recall.'

'Oh yes, by running away.'

'Not running away,' said Dawson, rewriting history. 'I was distracting Madam's attention, thus allowing you to fall on top of her and knock yourself out.'

'I didn't fall on her,' snapped Pat. 'I threw myself bodily at her to stop her shooting you, so, oh yes, I saved your pointless life twice.'

Before Dawson could reply, there was the sound of a car engine outside. Pat rushed to the front of the house, and was back almost as quickly.

'Is it Bigg?' asked Dawson, reverting to cowardice mode.

'Worse. It's the bloody cops.'

'By what possible reasoning could you think that the arrival of the police is worse than the arrival of three murderous bastards trying to kill us?'

'Stay here, then.' Pat led the way through the kitchen of the house and into a conservatory to the rear of the property. The door to the garden was locked but it flew open with a splintering crash as Pat put a sizeable right shoulder into it. 'I doubt if they'll take kindly to us having a middle-aged woman trussed up on the sofa.'

'But they won't shoot us,' responded Dawson, following Pat out into the almost pitch-black garden. 'Will they?' As he trailed the bulk of Pat Bootle through the darkness, he reflected on the fact that this was the second time in one night he'd hightailed it out of a house with people in hot pursuit, which was twice more than he'd accomplished previously in his life.

As they climbed over a low fence at the rear of the garden, torches could be seen coming around the side of the house fifty feet behind them. He and Pat found themselves in a narrow service road with a row of lock-up garages opposite. He was thinking that where there's a garage there might be a car, but Pat was ahead of him on that. Walking closely along the front of the garages, and feeling as much as seeing, he almost immediately found one without a padlock on the door, and bending down, he pulled the latch and the door moved surprisingly silently up and over. Inside was a smallish, rusty looking 4x4 Subaru. 'Trusting lot round here,' grunted Pat as he discovered shortly afterwards that the driver's door was unlocked. They eased themselves into the vehicle.

'What now?'

'Now we make our second getaway of the night,' replied Pat, fiddling with some wiring under the steering column. And he was as good as his word, gunning the aged Subaru through the garage doorway, spinning the wheel sharply to the right, away from the bobbing torches which were now only metres away, and off down the dusty service road with the confidence of a man who knew exactly where he was going.

'Do you know where you're going?' asked Dawson, twisting in his seat.

'To start with, away from here seems like a good idea. So, finding the main drag in this two-horse town would be an even better idea.' They rocked around a couple of corners and saw some streetlights ahead. 'Ah, this looks promising.'

Seconds later, they emerged on to a wide highway and a signpost informed them that it was the A39 to Shepparton and Melbourne. Pat grunted in satisfaction. 'Right then. Where to, Sunshine?'

'What do you mean?'

'You were headed somewhere last evening before Chuckles and Rambo borrowed you. You weren't just on a pootle around south-east Australia, taking in the sights.'

'I could have been.' Despite all the recent rescuing from the jaws of death, Dawson still didn't trust Pat enough to mention Yackandandah. 'I am on holiday, after all.'

'Holiday, my arse. Riley's Big League. You've got something he wants, or you know where that something is. One of the two. Now's the time to tell me which, and since you were going somewhere, the logical deduction is that that special something is in the place you were going to. Am I right or am I right?'

'You're wrong, but even if you were right, why should I tell you?'

'Apart from the fact that I've saved your life three times now?'

'I'll agree reluctantly to two times, okay? I doubt if my life was in danger from the cops. And at the moment, deportation has its attractions.'

'You're assuming they were police back there then.'

'I was just going on what you said. What makes you think they weren't?'

'Very convenient, wasn't it? Bigg's after us, police turn up, and I'd be staggered if long tall Sally hasn't got at least one or two bent cops in his pay.'

'Or, bearing in mind Riley doesn't know where we went, the police could have been called by a suspicious neighbour, knowing the house was supposed to be empty.'

'Yes, could be, but I prefer not to take chances. And remember, Riley's pretty much king of the Victorian underworld, so to assume he couldn't find out where we went pretty damn quick, would be foolish in the extreme.' He sighed and went on in a more conciliatory tone. 'Look, whatever or whoever you think I am, I'm not on Riley Bigg's side. The man's an utter bastard and if I can help bring him and his little empire down as a by-product of the bigger picture, then believe me I will. I pretended to work for him for the best part of two years, and it's two years I'm not going to get back.'

'So you're on my side?'

'What side's that? I'm not sure you know yourself. We've established that Alan What's-his-face sent you here and I'm assuming that he is probably something to do with British Intelligence, or Interpol maybe. Look, I'm all you've got for the moment, so you might as well trust me.'

Dawson thought for a long time. He didn't know what to do and he didn't know who to trust. But he was wary about tying his colours to Pat Bootle's mast, the man who had appeared out of the blue a few months ago, just after he'd made happy reacquaintance with Rachel, and had casually swept her away from him almost before he'd had time to say, "Hello, fancy seeing you again." It sounded irrational, but he was damned if he was going to lead Pat to Yackandandah. Somehow, he'd have to part company with the big non-solicitor and find his own way there, alone. However, the method of achieving that objective was not immediately apparent to him.

An hour later, the Subaru approached the larger metropolis of Shepparton and, with dawn starting to break in earnest, the traffic began to build up. Dawson noticed two black Toyota Land Cruisers headed towards them at speed on the opposite carriageway. As the cars sped past them, he saw a head in the passenger's window of the first Toyota turn to look at them. Then there was a screech of brakes and Dawson shot round in his seat to see both the big cars slew around in the road no more than a hundred metres behind them. Pat had noticed them too – it would have been hard not to as several other vehicles had been forced out of their way as the Land Cruisers swung through 180°.

'That's not good,' murmured Pat and put his foot to the floor. The Subaru shot forward like a scalded cat but, being old and not very powerful, it was unfortunately more like a scalded cat with a thorn in its foot. The two Toyotas closed the gap in a few seconds and, just when a few local vehicles containing people would have been useful as witnesses, there were suddenly none to be seen. With a terrifying crunch, one Land Cruiser crashed jarringly into the rear of the Subaru, and at the same time the second one drew alongside and swerved violently into the driver's side of the smaller vehicle. There was nothing Pat could do and the Subaru bounced sideways off the tarmac, its nearside wheels hitting the drainage ditch alongside the road. It flipped side over side three times, bounced through a fence and down a small embankment into a field, before coming to a rest back on its wheels.

Dawson had remained conscious throughout this brief fairground ride and he threw open the door and started running. His speed of movement seemed to catch the six occupants of the Toyotas unawares and by the time they'd drawn their guns, he had disappeared behind a solid-looking barn fifty metres away, the first in a series of farm buildings. Dawson imagined that Pat had not managed to escape as readily, but he found that he wasn't feeling too sorry for him. He assumed that Pat would take up the attention of some of the hoodlums, which meant that only six minus some would be available to chase him.

Running through the farmyard, he debated whether to seek sanctuary in the farmhouse itself, but it was in darkness and something told him that the sight of a farmer wouldn't cause his pursuers to draw breath. To his surprise, Dawson realised at this point that he was outpacing the chasing pack of three. Dawson, though he would not have kept Usain Bolt company for long down a hundred metres straight, had been something of a middle-distance runner through his twenties, and had briefly represented the South Surrey Spartans Athletics Club in the 400 metres. That, together with the fact that he was dodging in and out of various buildings, started to give him some breathing space. It would have given him a bit more had he actually been able to breathe: it was five years since his days with the SSSAC after all.

He emerged suddenly into a side road and there his luck took another turn for the better. Parked on the other side of the road for no apparent reason was a police car. He was fully aware of what Pat had said about Riley Bigg's likely hold over some of the local constabulary, but he had to take a chance. He went straight up to the car and rapped on the window.

___ In which Pat Bootle has a
   headache, and ponders an
   uncomfortable reality

Pat Bootle woke up with a raging headache. He could probably have lived with that had he not been sitting in a puddle of water on the floor of an empty basement, bound securely round the ankles and handcuffed by his wrists to an old radiator beside him. The radiator groaned encouragingly when he gave an experimental tug. So did Pat though, as the handcuffs bit into his chunky wrists. However, given the lack of radiatorial solidity, the handcuffing may not have caused him too much distress, were it not for the likelihood that Riley Bigg, accompanied by Chuckles and Rambo and goodness knows how many other possibly psychopathic acquaintances of theirs, were going to be the next people to walk through the door opposite.

The immediate prognosis did not appear favourable and, not for the first time during the last couple of years, he found himself wondering how he'd ended up here. He suspected that his superiors back home had only chosen him because of his complete fluency in English. They'd understandably been wary of sending anyone to Australia who couldn't blend in fully and had no natural-born Aussies readily at hand. They'd tried to train him to speak with an Australian twang but it had proved a fruitless exercise, and they'd finally come to the conclusion that there were so many Englishmen in the country anyway that one more wouldn't be a problem. And it hadn't. Armed with a couple of names and addresses and a nice line in references, he had inserted himself into the murkier parts of the Melbourne underworld and put it about that he was a driver with a successful background in rapid extrication techniques. When Riley Bigg's usual chauffeur had unexpectedly suffered a distressingly fatal accident involving a chain-saw, a garden hedge and the not altogether unwitting assistance of a "trade attaché" from the embassy in Canberra, one thing had led to another, and the job was his.

Bigg had also noted the potential benefits of having an apparently English-born-and-bred employee, so it wasn't entirely a surprise when Mutt Johnston had been packed off to Surrey when the need had arisen.

Pat was unsure how Riley Bigg had acquired the idea that Saul Dawson had something in his possession that he himself wanted to possess. Wanted to possess very badly indeed. So badly that any and all grades of mayhem and murder might be introduced to the proceedings to enable possession to change hands as speedily as possible. Pat's initial impression upon meeting Dawson for the first and indeed all subsequent occasions was that there was a serious case of mistaken identity at play. He had quickly come to the conclusion that Dawson was a bit of an idiot and an even bigger waste of space, so the way that the surveillance had stretched past Christmas into the New Year had rather distressed him. At least following him wasn't too demanding: flat to the am dram GODS to the pub and home again, rinse and repeat. The closest to anything interesting was an evening in September when the car got stopped for no apparent reason by a zealous copper who overly inspected Dawson's taillights.

Once Pat reported that back, Riley had seemed to think that the outlay of $900 for the Nissan Micra had been a more than worthwhile investment for the information retrieved from the car. Pat had been instructed to keep well clear while this transaction was taking place, so he did not know exactly what information had been acquired, but it was obvious that Riley would need more knowledge from somewhere else to join up the dots. It appeared that Dawson was the possessor of that additional knowledge.

Worming himself into Dawson's immediate purlieu had proved ridiculously easy. Early observations had revealed that his prey was infatuated with a tall, not completely unattractive woman called Rachel Whyte, so Pat had simply turned on the charm and inserted himself into the gap between them. From then on, however, he had been completely frustrated. Despite using all the subtle techniques of covert interrogation he'd been taught in his basic training, he had failed to elicit anything from Rachel that would give a clue as to who Dawson might really be, and where he might have secreted any extra information above and beyond what had been on Dawson's Nissan Micra. Climbing into Rachel's affections may not, on reflection, have been his best decision ever. He would have been better off cutting straight to the chase and climbing into Dawson's affections instead.

He reviewed his current state of trussedness one more time. A nylon rope gripped his ankles tightly, so he ruled out escaping from that for the time being. However, it looked like Riley and his pals could only run to one pair of handcuffs. Pat was squashed hard up against the old radiator to his left because his captors had had to loop the cuffs around a pipe at the top of it, with Pat's hands either side. It was an extremely uncomfortable position, but not an impossible one.

As he pulled at the radiator, trying desperately to loosen it enough to free his hands, he hoped that the next person to come in would be Rambo. Rambo he could talk to, he thought. Rambo he could persuade, if not to let him go, but to do something stupid that would give him a sliver of opportunity. Rambo rarely let twenty-four hours pass without achieving something stupid, after all.

However, when the door opened, Rambo didn't walk through it. Both Riley Bigg and Chuckles did, together with another man who looked scarcely less menacing, what with the vivid scar down his left cheek and the half ear alongside it. Oh, and the double-barrelled sawn-off shotgun. The shotgun was definitely quite menacing.

Chuckles was relegated to door-guarding duties as Bigg

approached Pat and stood a few feet away with his long arms folded and a grim look on his already grim-looking face. The man with the shotgun stood a little to one side.

'Aren't you going to introduce me to your attractive friend?' asked Pat.

'I think we can forget the pleasantries,' said Bigg. 'I need to ask you some questions, which you will oblige me by answering quickly, clearly and accurately.'

'And then?'

'And then my attractive friend is going to kill you.'

'I thought young Chuckles had first dibs on that sort of thing. Either way, it doesn't seem like much of a deal. I think I'll decline the offer.'

'They drew lots for the pleasure. Chuckles lost. Chuckles doesn't like losing, so if you aren't cooperative, Bunny here stands down and passes the baton on. You really wouldn't want that to happen.'

Pat knew that somehow he needed to take charge of the situation before either Bunny or Chuckles got to work. Having already discovered that the radiator was less secure than it had been when originally fitted, he hoped that a burst of adrenalin, together with a touch of abject fear, might enable him to loosen it a lot more. He wasn't confident about the outcome, but he'd signed the contract and there had been no clause in it that said it was compulsory for him to remain alive. What was missing, however, was the burst of adrenalin. He was thinking quickly and was only dimly aware that Bigg had started speaking again and had apparently asked him a question. The next thing he knew, Bunny's shotgun had come crashing down on his left kneecap.

With a yell of pain, Pat tried to grab the injured knee with his hands, which were of course handcuffed to the radiator. In so trying, and with a positively Samsonian effort, he succeeded in wrenching the entire radiator off its fixings and, almost without thinking, swung it bodily in a half-circle which was hardly interrupted when it came into that part of the room occupied by Bunny. Pat executed an almost perfect sideways roll, and when he came face upwards again, he saw that Bunny was out cold and had crashed heavily into Riley Bigg. He had dropped the shotgun and Pat, with a speed and efficiency honed by a mixture of training and fear, grabbed it out of the air by the barrels despite having both hands still connected to the radiator. He then tossed it up and caught it again by the handle, pointed it at the now rapidly advancing Chuckles and emptied both barrels in quick succession. Chuckles went down like a big sack of spuds, a sack with copious amounts of blood leaking violently from it.

Pat looked around at his handiwork. So far so moderately good, he thought. Chuckles was clearly not going to be doing any more chuckling, Bunny had at least temporarily gone to ground, and Riley Bigg was pinned to the floor looking dazed. Pat didn't want him to become undazed and start shouting, so he gave him an encouraging clump over his bald head with the shotgun, and then shuffled over to Chuckles, dragging the radiator behind him, which bumped usefully across the prone forms of Bigg and Bunny. Picking up Chuckles's automatic, he somehow managed to twist his hands around enough to loose off a successful shot at the chain looped around the radiator. Two more accurately placed shots removed the heavy bracelets from each wrist. He quickly removed the rope from his ankles and stood up.

He had no idea how many other villains were in the building but figured that it wouldn't be just Rambo. Rambo wasn't allowed to play by himself, after all. Pat was mildly surprised no one had yet turned up to investigate the gunshots but he suspected he didn't have much more time at his disposal.

__ In which Alan and Rachel look at
      computers, and Alan casts his
      mind back

Aardvark Amalgamations had been created to undertake work that wasn't currently covered by the mission statements of any existing British Intelligence bureau. Alan Flannery, previously muddling along in a middle-ranking capacity in MI5, had been offered the chance to set it up and run it in a quasi-autonomous fashion, and because he quite liked the sound of the quasi-autonomous bit, together with the extra ten grand a year offered for the job, he had accepted. He had been given such a wide remit that he had even been able to name the new outfit himself, hence Aardvark, it being a word that appeared to have been made up purely to get on to the first page of the dictionary. As a child, he'd believed that the actual animal was therefore made up too. As for the Amalgamations bit, he had discovered that a lot of the work he had inherited involved looking for things or people and once found, bringing these various different objects or parties together, either amicably or otherwise. He had never been allowed to recruit enough staff for the work, but in his ten years at MI5 he had made a lot of useful contacts and had seen to it that a number of people owed him favours. He had then been able to beg, borrow or steal additional temporary manpower on an occasional basis.

He had already hauled Rachel up to HR to recruit her on a one-month internship and to sign the Official Secrets Act, and they were now watching two geeky tech types in floral shirts doing geeky, techy things to test the memory stick to within an inch of its life.

'Okay, that should work,' said the geekier, techier, more floral one, turning with a gap-toothed smile peeking through his ginger beard. 'Shall we give it a whirl?'

'Please,' said Alan. The two techies slid their chairs in

unison from one workstation to the next and popped the stick into a port. Two buttons later and a set of numbers flashed up on the screen. All four of them peered at the numbers.

36.19.827

'Mean anything to you?' asked the slightly less techy, slightly less beardy one.

'No,' said Alan, while actually thinking, "Yes".

'Yes,' said Rachel. They all looked at her. 'Well, I think so. I'm not sure but aren't they half of a set of geographical coordinates?'

'Really?' Alan peered with apparently renewed interest at the screen, while wishing he hadn't brought Rachel along.

'Yes, I mean there's no Longitude or Latitude written down, no N, S, E or W, but that's what they look like. And it would make sense, wouldn't it, if this is supposed to be "a clue".' The two geeks stared at each other. Alan thought that they may never have heard the word "clue" in their department before, and certainly not pronounced with such force. It was all a bit Agatha Christie.

Alan shook his head as if to clear it. 'Assuming, for the sake of argument, that you might be right, I'm not sure how much of "a clue" it actually is. If I've got my GCSE Geography remembered correctly, all this will give us is a line round the whole bloody planet and we don't even know whether it goes vertically or horizontally.'

'Worse than that, I'm afraid,' said Rachel. 'It's going to give you four lines, not one: you know, north, south, east and west...' she trailed off.

'Never mind. Let's work with what we've got. It may be something, it may be nothing. Do any of these machines actually connect to Google?'

It turned out they did, and it took a matter of minutes to discover that Rachel was correct and, that if the numbers were indeed coordinates, then they could mean one of four lines circling the globe, meridians, parallels, call them what you will. They stared at the information in front of them.

36° 19.827 North produced a nightmare of over-information. The likelihood of locating one point on its axis brought to mind very small needles and extremely large haystacks. That parallel travelled through the United States and then on to the Mediterranean via southern Iberia. From there it passed through most of the more dangerous parts of the Middle East and on to China and Japan.

36° 19.827 East headed south from the Arctic through Russia and Ukraine and then on to the Middle East again before hitting eastern Africa and, eventually, Antarctica.

Rachel had a thought. 'Where do they cross each other? It looks like it could be somewhere interesting.' Gingery Tech was on it straightaway.

'Southern Turkey,' he said. 'A few miles from a place called Antakya and not a million miles from the Syrian border.'

'Okay,' said Alan. 'Note that and run off a map.' He was quite pleased that Rachel's idea appeared to point to potentially fertile ground. 'Let's go and do some research on Antakya. See if we can find anything anywhere that bears that out as a serious location for whatever it is we might be looking for.'

Rachel jumped in. 'Hang on. Surely we're only halfway there. That's east and north covered, not south and west, and pardon me for mentioning it but there's a bloody great clue pointing us to Australia, isn't there?'

Alan couldn't immediately see a way of diverting her from the scent and by the time he'd even started trying, Rachel had come up with confirmation that **36° 19.827** South ran through the south-eastern tip of Australia. She could barely contain her excitement as she looked up **36° 19.827** West, only to find that it ran virtually the whole length of the Atlantic Ocean. Neither that nor the eastern meridian went anywhere near Australia.

'Still,' she said. 'It's a start.'

For Alan though, it was merely a new complication.

Alan had received a phone call from Séan MacGuffin late last summer, over six months ago. 'How are ye, then?' MacGuffin had started in that Emerald Isle voice which Alan always thought sounded a bit too over the top to be genuine. He had nonetheless listened, as MacGuffin only called when he had news to impart. 'I'll be sending ye something through the mail then, Mr Flannery. Ye might find it of use.' When Séan said "I'll be sending", he usually meant "I have sent", another Irishism which needed some translation. 'Have ye received it yet?'

'What sort of something, Séan?' Alan had asked.

'Oh, a tiny little thing, to be sure. Teeny, tiny little package.'

'Hang on, Séan, I'll take a look,' Alan had said, and put MacGuffin on hold. 'Juliet?' he'd called. 'Has the post come yet? Anything from our pals across the Irish Sea?'

Juliet's slightly severe head had appeared in the doorway. 'I am just sorting through it, Napoleon. Everything has to be properly logged, as you know. However, is this the item to which you are referring?' It was a small padded envelope with a Republic of Ireland postmark.

'Okay, Séan, I have it here.' Holding the phone uncomfortably up to his ear with one shoulder, Alan had slit open the envelope. Inside was a clear plastic bag containing a basic memory stick. 'What's on it?'

'Stick it in one of those computer thingies and find out. To be sure, I think you might find it interesting. Have a nice day now.' And Séan had rung off.

So Alan had gone across to the door to the adjoining office and locked it, although he trusted Juliet implicitly, didn't he? Still, better to be on the safe side. The memory stick had revealed a very short message. "Diamonds. Cache **#43290BV**. 24th February 1943. Yack."

A couple of years earlier, Alan had shared a long, drunken evening with Séan in a hotel in Paris at the conclusion of a complicated joint reconnaissance exercise involving various agencies of British and Irish intelligence. It had been a nerve-wracking couple of weeks which, although ultimately successful, had aged the participants by what felt like several years each, so they had all fancied letting their hair down. Alan and Séan had gone on to a club after the main party had broken up and, being naturally garrulous, considerably more so than was usual in intelligence circles, Séan had opened up about his past life, including the three ex-wives and various other indiscretions. Alan, as a natural listener with an ear always cocked for useful information, had stored these away for future use should it prove helpful. Most of it had been the usual flotsam and jetsam attached to a middle-aged life, but the drink had helped Alan to keep listening and at about two in the morning he suddenly became glad that he had.

It appeared that Séan had left out some information on his original application to join the Irish Intelligence Directorate, G2. This related to his time as a captain in the army, where a couple of prisoners in his care had met mysterious deaths. Séan had insisted to Alan, even in his over-lubricated state, that these had been the result of an unforeseen accident, although what the three of them were doing being rowed across the Liffey in the dead of night he was unable to fully explain. The whole unsavoury episode had been hushed up and had not been on his record when he had left to join the Intelligence Service. Séan's current bosses would be extremely interested to hear about that, Alan had thought. And that wasn't all. Apparently, according to Séan, the Russians had somehow also heard about the boating incident and had tried to put pressure on him to do a few bits and bobs for them. Which Séan, being an Irish patriot, had naturally refused.

Or had he?

The following morning, Séan had been unable to recall fully how much he had inadvertently let slip to Alan in the wee small hours, but Alan, being generous in all things, had been happy to tell him and to drop hints that Séan might care occasionally to remember that Alan wouldn't dream of revealing his faux pas should a few mildly interesting titbits of information pass back and forth between them. Well, not back and forth, just forth.

Little of anything very worthwhile wended its way from Dublin in the intervening time. But this message had looked altogether more interesting. The mention of diamonds and a date slap bang in the middle of the Second World War screamed stolen Nazi horde to Alan, although the word "Yack" had meant nothing to him.

He'd lodged the memory stick in a safe spot in his office that even Juliet knew nothing about, and had spent the train journey home to leafy Surrey trying to decide what he would do if, or when, he discovered what "Yack" signified. In that case, he could find the diamonds and simply turn up at the MI6 mothership loaded down with the gems and an overwhelming sense of achievement tinged with smugness.

Late that night, once he had ascertained that there was only one possible Yack in the gazetteer at the back of his atlas, and with two fingers of whisky from the bottle he kept in his desk for emergencies warming his insides and a small smile playing about his lips, he'd dutifully passed the information, or a version of the information, up the chain of command where it had disappeared into the mysterious bowels of Vauxhall Cross.

Not for long though.

'Flannery?' Down the phone had come the sharp voice of a man he knew only as Jason. The "Flannery" was discouraging. It was usually "Alan", MI6 also scoffing at his internal use of "Napoleon". He had started to get the message about that. 'Did you do any checking, any checking at all, before you sent us this pile of old horse shit?'

'Not really, no,' he'd ventured, hoping his expression of wide-eyed innocence would travel along the phone line.

'Those map coordinates you sent. Did you bother looking them up? Do the words Atlantic Ocean mean anything to you?' Jason had continued.

'Big wet thing to the west?' volunteered Alan, hoping that Jason's tone might soften. It hadn't.

'You got this from your paddy friend, didn't you? He's having a laugh. You should cross him off your list of contacts.' And he'd put the phone down.

Alan didn't have to look up the coordinates. He'd done that already, just before deleting the "Yack" and adding them in its place. They pointed to a spot very close to where the Lusitania had been sunk. Perhaps MI6 would think the diamonds were on board? Even though the Lusitania had gone down in the wrong war? He'd thought he was being clever but needed confirmation of exactly how clever.

Next he'd phoned MacGuffin. Had the Irishman read the message on the memory stick and taken note of it before passing it on?

'Right, this bollocks you've sent me, Séan. I've just had my ear chewed off. Are you trying to tell me there's Nazi loot sitting undiscovered on the seabed?'

Séan had paused for a moment, and then laughed for quite a long time, but finally saying: 'Have ye not got a snorkel, young Alan? It's a little bit of intel of the kind ye've been pressing me for, isn't it, but I hadn't had so much as a wee look, to be sure.'

So either Séan had forwarded the stick sight unseen, or he was lying through his broken teeth. Alan had found he didn't care. It was about time he did something for himself.

'Is Moscow aware of any of this?' he'd asked.

'Ah, now, I wouldn't know about that, would I?' Which probably meant, "Yes".

'Okay, then,' he'd said, apparently conceding defeat. 'Thanks and no thanks. I guess we'll need some diving suits. I'll park this for the time being but don't think I'm not grateful. If you come across anything else, you'd tell me, wouldn't you?'

'My life is in your hands,' MacGuffin had replied, laughing uproariously again.

Maybe that's not so far from the truth, Alan had mused, and the next day had found himself in Dublin, tracking MacGuffin to his flashy docklands apartment and mercilessly plying him with Jamesons until he had got all the information he wanted. He had left MacGuffin a beaten man, but even so was surprised to learn within three days of that conversation that the Irishman's body had been dredged from Dublin Bay. Alan's mistake was in assuming suicide.

While he'd been in Dublin, Alan's hard drive had been removed by two silent men in white overalls and replaced with one that he instinctively mistrusted. He'd hypocritically resented the lack of faith it implied. The strong subversive streak that had lain undetected below his generally affable exterior had now surfaced and was not about to sink back beneath the waves.

So now he had a complete picture. But he also knew he was now under surveillance from above, so retrieving the diamonds was an apparently insurmountable problem. Or was it? He could send someone in his place, someone MI6 was unaware of, someone who could be persuaded, someone who needed a job and money, someone who could take the fall with some planted information (if need be). Someone called Dawson.

__ In which Dawson meets various
    police officers and a man from a
    Consulate

Dawson was momentarily disconcerted to find that the police car contained two female officers who both possessed visible firearms. The suspicious looks they were giving him were probably understandable in the circumstances. However, they were polite enough to wait while he caught his breath after his fear-induced exertions. And they certainly did not waste much time once Dawson had told them how he'd been a hitchhiker in a Subaru that had been rammed and driven off the road by a couple of black Toyota Land Cruisers just around the corner. He was quite proud that he had managed to keep his tale brief and as close to the truth as possible. Ordering him into the back of the car and switching on their blues and twos, thus thrilling Dawson, they raced the short distance out on to the main road, swung right and almost immediately came to a completely empty stretch of road.

Dawson couldn't help noticing that the two hefty Toyotas, which were a fundamental part of his story, were missing. What had happened to the men who had been chasing him, Dawson had no idea. Having pulled up where Dawson directed, the two policewomen got out of the car, walked to the verge and peered down through the broken fence and some scrubby low bushes to the field below. There had been no obvious sign on the road surface of the somersaulting that he remembered the Subaru executing, so Dawson, trailing behind, was relieved to see the small Subaru sitting in the field down below, looking understandably sorry for itself.

'This is the vehicle you were in, is it, sir?' asked policewoman number one, the taller and broader of the two. Her colleague meanwhile, had pulled out her radio and was speaking indistinctly but firmly into it. 'You say you were a hitchhiker,' number one continued.

'Yes,' murmured Dawson. 'That's right.' He was peering down at the Subaru but couldn't see Pat in the driver's seat. It would be quite hard not to spot him had he been there, he reflected.

Number one turned to number two, who had finished speaking into her radio, and raised her eyebrows. 'On their way,' number two said. 'We'd better pop down and take a look. Can't see a driver anywhere. May have been thrown out of the vehicle.' Dawson had already explained that the driver, "and no, I don't know his name, we hadn't introduced ourselves, sorry", had appeared to be slumped, probably unconscious, in his seat but that he, Dawson, hadn't hung around to check, given that several men brandishing guns had been determined to chase him down and do him serious injury, or worse, and no, he had no idea why. But he simply shrugged and joined the two policewomen as they edged down the embankment to the battered Subaru. It was a mass of dents, scratches and broken windows, but because of the multiple rolls and collisions, not only with the fence but also with a couple of small but tough-looking trees, there was no obvious proof that the Subaru had been impacted by another car, let alone two. This had clearly been noticed by the officers as well, number two in particular, who had taken her notebook and pencil out of a pocket and whose sharp-looking face was giving the impression that she might shortly be asking some potentially uncomfortable questions. Number one, meanwhile, who possessed a slightly less suspicious natural facial expression, had done a quick but thorough recce of the immediate area without coming across, or falling over, any recumbent bodies. Pat was not there.

At that point, two more squad cars pulled up on the road above them and four cops, male this time, got out and put on their hats. One had some gold braid on his. They were followed by a police van from which a motley crew of what seemed to be a forensic persuasion emerged. Number two policewoman tapped Dawson on the shoulder. 'We'd like you to come down to the station, sir, if you don't mind.' Dawson doubted that it would have mattered whether he'd minded or not. He tried to leaven the atmosphere in his usual semi-facile style.

'Thank you,' he said. 'Where do the trains go to from here?'

The leavening was an abject failure. 'Police station, sir,' she said grimly. 'There are a few things you can help us with.' It wasn't a question. Dawson shrugged and started to climb up the bank with number two close behind. Number one remained by the Subaru, awaiting the imminent arrival of the forensics team.

Back on the road, the cop with the gold trim on his hat met them. 'Inspector Innes,' he said. 'Are you Mr Saul Jeremy Dawson?'

Dawson could not remember referring to himself by name to the two policewomen and if he had he would not have mentioned the Jeremy bit. He would only have mentioned the Saul bit under duress. This, therefore, was not an encouraging development. As his passport was, miraculously, still in his pocket, he had little option but to concur that he was indeed named Dawson and, through gritted teeth, a Dawson of the Saul Jeremy variety. He was clinging to the increasingly unlikely scenario that the police still believed him to be an innocent hitchhiker.

'In the car please, sir,' said the Inspector. Dawson was ushered into the back seat and was joined by number two policewoman, while the Inspector got into the front and nodded at the driver, who set off at a fair lick towards the centre of Shepparton. For once in his life, Dawson decided it might be for the best if he kept his mouth shut for the time being, and he cast his mind back to a similarly uncomfortable journey in the back of a car accompanied by Rambo and Chuckles, which, unbelievably, was only the previous day. This trip had the slight advantage of being with people who he was pretty confident wouldn't be shooting him for no reason at all and who smelled considerably more fragrant than either Rambo or Chuckles had done.

Shepparton Police station turned out to be a modern two-storey construction painted an interesting shade of crimson. Dawson was ushered rapidly inside and through a small reception area by number two, Inspector Innes following. Not much sauntering going on here, reflected Dawson. He was shown into a small interview room and invited to sit down on one side of a table.

'Do you have your passport on you, sir?' she asked. Dawson handed it over. No thanks were forthcoming. She glanced at it and left the room. 'Wait here,' she commanded unnecessarily as she walked out.

He was left alone to stew with his thoughts for more hours than he could put a number to. At one point, he was brought a cup of tea and the world's smallest biscuit. Finally, Inspector Innes walked in without his gold-braided hat, but with a rotund, jolly-looking man with receding hair, who was wearing a dark suit, a crisp white shirt and what looked like an old school tie. The Inspector failed to introduce the fat man.

'Do I need a solicitor?' asked Dawson.

'Do you have a solicitor?' responded the Inspector.

'Good point. Do you do legal aid?'

'Do you think you're under arrest then?'

'Aren't I?'

'No. Do you think you should be?'

'I haven't done anything wrong.'

'Just lying to a police officer, and aiding and abetting the stealing of a motor vehicle. But I think we can overlook those. Oh, and my colleagues in Jerilderie are a bit pissed off that you ran away from them. Particularly leaving a poor defenceless woman bound hand and foot in the house you broke into. Oh yes, add breaking and entering to the list of felonies.' But there was a small smile lurking at the corners of his mouth as he spoke: 'Anyway, we have a few questions we'd like to ask you, and then you're free to go with Mr Jeffers here,' and he nodded at the plump man in the suit who, unbelievably, bowed slightly in response.

'Okay,' said Dawson, considering the ramifications of what Innes had just said. 'And who exactly are you, Mr Jeffers?'

'Mr Jeffers is from the British Consulate in Melbourne,' said the Inspector. 'He'll look after you but first, in your own words, perhaps you can let us know exactly what's been happening to you?'

'Where from?' asked Dawson.

'A clue then. Tell us what you know about a gentleman named Riley Bigg.'

'Oh, him.' Dawson had decided that more lying, although he hadn't actually lied very much, probably wouldn't be the wisest course of action. Besides which, he was very tired and he was hoping that if he could get out of Shepparton Police Station reasonably quickly, then the British Consulate in Melbourne might possess a nice comfortable bed he could fall into. 'Yesterday...' he began. Was it really only yesterday? 'I'd stopped for a snooze and a bite to eat in a place called...' he'd forgotten. 'Sorry, I've forgotten what it was called, I'm a bit short of sleep, truth be told.'

'Gundagai,' said the Inspector.

'Sorry, yes, Gundagai. I was leapt upon by two big, nasty types who threw me into a car and drove me off to a house where this Riley Bigg chap was waiting.'

'Good. The car. Was this the Mercedes later found in Jerilderie outside the house you broke into?'

'It wasn't me doing the breaking. But yes, that was the car. I think it belongs to Bigg.'

'Strangely it does, registered in his name and everything. And as for the breaking and entering, I'm guessing that that was instigated by your travelling companion, Mr Patrick Bootle, aka Mr Mitchell Johnston. Can we take it that you are misremembering the bit where you hitched a lift later on in the proceedings?'

'You seem to be doing all my confessing for me. Is there actually anything you don't know?'

'We don't know where Patrick Bootle is now. Nor Riley Bigg. Nor indeed, the men you say chased you through the farmyard back there with guns. We suspect they were picked up by the cars you say forced you off the road.'

'You accept that then, do you?'

'It makes sense, but we'll know for sure when we get the forensics report. Whatever the case, find Bootle and we find Bigg. Find Bigg and we find Bootle.'

'Talking of Pat, who is he really? I'm beginning to think he may not be an overgrown provincial solicitor with designs on my future wife.'

'We're not completely certain yet, but we've an idea and we're trying to find out for sure. It's not easy though. There are, er, diplomatic obstacles to overcome.' He left it there, so Dawson tried another tack.

'What does Mrs Bigg say?'

'Mrs Bigg hasn't yet calmed down enough to say anything, unfortunately. There's been a lot of spitting.'

Dawson did some thinking and surprised himself by coming up with an idea. 'You presumably know about the house outside, where was it? Gundeega?'

'Gundagai. And yes, we're there, they're not.'

'Well, Pat and I were accosted' – was that the right word? – 'by the lovely Mrs Bigg in Wagga Wagga.'

'Go on.'

'We hadn't stopped to tell Bigg where we were going, as you can probably understand, and we hadn't exactly dawdled in getting there, so where did she come from and how did she find us so quickly?'

The Inspector inspected him for a few seconds, then got up, went to the door and called out. Number two policewoman turned up and he spoke quietly to her for a minute before she moved back into the bowels of the crimson police station. 'You're not just a pretty face, are you, sir? We don't know if Bigg has a place in Wagga Wagga but, if he does, we'll find it.' Dawson felt quite pleased with himself and completely willing to overlook the lack of actual thanks. The Inspector looked at a notepad in front of him and made a few squiggles. 'Just the big one now, if you'll forgive the pun. Why exactly are you in Australia and where were you on your way to when you were waylaid?'

Dawson had not come up with a satisfactory answer to this question, despite the fact that it had obviously been coming. Before he could think of anything, the fat British Consulate guy decided to join the party and, coughing slightly, he murmured, 'I don't think we need to go there, do we Inspector?' He looked apologetically at Innes and then smiled at Dawson. 'If that's about it, we can probably wrap things up here now, don't you think?' and apparently brooking no argument, he pushed his chair back and got up from the table, pulling his capacious jacket down over his extensive stomach.

Inspector Innes failed to look anything like a man who had finished wrapping things up but he pursed his lips, raised his eyebrows and shrugged his shoulders. He clearly had instructions from above. 'Okay, then, you're free to go. But if you have any more bright ideas like the one about the house in Wagga, give me a call.' He handed Dawson a card. 'I think we should talk some more some time. Good luck, Mr Dawson.' And he stood up.

So did Jeffers. Sensing a trend, Dawson stood too. The Inspector accompanied them back to the small reception area, shook hands and left them to step out into the burning Australian sunshine.

'My car's this way,' said Jeffers, leading Dawson around a corner to where a white Ford Escape SUV was sitting.

'Where are we going?' asked Dawson. 'Melbourne?'

'Yes, that's correct. It's a couple of hours away, so you

might want to get your head down. Unless I'm mistaken, you probably haven't slept since Gundagai. Put the seat back; there's a handle down there,' and he pointed to the side of the passenger seat.

'You're a mind reader.'

Dawson fell asleep almost instantly and found himself having slightly disturbing dreams about men pointing guns at him. When he came to, there was a man pointing a gun at him. He immediately noted this unpalatable truth, together with the fact that it was now growing dark outside and the car had stopped moving. The man holding the gun was fat Mr Jeffers, who had instigated Dawson's new state of wakefulness by prodding him in the arm with the barrel of the weapon.

Now, Dawson was at heart a gentle sort of soul. For most of his life he'd wanted little more than a few good friends, some decent, enjoyable sport, some decent, enjoyable sex and a drink or two. But here, now, he was getting mightily fed up with having people point pistols at him, even if none of them might actually have been pistols given that he had no idea what the difference was between a pistol and a revolver and any other sort of bloody handgun. Frankly, enough was enough.

When he'd fallen asleep, his hand had still been hanging by his side in close proximity to the handle that moved the back of the seat from the upright to the almost horizontal and vice versa. Opposite that handle was another, identical one operating the driver's seat. Despite lounging at an angle of 45° himself, he didn't think twice. He moved his hand quickly across the ten-centimetre gap and yanked the handle controlling Jeffers' seat sharply backwards. Jeffers, hampered both by the size of his stomach and by being turned somewhat awkwardly sideways in his seat, was catapulted backwards as his rear support vanished. He managed to get a shot off but it disappeared through the roof, thus significantly reducing the sell-on value of the Escape. Although Dawson was still hampered by his seatbelt, he managed to scramble across the gap and grab Jeffers' plump right wrist with his left hand while simultaneously thumping him as hard as he could across the bridge of the nose with the back of his right hand. Jeffers lost his grip on the gun and Dawson, to his surprise, managed to catch it before it dropped into the footwell. Must be all that rugby I've played, he thought, quite pleased with his efforts and, with adrenalin still surging through his body, he brought the gun hard down on Jeffers' balding head. Jeffers slumped back in his now virtually horizontal seat and lay still.

Having thus rendered unconscious the man who it appeared may not after all hail from the British Consulate in Melbourne, Dawson wasn't sure what to do next. The dashboard clock showed it to be just after 7pm and he had no idea where he was. He no longer had a phone on him. The official Aardvark mobile had been purloined by Rambo and he believed he had left his own old phone in the hire car left abandoned when he was snatched. He examined the gun in his hand and, after fiddling with it for a while, accidentally worked out how to eject the clip of bullets from the handle. He managed to get it back in again too, quite easily, and since he couldn't find anything approximating to the sort of safety catch he'd seen on Mrs Bigg's gun, he started to feel much more confident.

He quickly relieved his companion of his wallet, a few sheets of official-looking paper and a mobile that he found in an inside pocket of his jacket, then shoved him out of the car and laid him none too gently on the ground. He looked at the mobile but decided that it would be too much of a risk to use it, so he reluctantly hurled it out into the night. Looking around in the dark, he could see no signs of civilisation and no cars had passed them since he'd woken up. The road looked small and rarely used so they had clearly turned off the main Shepparton to Melbourne highway. He got into the driver's seat and, turning the car with some difficulty back the way they had obviously come, he drove off into the dark.

After a few minutes, he came to the M31 and a signpost informed him that Melbourne was to his left and Shepparton and Albury were to the right. He pulled onto a small patch of gravel by the junction, switched off the engine and considered his options. He didn't want to hang around in case Jeffers woke up and came looking for him. Mind you, he would have to use Shanks's pony, and frankly the size of him suggested he would be unlikely to be able to walk the five or so kilometres that Dawson had driven in much under two hours.

His choices seemed to be to carry on to Melbourne, find the British Consulate and report Jeffers as a bad egg of the most curdled variety; to return to Shepparton and place himself back in the hands of Inspector Innes; or to make use of the vehicle he had acquired and proceed to the town where he was supposed to have been going in the first place – Yackandandah. He immediately ruled out the first of these alternatives. Either Jeffers was a genuine British Consulate official turned rogue, or he was someone they had never heard of. Whichever the case, he could only see hours, if not days, of questioning followed by deportation back to England lying in store. As for Shepparton, much the same. He thought that Innes was a good guy, but he couldn't be sure he wasn't in cahoots with Jeffers, so the inevitable questioning might be followed by a more permanent disappearance than simply boarding a plane home. It had to be Yackandandah, then.

Aware that he had yet to examine the wallet and papers he had borrowed from Jeffers, he restarted the engine and turned right on the main road. The next place of any size was Broadford and, approaching the town twenty minutes later, he spotted a petrol station and diner lit up on the left-hand side of the road and, on an impulse, he pulled in. Carefully parking the SUV so that it was hidden behind a couple of articulated lorries, he wandered inside, went to the toilet and splashed water on his face, then visited the onsite shop and bought some deodorant and a road atlas covering Victoria and New South Wales. In the cafe, he ordered a bacon and egg roll and a cappuccino, both of which turned out to be large and delicious. Feeling somewhat restored, he opened the road atlas and discovered that Yackandandah lay about 225 kilometres away. He would have to turn right, or east, a way up the road at a place called Wangaratta. He decided to make the journey that night and sort out what to do when he arrived.

First, he ordered a second cup of coffee and dug out the wallet he had taken from Jeffers. It didn't tell him much. There were a couple of bankcards and an Australian driving licence in the name of Maurice Jeffers. Nothing else apart from a wad of just over 200 Australian dollars. He had no compunction about transferring the cash into his back pocket; call it payment for slights and discomfiture suffered, he thought. He could also use it to pay for his meal, which he did. Next, the sheets of paper, which were folded into quarters. There were three of them, A4 size, and they were covered in closely written script. Unfortunately, Dawson had no idea what the subject matter was as it was not written in English or any other standard western text. He wasn't an expert but the word "Cyrillic" jumped into his brain, closely followed by the word "Russian". If so, that put a whole new complexion of a rather rubicund colour on proceedings. So Jeffers was Russian? Or working for the Russians? What other explanation could there be? Given everything that had occurred, Dawson couldn't think of a better one. He slid the papers thoughtfully into his pocket and left, heading north-eastwards.

___ In which Martin looks out of a
window, and meets a girl in a
bar

Martin Evans gazed down out of his hotel window, being careful
to keep as hidden as possible behind the half-drawn curtains.
He was keen to see how long Greta would hang around on
the pavement outside and he was debating whether or not
he should or could follow her if she showed signs of moving
off. He had thought the whole business of her taxi following
his from the airport to be a hoot of the first water, but if
nothing else it meant that he had been right to make the trip
to Australia. Something was definitely going on, and being a
top newshound with an estimable record exposing fraudulent
car dealerships in the Rhondda – well, okay, one fraudulent car
dealership, although there was that hairdresser in Cwmbran
who was pocketing cash from the till, not to mention the so-
called bed and breakfast in Stallford that had turned out to be
a not very successful attempt at minor brothel keeping – he
felt more than qualified to discover what exactly it was that
was occurring.

He'd been aware of the taxi following his almost from the
moment they had pulled away. Greta just wasn't very good at
her job, he thought, whatever her job was. Not only had she
obviously given him a false name on the plane but her attempt
at shadowing him through Sydney Airport was so amateur
that he'd felt sorely inclined to go up to her and suggest
that they pool their resources. The fact that she was easily
the most attractive girl he'd met for years had reinforced that
inclination, but he had concluded that more was to be gained
from acting the innocent. He was sure that Greta's presence
was linked to Dawson, and finding Dawson was his number
one priority.

As the blonde girl, wearing the same green hoody that

she'd had on in the plane, but with the hood up despite the heat and humidity, continued to mooch aimlessly around opposite, Martin finally decided that progress would be improved if he were a bit more proactive, so pausing only to sloosh water onto his face, he hurried down the stairs and out into the street. Greta was nowhere to be seen.

Martin had a good look around but she could have gone anywhere in the few minutes since he had last seen her from his room. Bugger, he thought, what now? However, he quickly realised he was no worse off than he'd been before the girl had turned up and tweaked his suspicion buds. After ten minutes or so spent peering around corners in case she was hiding, he decided he needed a drink so returned to the hotel, where well-honed instinct led him unerringly to the bar. There were only about a dozen people in the room. One of them, leaning casually against the bar counter and eyeing him quizzically, was Greta. She had removed the hoody, which lay in a pile on the barstool next to her, and she looked, well, extremely pretty.

'I thought you'd never show up,' I said as Martin walked into the bar and looked at me. 'Can I get you a drink?'

He nodded and came over. I was trying to read the expression on his face. Was it relief, or something more? I was usually fairly adroit at reading men's expressions, especially when they approach me in bars, which often happens, but I was struggling here. Relief, definitely, but also determination, I decided as he shook my hand and perched on the next-but-one bar stool. The stool with my hoody draped across it was between us, acting as a barrier. He could have moved it but hadn't, showing unaccustomed respect for a female, staying out of my space. A good sign. He made eye contact, another good sign.

'I'll have a light beer,' he said. 'I don't think Australia does heavy beer very well. You certainly owe me one; it's quite rude to go around stalking people.' If he was just on the pull, he'd have offered to buy me a drink, but was obviously quite happy for me to do the buying. Yet another good sign. After all, I needed information from him and really didn't have time to be fighting him off.

'I wouldn't call it stalking, exactly,' I said, while waving at the young barman who hurried over as if my summons was something he'd been waiting for all his life. 'Following, I will admit to. I've always wanted to do that, and my mad Greek taxi driver made it even more fun. But how did you know I was behind you?'

'Journalistic sixth sense, probably.'

'Ah, yes, the sleuthing hack! I remember. And what does the sleuth think he's hacked into exactly?'

'Well, for starters, I don't think your name's Greta.'

You don't say, I thought. 'Really? Why not? Don't I look

like a Greta?'

'You know why not. You said your name was Lucy and then immediately changed your mind.'

'Every girl's prerogative,' I replied, and pulled a slightly bent passport out of my jeans back pocket. The jeans were pretty tight and Martin looked as though he wasn't sure how I'd got it in there in the first place. He opened the passport and read the name, Greta Morgan. He looked far from convinced but let it go.

'Hmm, good Welsh name,' he remarked, handing the passport back and watching me slide it deftly back in my pocket. Not so much eye contact now, I thought.

'Exactly. We Welsh need to stick together.'

Martin drew a breath and plunged in. 'Dawson?' he asked with raised eyebrows.

'Dawson,' I replied, ecstatic that my instincts had proved correct. As had Martin's, I guess.

'Do you know where he is?'

It was clear to me that we needed to pool our resources. I knew where Saul was, or at least, where he was supposed to be, and Martin was obviously in possession of some information or other. 'I do know where he was supposed to be going, but that was a few days ago and I suspect he may not have got there. I was hoping you might know a bit more than me, given that you've admitted jumping on a plane at very short notice because you were worried about him. I take it Saul's a friend of yours.'

'If you're calling him Saul, I doubt if he's a friend of yours and, frankly, if you are, I'm astonished he hasn't mentioned you.'

I ignored the implied compliment. 'I've only known him a couple of weeks.'

'Not a friend then. Or at least, not enough of one to be following him to Australia at the drop of a hat. So I'm guessing you work together.'

'OK, yes, we'll go with that.'

'Except that he's out of work.'

'He's not now, and we're worried that he's got himself into some sort of trouble and we can't reach him.'

'That makes two of us. Which, as you point out, is the reason I'm here too.' He paused. 'That and the phone call, of course.'

'Phone call?'

'I was due to meet him for a drink the other night, but he never showed up, and then he called me on an unknown Australian number and made a very odd request.'

'Go on.'

'He asked me to go and get some old discarded wrappings, paper, cardboard box, that sort of thing, from his dustbin.'

'Okay, that is odd. Did he say why?'

'Nope. Just asked me to keep them safe. He said he couldn't talk on the phone.'

That sounded worrying. 'Did you find the stuff he was talking about?'

'Absolutely, but I've no idea what it's all about and I haven't been able to reach him since. I don't even know what was in the packaging to start with. Also, his flat's been broken into.'

I was shocked and annoyed, but there wasn't a great deal I could do about a burgled flat in Surrey from the other side of the world. What sort of tinpot secret intelligence operation was I working for that couldn't even keep tabs on this sort of thing? Why did it take the local newspaper editor to tell me about it?

'What did you do with the packaging? It's not still in his flat is it?'

'What do you take me for?' Martin seemed genuinely affronted. 'It's upstairs in my room. Do you want to see it?'

'I certainly do. Let's go.'

'So, anyway, who's we?' he asked, as we were walking up the stairs. 'You can take it I'm not wholly convinced by the publisher story.'

Napoleon had been annoyed that I'd opened up too far with Rachel, but Napoleon wasn't here and Martin was clearly going to be a help – had already been a help. So out came the business card again. Martin looked at it and handed it back with a smirk. 'I see,' he said. 'I thought as much anyway, but unless I'm very much mistaken, we're talking about some quasi-official government agency not too many pages away from MI6. Am I right?'

'Yes, of course you're right.' When it came to the words "Secret Service", I seemed to be having terrible trouble keeping the "Secret" bit "secret". 'God, you really are a newshound aren't you? Okay, are you still with me?'

'I think we'll both be better off sticking together. We need to find young Daws fast, and what with my acute sleuthing brain and your finely tuned combat skills, we'll more likely achieve that together than apart.' I didn't pick him up on the finely tuned combat skills part; I'd really have to sign up for some courses when I got home.

We reached his room. 'So, where's this packaging?' I asked. Martin tipped the contents of a backpack on to the bed. Brown paper with Dawson's name and address on, together with some stamps, a white cardboard box, squashed flat and folded in two, and some bubble wrap. And that was it. Two things sprang to my mind straightaway, neither very original. I'd heard of full stops hiding tiny, miniaturised pieces of data, unless that was just in James Bond. However, there were no full stops. So I looked at the stamps, but there was nothing foreign or unusual about them. They were just a selection of plain old British ones bearing the familiar silhouette of the Queen's head. I couldn't believe they had any importance but tore them carefully away from the paper and stowed them in the opposite back pocket to the one containing my passport.

'Ah, yes, stamps,' said Martin. 'The old Charade trick. I'd already thought of that and discounted it.'

'Hmm, yes, philately will get you nowhere.' So where did that leave us? Despite Dawson's call to Martin, the packaging looked more and more like a blind alley. 'Do you know what was inside all this?' I asked.

'I've no idea. Daws didn't mention it and he clearly didn't want to hang around on the phone. Whatever it was, look at the box,' and he opened the cardboard out to an approximate cube. 'It was quite big.'

'And I think we can put two and two together and guess that whatever it was, it was the reason for the break-in at his flat. So, either it's still in the flat or, more likely, it's in the possession of person or persons unknown. Either way, there's no point us worrying about it. There are people – not a lot of people, admittedly – 12,000 miles away, who can have a think about that. Excuse me a mo,' I added, slipping a phone out of another pocket.

'You're like a small blonde magician,' Martin said. A bit of magic might be quite useful now, I thought.

I got straight through to the rather severe tones of Juliet. I explained the situation as concisely as I could, and Juliet agreed to get someone round to take a look at Saul's flat. We both felt that going to Yackandandah was still the best thing to do and then take it from there. I failed to mention Martin. I wasn't entirely sure why, but he picked up on it.

'Ashamed of me, are you?'

'No, but the fewer people who know you're helping me, the safer it might well be for you.'

Martin seemed to accept that, although it appeared slightly implausible. 'So, what was that place you mentioned?' he asked. 'Yackandandy? Where's that, and *why there?'*

I answered as honestly as I could, although I had no idea myself why Napoleon had considered it important. Not on the right pay grade, presumably. Next time, I'd want a lot more information up front, or Napoleon could stick his bloody Boy Scout troop up his arse. 'We'll need a car,' I said.

'Already on its way,' replied Martin, which took me by surprise. 'Should be about another thirty minutes. I ordered one as soon as I arrived. I've heard this is a big country and I don't like walking. By the way, don't you have luggage? I mean, I'm amazed how much you can fit into those non-existent pockets, but you seem to be taking the phrase "travelling light" to new extremes.'

'No, no luggage,' I replied.

I had had luggage but that had been in the safekeeping of Laurie since I'd left Sydney less than four days ago. I reckoned I didn't need it yet. It would just slow me down. I was a resourceful girl, after all.

___ In which Dawson discovers that
Yackandandah is older than it
looks, and a reunion takes place

It was past two in the morning when Dawson arrived in Yackandandah. He parked in a layby on the outskirts of the town, put his seat back (carefully) and tried to grab a couple more hours' sleep. The temperature was still in the mid-twenties with humidity to match, but he didn't want to attract attention by turning the engine and air con on. He wasn't sure if there was a search being undertaken for the Ford Escape, although as he did not know who actually owned the vehicle – British Consulate? Russian Intelligence? Neither of the above? He had no idea who specifically might be looking for it. The Police? Riley Bigg and chums? So all in all, he didn't sleep much and when he did manage to drop off, he was jerked awake again by every little noise out in the darkness. There seemed to be a lot of wild fauna prowling around outside his vehicle. Most of it would probably want to eat him.

However, he did eventually doze off and when he came to, the sun was rising. By his reckoning, it was now Friday morning, less than four days after he'd landed in Australia. He'd not expected to make it to Yackandandah in a matter of hours, but he imagined that Alan Flannery might be a bit disappointed to learn that it had taken him well over half a week to get there. Whatever he was supposed to be doing there, he might be too late to do it, or if he was expected to meet someone, they would probably have long since gone. It could be the scariest wasted journey ever undertaken by anyone.

He got out and stretched his legs, and had a discreet pee behind a nearby tree. He couldn't see any sign of the animals who had been making such a racket in the night. He drove slowly into the town and parked in the centre. It was still too early for many people to be up and about, so he had a walk around.

Yackandandah turned out to be, if not quite a one-horse town, then pretty much a one street town. For all that, by 8 o'clock it had transformed itself into a bustling, if dusty, little community that amongst many fine colonial buildings, boasted an old school house that proudly proclaimed to having been built in 1103. This was either an out-and-out lie or the original inhabitants of the country had been more proficient in construction techniques than Dawson had previously imagined. He had managed to forget about the forthcoming folk festival, but notices pinned to boards and trees and in every shop window reminded him. He looked at the dates and was relieved that he still had a few days before the nightmare was due to begin. Despite that, the largest tent in the southern hemisphere was in the process of being erected on the green at the top of the High Street. Not only was it a High Street, but it had a few high street shops and he was able to buy a couple of shirts, some fresh underwear and a toothbrush.

He managed to find himself a room in The Sun Hotel ('You'll have to be out in four days, cobber, we're booked solid for the festival; everywhere else is too.') and after cleaning himself up, he wandered downstairs for a drink and to ponder his next move. He supposed that, despite carelessly mislaying both mobile phones, he should try and call Alan. So, using the phone in the lobby and without concerning himself too much about what time of the night it might be back in England, that's what he did. An unfamiliar female voice answered.

'Aardvark,' it said in a clipped, Home Counties accent.

'Oh, er, hello, I'm trying to get hold of Alan Flannery. I thought this was his phone.' Dawson half expected Riley Bigg to come on the line but he didn't.

'Mr Dawson, I presume?' Dawson concurred that yes, he was indeed Dawson. 'Good. My name is Juliet and I will tell Mr Flannery that you called. Where are you calling from? And you are not using the secure phone you were provided with, so I will have to keep the call brief.'

'I'm in Yackandandah, as requested. What do I do now?'

'You wait.'

'For further instructions, yes, I know. How long for?'

'Are you all right?' asked Juliet, her tone softening a little. 'We were expecting your call at least two days ago.'

'I'm fine, just a bit tired. I had a, let's say, difficult journey –'

'Don't say any more,' interrupted Juliet. 'Walls have ears. You're there now anyway. Does anyone know you're there?'

Dawson thought that was a slightly odd question. 'You do, but if you mean anyone out here in the wilderness, then I hope to God not. I wouldn't bet on it though, so I'd really like to know what I've got to do now so that I can get the hell out of here, preferably before all the insane folkies turn up.'

'Someone will contact you shortly. Just lie low and don't draw attention to yourself.'

Dawson put the phone down and returned to his room where he lay down on the bed and almost immediately dozed off. The light was fading outside his window when he woke up, so he realised he must have been asleep all afternoon. He found his mind was considerably clearer for the sleep. He had been told to wait for further instructions, both by Alan and now by the Juliet woman, although he had no idea how short "shortly" meant. As he had no alternative plan, he resolved that that was what he had to do. And there were worse places to wait. Yackandandah seemed to be a nice enough town, folk festival or no folk festival.

It took him a day and a half of fruitless waiting, in and out of the hotel and wandering aimlessly around, before the realisation hit him that he had no idea who Juliet was. Judging by what he had gone through over the past few days, she could be anybody. Or was he being paranoid? And if he was, why shouldn't he be? Panicking, he decided he had to get out of the hotel sharpish. Go somewhere nobody would expect. Buy a throwaway phone. Suddenly, he could feel the net inexorably closing in. He was halfway down the stairs when two people entered the lobby from the street. Two people he recognised straightaway.

He stopped mid-flight, managing somehow to retain his balance and not fall down the rest of the staircase, and stood staring. The two people in the lobby stared back. Then the smaller of the two, the pretty blonde one, pushed her sunglasses up on to the top of her head and said, 'Are you off somewhere, Saul? Can you get us a drink before you go? We're as parched as a camel's backside.'

'Wha...?' managed Dawson, carefully negotiating the rest of the stairs. 'Unggh,' he continued, unable to get his tongue or brain around the fact that a girl he'd met once at a party in Surrey, together with one of his best mates from Stallford, had turned up at a hotel he was staying at in a hick town in Australia, a place where nobody apart from Alan Flannery and Juliet should know that he might be.

'Well, Greta, you were right,' said Martin Evans. 'He is in Yackandandy.'

'Trust mummy,' the girl replied, smiling. 'She's always right.'

'Who's Greta?' asked Dawson, leading the way to the bar. 'I thought your name was Lucy?'

'Ah, ha!' exclaimed Martin in triumph.

'It doesn't matter. Lucy, Greta, call me what you like. Actually, no, cancel that. Apart from where Passport Control is concerned, I think the lovely Greta has probably run her course. I've got too much to think about without having to remember what my own name is. Right, we've got some serious talking to do. How long have you been here?'

'Couple of days,' said Dawson.

'Is that all? What the hell have you been doing? I've been to England and back since you've been in Australia.'

'Now I'm even more confused. You already *were* in England, weren't you? And you, Evans, what on Earth are you doing here? No, don't answer that, back to you, lady, who exactly are you?'

'Can't you guess?'

'I'm not in the mood to play games, but I do know you're not who you claimed to be back at the party. Let's see, does the name Aardvark mean anything to you?'

'Got it in one. I'm supposed to be your shadow but I've not been doing a very good job of it.'

'Just as well. You might have struggled to stay alive if you had been.' And he ran through a potted version of his last few days.

'That explains where Pat Bootle is, then,' said Lucy. 'But it doesn't tell us who he is or whose side he's on. He's clearly been planted on Riley Bigg – Riley Bigg? Is that his actual name?' Dawson decided not to go through the whole Really Big rigmarole again and just nodded. 'Okay, if you say so, Riley Bigg it is. So who does Bootle really work for?'

Dawson counted on his fingers. 'Not you lot, not Bigg, so someone else. Perhaps if we had some idea why we're all here and what we're all looking for, if that's what we are doing, then we might have a better idea of who else is involved.'

'This whole thing seems to be getting murkier and more complicated than I'd expected.'

'So, Martin, you old reprobate,' said Dawson, turning to the Welshman, who was already most of the way through a litre of local beer. 'I assume you're here because of that thing I asked you to do. Although I don't recall asking you to get on a plane and tell me in person.'

'It seemed the polite thing to do, particularly since you couldn't be arsed to answer your phone.'

'I don't think you've been listening to what I've just been saying; presumably the sound of beer running down your throat drowned me out. "Arsed" has got nothing to do with it.' He realised how irritable he sounded. 'Sorry, that was uncalled-for. I'm really pleased to see you. Both of you.' There was safety in numbers, he thought, especially now he knew that Lucy, or whatever her name might really be, was a professional. What with her martial arts training and Jeffers' gun, which he still had in his possession, he felt a bit safer. Not a lot, but a bit. 'Did you manage to get hold of all that packaging?'

'Yes,' said Martin. 'Just. Bit scary, your old neighbour, isn't she?' He paused. 'There's something you need to know, mate. You've been burgled.'

Dawson tried to summon up some outrage, or even a modicum of surprise at this news but failed dismally. 'What did they take?'

'Nothing obvious, so we think they were after what was in the packaging.' He raised his eyebrows but Dawson was thinking. 'Well?'

'Well what?' asked Dawson.

'What was in the packaging, you clown?'

'A tea service.'

'Pardon?'

'A porcelain tea service. And yes, I know it sounds ridiculous.'

'Wait a minute, that was us,' said Lucy.

'What do you mean?' asked Dawson, while Martin looked blankly at the pair of them.

'Aardvark. We needed someone, Alan knew you were out of work and were available, so he set the whole fake timeshare thing up. You were meant to pick up the tea service, but then you had your accident and it didn't happen. He must have arranged to get it sent to you instead. I didn't know that, but the plan was definitely to plant it on you.'

'So the whole timeshare thing was invented?'

Martin chipped in. 'Surely there isn't any timeshare stuff going on now? It's a bit 20th Century I'd have thought.'

'That's what I told Alan,' said Lucy. 'I certainly said no one would fall for it.'

'Er, excuse me,' said Dawson. 'I'm still here.'

'I'm sorry. But really? I mean, I know you needed work but didn't it at all strike you as a bit far-fetched?'

'Is there any chance of us moving past how stupid and

gullible I am to the next big question? Why a tea service? What about it? Looked just like a tea service to me, not that I'm an expert.'

'I don't know exactly what, but it's the teapot. There's some information that needed hiding, so Alan came up with some hairbrained scheme to plant it on you. You didn't bring it with you, by any chance?'

'The teapot? Oh, yes, it was the first thing I packed. No, of course I didn't.' He was aware that his voice might be giving the lie to the lie he was spouting, and a trained intelligence officer like Lucy would probably spot it. He wasn't sure why he was hiding the truth. Surely he could trust Lucy. Or was he just being deceived by a beautiful face? He wouldn't be the first. He decided to keep this card close to his chest, just in case. 'So there may be a teapot sitting in my flat with something, we don't know what, hidden inside it. Or, more likely, it's now in the hands of someone we probably don't like. Possibly Mr Riley Bigg and his mates or possibly, if we're right about fat Jeffers, somebody of a Russian persuasion. Not forgetting whoever Prat Bootle's working for.'

'We need to talk to Alan,' said Lucy. 'He must know what's in the teapot. And we need to tell him about the flat. He can go round and check it out.' She dug her phone out of one of the almost non-existent pockets in her jeans and started dialling.

'I spoke to someone called Juliet earlier,' said Dawson. 'Do you know a Juliet? Thought she might be fake, but I'm getting understandably paranoid.'

Lucy nodded, listening to the dial tone, then, 'Juliet? It's me. Listen. I need to speak to Alan.' There was a pause while she listened. 'Well, where is he? Look, it's quite urgent. The teapot that was sent to Saul... Alan needs to get someone round to the flat pronto – it was burgled a couple of days ago. The ungodly may well have it. Oh, and if he could possibly call me back when you manage to get hold of him to let me know what was in the teapot, and what we're all supposed to be doing here with half the Australian underworld and the nastier representatives of several foreign powers on our tail, that would be good too.' She listened again. 'Yackandandah, yes. Well, shadowing him might have seemed like a good plan yesterday but events have overtaken us. Oh, and we have a civilian with us too and we probably need to be making a move before he drinks the town dry.'

She hung up. 'Juliet will get on to it, she's great. Now then, Saul, you seemed to be on your way out when we arrived. Why's that? I assume you have a room here, since you were coming downstairs.'

He cast his mind back. He had been getting the hell out of Yack, hadn't he? 'Well, I may be overreacting,' he replied with a hardly noticeable trace of sarcasm in his voice, 'but I remembered that I came here in the car belonging to the guy with the Russian papers in his pocket, so he or his mates are probably on their way to retrieve it – and me. I was going to check out of here and get as far away as possible. England, for example. The Cricketers in Stallford holds a certain attraction.'

I could understand Saul wanting to head for the high hills but he had, at least unwittingly, moved things along and I was beginning to feel that my job now was to embrace that and not simply run away. Maybe there was nothing in Yackandandah at all, but we hadn't ended up there by accident and if we were indeed about to be joined by various known and unknown forces of ungodliness, we would be better off confronting them, however dangerous that might turn out to be. At least we'd have a better idea of what we were up against.

First though, Saul was right about Jeffers' car. Bringing to bear all my six months of not exactly extensive experience at Aardvark, it appeared unlikely to me that Jeffers really worked at the British Consulate and if he did, then someone considerably higher up the MI6 food chain than Alan Flannery would need to know that he was a bad apple. It struck me that here, twelve thousand miles away from London, I was well and truly in charge. I was definitely up for the challenge. This was what I'd joined for in the first place.

The first decision was to ditch the big, obtrusive Ford, but the second decision had to be to retain the hotel room that Saul had been about to relinquish. It would give us somewhere to lie low and catch up on some sleep. Martin and I had certainly not had much and if the ordure really was going to be colliding with the wind machine soon, we might not get much more for a while. Of course, Saul had mentioned that he only had the room for four days before hordes of folk festival visitors arrived. The thought crossed my mind that a combination of feminine charm and the wielding of a firearm might help to extend our stay if necessary. But it only crossed my mind for a moment. The firearm bit, anyway.

It was dark by now but even so, as we headed out onto the high street, I reckoned that Yackandandah was already looking a lot busier than it had been when Martin and I had arrived. All in all, Saul had probably done remarkably well to get the room for as long as four days.

The small Toyota that Martin had hired was only a few spaces away from the larger Ford Escape, so we drove out of the town in convoy and, twenty minutes later, left the Ford in the car park of a small industrial unit in a place called Beechworth. It didn't seem likely that it had any sort of tracking device fitted to it, or unwelcome company would surely have already turned up.

Back in The Sun Hotel, we settled down to wait, unsure exactly what we were waiting for. Of course, there was only the one double bed so, fully embracing the duty of care I had to the two boys, I told them to take it while I stood the first three-hour watch. Me first because if the bogeyman was going to show up, it would more likely be sooner rather than later.

And then my phone rang.

__ In which Pat walks upstairs, and
a Chinese man falls down some

As an employee of German Intelligence at the Bundesamt für Verfassungsschutz for several years, mainly concerned with fairly routine intelligence operations within the federal border, Pat Bootle had rarely had to make use of the combat skills that had been drummed into him during weeks of intensive training in Cologne. When offered this opportunity, therefore, he had jumped at it. As he'd said to Dawson, Bootle really was his name. True, he had been born Patrick Augenthaler, but had been adopted as a baby by a German schoolteacher and her English airline-pilot husband, Ron Bootle. He was therefore completely bilingual, and indeed idiomatically fluent in flat Home Counties English, having spent three of his teenage years living near Heathrow. Because of this he had felt he would be far better off working for foreign intelligence, preferably in some warm, sunny, ex-British colony with a reputation for good food and drink, and had applied more than once for such a transfer but with no joy. It had always come down to his size. It was felt that a desired level of unobtrusiveness and Pat were not closely related items. This was his big chance, therefore. So far, he was aware he had not covered himself in glory. Even disposing of a few members of the Australian underworld, while probably helpful to the Victoria State Police, would not garner any accolades back home. It was not what he was being tasked to do.

As for what he *was* tasked to do: after all this time he was no closer to discovering what had happened to Heinrich Baumgartner, who had disappeared shortly after making contact with Riley Bigg while on the hunt for the missing diamonds. Making contact with Bigg with a substantial amount of loot waiting to be found was not a great idea, even for someone as experienced as Baumgartner or as seemed certain, the late Baumgartner. It appeared an even worse idea to Pat.

He still had no proof that Riley was involved of course, nothing that could be run successfully through a criminal court at any rate. Even plying Rambo with strong liquor on more than one occasion had failed to elicit anything more helpful than discovering that Rambo could down vast quantities of strong liquor without any noticeable effect on his cognitive processes. Mind you, it was hard to make a significant dent in an IQ that was starting from such an imperceptible height. As the disposal of unwanted deceased bodies was definitely in Rambo's job description, Pat had been hopeful of a result for some time. Australia had a land area of approximately 7.6 billion square metres, only two of which would be needed to hide a German agent, so finding Heinrich without a semblance of a clue would be tricky.

—

Now, down in the dank and dreary cellar surrounded by one dead Chuckles, one unconscious Bunny and one similarly sleeping Bigg, Pat realised he would be better off somewhere else. He could try and achieve that alone and take his chances with Rambo and any other of Riley's cohorts who might be lurking upstairs, or he could do it while lugging the aforesaid Riley bodily along, both as security and because any information he might be able to wring out of him might start counting on the currently very empty credit side of the ledger back in Germany. Easier said than done, however. Pat was big and strong, but Riley was a ridiculously awkward shape to carry while asleep, and unlikely to be very compliant if and when he regained consciousness.

Still, awkward shape or not, Pat had his career to think of, so he dug Riley out from under Bunny, none too carefully, and tied his hands together behind his back using Bunny's belt. It took Pat only half a dozen slaps around Bigg's face before the cadaverous gang leader started mumbling and blinking his way back to consciousness. Pat made sure that Bigg had full vision of Chuckles' gun, and to further emphasise the point that silence might be a life-preserving tactic at the present time, Pat also put the forefinger not attached to the trigger of the gun to his lips and then ran it theatrically across his own throat. Bigg got the message and nodded in a sullen manner.

'Okay, Riley,' said Pat. 'You and I are going walkabout, to use the vernacular. How many other goons have you got upstairs?'

'I could tell you that, of course, but how would you know if I was telling the truth?'

'Try me.'

'One.'

'Wrong answer. Too low. And you wouldn't leave Rambo up there on his own.'

'You don't think much of him, do you? You'd do well not to underestimate him.'

'I'm not sure if that's possible. Whatever the case, the only way is up. Off we go then, you first. The door's over there.' Riley, seemingly unconcerned, led the way through the cellar door and then, carefully, with his hands tied and unable to help himself with the banisters, up a flight of uneven steps to a second door at the top. There he paused.

'Keep going,' said Pat. Bigg shrugged and pushed the door. 'Wide open, please. Flat against the wall if you can.' Bigg did as he was told and stepped into the corridor beyond. There was another staircase opposite, with the foot of the stairs to their left. No one was in sight, but suddenly Bigg flung himself to the floor and a hail of bullets rained down from somewhere in the darkness at the top of the stairs. Had Pat still been standing behind Bigg, he would have become the second dead German agent in a few months. But he wasn't. With a speed belying his bulk, he had followed Riley Bigg to the ground but slightly to the left, where he rolled over twice and came up on his knees facing up the staircase. One bullet was enough to account for the small Chinese man who had been firing from above. Pat leapt adroitly to his feet and stepped to one side to avoid the body of the gunman as it rolled down the staircase and ended in a heap at the bottom.

'Hmm,' said Pat to the still prone Bigg. 'One down. So, if you're to be believed, none to go. But we don't believe you, do we?' He scanned his surroundings. Despite what he had said, the sound of gunfire had not brought anyone else running. Not even Rambo could have mistaken it for a fleet of cars backfiring. It was all very strange. However, the opportunity to make good his getaway without becoming embroiled in a pitched battle that he would almost certainly lose was irresistible. The light in the corridor suggested they were above ground and there was a corner behind him that looked encouraging. Too encouraging. He had been brought up not to trust blind corners. He stepped cautiously over Riley Bigg and said, 'This is where we part company. Just for a while. I haven't finished with you. Heinrich was a friend of mine. You'll be seeing me again.' He turned and walked away, through the first door he came to, and was gone.

___ In which Maurice Jeffers dreams
      of diamonds, and Inspector Innes
      smells a rat

It was the mozzies that finally woke Maurice Jeffers. He had been unconscious for quite some time, two hours according to his watch, and now he was cross. And itchy. He didn't appreciate being made a fool of, especially by amateurs. He would have to come up with a story that was less embarrassing than the reality. That, however, was something for the future. The here and now found him lying, dirty and scratching himself, on a roadside verge in a part of the world that he had deliberately chosen for its distance from civilisation. He was carless, phoneless and walletless. And the papers were missing. That wouldn't go down well. He was supposed to memorise stuff like that, but found it hard to do, especially with Russian not being his first language. Saul Dawson had proved to be trickier than he had expected, not that he had really known what to expect when the call had come.

It had not been a call he was anticipating. During twenty years and seven overseas postings, the likelihood of picking up the telephone and hearing the words "Come and drink vodka on the beach" had diminished almost to nothing. In fact, it had taken him a couple of minutes to work out what he was hearing, and once he'd realised, a cold chill had run down his spine.

How had it all started? He still wasn't 100% sure. In the early 21st Century, his homosexuality should not have been a problem, but it was and always had been. It was a common enough story, he supposed. His father would have cut him off from the family fortune without a second thought had he found out, and the wife he had met and married at university would also have been less than enamoured by the revelation. Mind you, her string of subsequent affairs with more sexually active and, frankly, slimmer men probably gave the lie to her ignorance. Whatever the case, they had been a huge relief to Jeffers and had allowed him to divorce her without raising suspicions amongst his family.

The visits to various clubs of differing levels of seediness had followed and become an addiction, and he supposed it was inevitable that one of the bewitching young men he had fallen in with had turned out to be after him not just for his body, which would after all have been ludicrous, but for possible future use should it be required. And now, many years on, he was required. When he had finally landed the posting in Australia, splitting his time between the embassy in Canberra and the consulate in Melbourne, he had smiled with relief. Russia was a long way away.

However, having overcome his initial shock, and realising that he could not just tell the Russians to go fuck themselves, he had entered into this apparently simple task with gusto. Even more gusto once he understood there were diamonds involved. If he could find and divert some of those into his own capacious trouser pockets, he had naively concluded that he would be forever free of unbending fathers and the threat of prison for treason. Or were they still allowed to hang you for that?

The job had been to extricate Saul Dawson from the Australian police and deliver him to an address in the backwaters of northern Victoria. Simple. He had the official paperwork and he had undertaken similar tasks on several occasions over the years in a genuine British Embassy capacity. But the diamonds had gnawed away at him. He had supposed that this Dawson fellow either had them or knew where they were, and when he had heard from the police about the connection with Riley Bigg, he had become convinced. Hence the small diversion from his official route, the production of the gun and, unfortunately, the subsequent catastrophic outcome.

Anyway, things were not going to get any better if he stayed where he was, so, with a deep sigh, he started walking. It was not something he was especially good at but there was no alternative. He spent the time trudging along the road trying to decide what to do next. The Russians were unlikely to be too forgiving of his failure to accomplish the first task he had been set and he could foresee a future involving bricks and deep water. And the Ambassador would also be asking questions about his movements and the loss of his official car. He really should have hired one, but it was too late now. So, either disgrace or unpleasant death awaited him.

Or… Diamonds. Diamonds gave him freedom. Diamonds gave him a new start somewhere entirely else. Dawson had the diamonds or could lead him to them. And he believed he knew where Dawson was headed. He had not memorised much of what was on the papers he had been given, but the word Yackandandah stood out whether it was written in English or Russian.

It took him another two hours to reach the junction with the M31. Which way to go? He vaguely remembered passing through a small town not long before he'd left the main road so turned to the right, back the way he had originally come. There was hardly any traffic about but whenever he heard an engine approaching from behind him, he stuck a chubby right thumb out more in hope than expectation. Thirteen cars and a flatbed truck passed him without slowing down, but finally there was the sound of brakes and a brief parp on a horn and he turned around to find a small pale van slowing down in the darkness.

'You okay, mate?' came an Australian twang from the driver's seat as the passenger door swung open beside him. Jeffers eased his bulk with some difficulty into the van, the driver helpfully brushing a collection of old food wrappings off the seat as he did so.

'Thank you,' said Jeffers in his plummy English accent. He

turned to the driver, a scrawny man of middle years dressed in some old cast offs he may have found in a skip somewhere.

'Don't expect to see blokes walking along here in the middle of the night,' said the driver, chewing on what seemed to be a knot of tobacco. 'You want to be careful. Could get knocked sideways by marauding roos crossing the highway in the dark. They're funny like that,' and he chuckled.

Jeffers had his story ready. 'Yes, unfortunately I dozed off at the wheel and my car's in the ditch a couple of kilometres back. I'm perfectly all right, just a small cut to the head, but a lift to the next town would be much appreciated.'

'That'd be Broadford,' said the man. 'Not far. No worries.' He didn't ask any more questions, for which Jeffers was grateful.

Approaching Broadford, lights appeared ahead, and the driver slowed the van and pulled into the car park of a diner and petrol station, both of which appeared to be open. 'Truck stop,' the driver said, spat a wad of tobacco out of the window and drove off, leaving Jeffers alone.

He needed a phone and there would be one in the diner. He still had a few dollars in his pocket, enough to call Domingo and buy a coffee at least. Domingo would come and collect him. Domingo would always come.

———

Iain Innes was at his desk in Shepparton Police Station. He hated the early shift – the dog shift as he called it – four in the morning to midday. It forced him to drink too much coffee and, given that not much went on in Shepparton at that time of day, to do too much thinking. And what he was thinking about this morning was Saul Dawson and the man from the British Consulate. Innes had been kept awake most of the night, partly because he never slept when he knew the alarm would be going off at three, but partly because something had been worrying him. And now he knew what it was. The timing.

Jeffers had turned up at the station far sooner than he had a right to. It was a two-hour drive from Melbourne, and two hours before Jeffers' arrival neither Innes, nor anyone else in Shepparton, had even been aware of Saul Dawson's existence.

Constable Bates walked in with Innes' fourth cup of coffee. 'Sir,' she said without preamble. 'Something's been bothering me about that business yesterday.'

'Go on,' said Innes. Elaine Bates was good, definitely Sergeant material, and would probably have his job one day. He remembered her raising her eyebrows at him when Jeffers had turned up fifteen minutes after the two of them had brought Dawson in.

'I phoned the British Consulate yesterday afternoon after you'd left.' She'd been working late then, thought Innes. Again. He didn't think there was an implied criticism in the "after you'd left", but it was possible.

'Don't tell me. They'd never heard of him.' It was about time he took the lead here.

'Oh no, he definitely works there. Quite senior attaché apparently, been all over. But here's the thing. He's on annual leave. From yesterday through to the end of next week. Gone fishing, his secretary says.'

Innes sat there silently for a few seconds, staring at Bates. Then, 'Fuck!' he said.

'Absolutely fuck, sir,' she agreed. 'So, what now?'

___ In which Alan has two uncomfortable
  phone conversations, and Dawson
  resigns himself to going to a folk
  festival_

Alan Flannery's phone buzzed in his pocket. He noted who the caller was and debated not answering, but in the end he did.

'Hello, Juliet.'

'Mr Dawson and Miss Morgan are in Yackandandah and for some reason which I could not quite understand, they appear to have a friend with them. You need to call them. They are concerned that there may be people after them. Mr Dawson in particular seems to have acquired a few enemies this week. Also, they tell me that Mr Dawson's flat was burgled a few days ago. I was not aware of this.' No reason why you should be, thought Alan. 'This is clearly not a coincidence, so you may wish to look into it.'

'And good morning to you too,' thought Alan. He said, 'Is there any good news?'

'No.'

Of course not. 'I'll get on to it straight away, Juliet. Remind me again. Miss Morgan?'

'Greta Morgan. Please keep up, Napoleon.'

He remembered. He'd always thought the business with names offered improved security and a sense that Aardvark was more involved with actual spying than it truly was, but it was probably time for a rethink. 'Thanks.' He rang off.

The morning was well advanced, but Alan was still in his study at home and had yet to bother getting dressed. So, shower first, he thought. More coffee second and phone call third. Maybe round to Dawson's place with Rachel fourth, just to keep up appearances. He knew exactly what he would and, more pertinently, would not find there. That had been a nice touch.

Thirty minutes later, he dialled Dawson's phone. He was greeted with a single drawn-out sound that indicated a disturbing degree of deadness. He frowned and tried Lucy's – Greta's – phone, and she answered.

'About time,' she said. 'Have you been in bed?'

'Certainly not. I don't know what time you think it is but I've been up for hours.' Up, yes, but not dressed. The women who worked for him seemed to be getting a bit ornery. 'Why isn't Dawson answering his phone?'

'Yeah, I'm not sure that Saul's phone should be number one on your list of questions, actually. Listen, this is what's been happening here,' and she ran through the events of the last few days, particularly those involving Dawson. She possessed a happy knack for clarity and conciseness. He found himself growing more and more impressed, both with her ability to distil and impart salient information and with the way that Dawson had risen to the challenge, or several challenges.

'So, that's us,' finished Lucy, and paused waiting for Alan to make some sort of helpful reply. After a while, she realised that wasn't going to happen without a further prompt from her. 'Alan? Are you still there? We'd really quite like to know what we're doing here before Bigg and Jeffers show up, and they won't be the only ones, will they?'

'Yes, I'm here,' said Alan, whose respect for and irritation with Lucy Smith or whoever she was these days, seemed to be growing at the same rate of knots. 'I'll have to do some digging and come back to you.'

'That's not good enough.' The respect didn't seem to be mutual. 'There's a lot you're not telling us.' It wasn't a question.

'I can't tell you much,' he replied eventually, 'but you should send this Evans fella home out of the firing line before you do anything else. You're going to have to stay put for a while and I suggest you try and get tickets for the folk festival that's coming up. There's someone you'll need to make contact with, but they won't be in Yackandandah yet.'

'Who?'

'I'm not able to tell you over the phone. Not secure enough. You might find something helpful in your app store.'

'My what?'

'Oh, no, sorry, not yours, Dawson's. Be resourceful. I'll be in touch.' And he was gone.

—

Lucy stood staring at her phone blankly for a few seconds and looked up to find Dawson's and Martin's faces mirroring her blankness.

'What did he say?' asked Dawson from the bathroom doorway.

'Virtually nothing. Positively Trappist in fact. However, it seems we need to look at the apps on your phone.'

'My phone?' echoed Dawson. 'What, *my* phone my phone or *your* phone my phone?'

It turned out that Lucy was becoming fluent in Dawsonese. '*Our* phone your phone, I should think.'

Dawson raised his eyebrows. 'Bit of a problem there. Bigg's red-faced goon has it. Or had it. I'm not sure that technology is altogether Rambo's boon companion.'

'That's helpful,' she said, trying to think. Alan had told her to be resourceful but there was a big difference between resourcefulness and magic. 'Martin, you're to make tracks. Get out of the firing line, in the words of the master. Us two,' pointing at Dawson, 'we're staying here for the folk festival.'

Dawson didn't like the sound of either "firing line" or "folk festival", but Martin simply grimaced and shook his head. 'I'm not going anywhere. I haven't come all this way just to turn round and scuttle off home again at the first sound of a bit of folk music. Who's performing? I'm partial to a bit of Steeleye Span myself.'

Lucy, meanwhile, was shunning resourcefulness in

favour of practicality and, since Alan's call had come from an unidentified number, had rung the number that was supposed to be his but which again was answered by Juliet.

'That telephone is mislaid, is it not, Miss Morgan?' said Juliet before Lucy had a chance to open her mouth. 'I am emailing you a code. You have your book, I take it?'

'Er, yes, I do, thanks,' and Lucy, for the second time in two minutes was left staring blankly at a disconnected phone in her hand. 'The bloody woman's psychic,' she muttered.

Almost immediately, the phone vibrated and an email popped up. Dawson and Martin were staring over her shoulder as she opened it to reveal the figures **2150315141**.

'What does that mean?' asked Martin, who was beginning to look like a man on the hunt for a Pulitzer Prize. If he was still alive to collect it, of course. And if, as a Welshman, he actually qualified to win a Pulitzer in the first place.

'I've got a code book somewhere,' said Lucy and pulled a thin, green paperback volume from her back pocket.

Martin shook his head in wonderment at this further example of prestidigitation, but Dawson was still looking at the figures. 'Lemon,' he announced out of nowhere.

Lucy, who had consulted her code book with lightning speed, looked at him. 'You're right. Lemon. How did you know that?'

'It wasn't hard. Maybe you guys need to come up with better codes: Enigma it ain't. I once scored 152 in an IQ test, I'll have you know.' Lucy and Martin were looking at him questioningly. 'Okay. Reverse each set of numbers and correlate them to the correct letter.' He paused, but there was no obvious change in their expressions. 'Thus, 21 becomes 12 becomes L, the twelfth letter. With me now?'

It seemed to click with his audience at the same time. Lucy said slowly: 'So 50 is 05, five, which is E, 31, 13, M, and so on. Lemon. Who needs a code book? You're a genius.'

'Well, I'm not exactly Alan Turing and anyway, it doesn't

really get us much further, does it?'

'Of course it does,' said Lucy. 'We're here to meet someone at the festival, aren't we?'

'Are we?' asked Martin, who was thinking that his journalistic training had been far too inadequate.

'That's what Alan said.'

'Did he?'

'Yes,' said Lucy a little exasperatedly, before realising firstly that she had been the one having the conversation with Alan, and secondly that she was actually the only professional in the room. 'Sorry,' she continued. 'There'll be a Lemon at the folk festival, mark my words.'

This came as no surprise to Dawson, who thought it probable that there were going to be hundreds of lemons at the festival, many of them holding musical instruments.

'So, sleep first, and then we need to get cracking, gentlemen.' Lucy stood up, looking like she was relishing the opportunity to lead whatever was going on through to a conclusion. Dawson could only admire the way she had taken charge. It was something of a relief.

—

After an eventless night, during which Lucy had stood two watches, Dawson one and Martin none, they all trooped downstairs the next morning and up the High Street, which was becoming noticeably busier. Stopping only for bacon rolls in the Dusty Duck cafe, they came to a small low-slung white building with a sign outside proclaiming it to be the Festival Ticket Office. There were quite a lot of people, not all them with beards, milling around a small room, in which there was a desk at the far end, accessible only by running the gamut of festival T-shirts and assorted other merchandise laid out on tables inside the door. Taking her leadership responsibilities seriously, Lucy barged her way through the crowd, and managed to acquire three all-access tickets and the same number of wristbands in a delightful shade of orange, for an exorbitant price which she'd been uncertain that the company credit card could cover.

Outside again in the shimmering heat, she started scanning the programme that had come with the tickets and wristbands. 'Oh, Poppy and Treacle,' she said. 'I've heard of them, they're really good. Who'd have thought they'd be playing out here in the back of beyond?'

'They sound like cats,' said Dawson.

'They certainly do not! Couple of girls, one's a flautist.' She paused. 'Oh, I see what you mean. Yes, I suppose they do a bit.'

'Moving swiftly on. Is there a lemon mentioned anywhere in there?'

Lucy turned a couple of pages. 'Oh, my god,' she exclaimed. 'Yes, there is. There's a group called Balaclava Lemon performing. Um, three times in fact. First on Wednesday, in the garden behind The Sun as it happens. If they're our boys, we won't have far to go.'

'Although we'll have been turfed out of the room by then, won't we?' Martin chipped in.

Lucy considered this. 'We're okay in The Sun until the day before. Sleep in the car one night, accost the Lemons the next day – job done – get out quick leaving the hordes of the ungodly trailing hopelessly in our wake.'

'I love an optimist,' laughed Dawson. He was beginning to remember why he'd been so attracted to this small, spiky blonde girl back at the party. When had that been? It felt like several centuries ago.

There were two things worrying me. Firstly, I was increasingly baffled by Alan Flannery's obfuscation. Or was it more than obfuscation? Was it downright lying? I was damn sure he knew more about what was going on than he was telling me, and it was me here in Yackandandah, not him. If I couldn't trust Alan, then who could I trust? Juliet? I wasn't sure. There were three possibilities. Either she was in cahoots with Alan, so reporting my anxieties about him, well, that would simply go back to him and no further. Or, she was in cahoots with someone else, and I didn't like to speculate on who that someone might be. Or, she was absolutely the level-headed, entirely trustworthy Aardvark and, by association, MI6 employee she seemed on the surface to be. That last was probably the most likely but I couldn't afford to take the chance.

Secondly, I was worried about Martin. Not Saul, strangely, who I was beginning to think had a hell of a lot more about him than had seemed apparent. First off, Martin looked as if he was intent on drinking Australia dry. I could tell him to stop but he didn't work for me so he probably wouldn't. Maybe couldn't. His excuse on the plane had been his fear of flying, sorry, crashing, but Australia itself was highly unlikely to fall out of the sky so that didn't wash now. And he'd refused to go home. Presumably, he had his eye on some sort of scoop when all was done and dusted, but the powers that be would certainly find a way of stopping that happening, so any journalistic dreams he's been harbouring were mere pie in the sky. Perhaps I'll tell him that. Perhaps I should just ship out with Saul and leave Martin pickling himself until whatever is going to happen actually happened. Or I could overpower him, tie him up and stick him in a cupboard for three days. Despite my lack of size, training, brawn and experience in such matters, I actually have little doubt that if push came to shove, I could push and shove one smallish, less than sober Welshman into submission without too much trouble. And Saul might help too. Or he might not, as he's been friends with Martin for a lot longer than he's known me.

—

We'd somehow managed to keep ourselves busy for the past twenty-four hours, doing touristy things in an attractive part of the world we almost certainly wouldn't visit again. Nothing out of the ordinary had yet occurred, but it was now Tuesday morning, and my spidey-sense told me that this state of affairs couldn't last much longer. I'd lain awake for most of the night, even those parts of it when I had not been keeping watch for unwelcome visitations. Visitations? That may be the wrong word. Tends to imply something ghostly. Ghosts I could cope with on the grounds that they don't exist. Visitors of a more solid variety I wasn't too sure about despite my outward bravado.

It was another in a long succession of hot, sunny mornings and I was taking a stroll around the town, sunglasses firmly on nose and sunhat firmly on head. I wasn't sure how accurate Alan's assertion that I was "known" actually was, but I wasn't taking any chances. I had Saul's descriptions of both Riley Bigg ("very tall, thin, bald, smart, possibly a little overdressed") and Maurice Jeffers ("fat, possibly suited, average height, probable bruise on head, likely to look very cross") safely stored in my head, but that wouldn't stand me in much stead if either or both had thought to employ minions to finish Saul off and therefore, as I wouldn't be about to stand idly by and let that happen, finish me off too.

Something was about to go down in Yackandandah, and it wasn't just a couple of banjos and a mouth organ. Alan knew what that something was but hadn't bothered to let Saul or me in on the secret, nor had he hopped on a plane himself to pursue the matter. So Saul had been the patsy. Or, perhaps, not the patsy, but a diversion. Riley Bigg and Maurice Jeffers had both been aware that he was coming here. Who else? Well, Pat Bootle, obviously. So, an Australian gangster, a British consular official who was surely in the pay of Russian Intelligence, and a Bootle whose allegiances were as yet unknown but probably not to the United Kingdom, had all been pointed at Saul like gundogs. In the meantime, Alan, or an accomplice of Alan's, had quietly been left free to pick up or uncover the answer to what was still a riddle to me. I ran that over in my mind again over a coffee in the Dusty Duck and found no obvious flaw. I wasn't stupid; I had a first from Cambridge hanging on my toilet wall to prove it. And I could not see any way around the fact that Alan was not the man I thought I was working for. If that was true, who could I tell? There was a man called Jason who I'd vaguely heard might be Alan's superior at MI6, but I wasn't sure how to contact him securely and I was sure as hell not going to go via Juliet, not until I knew more about her.

In which Pat finds a telephone, but loses Riley Bigg

Pat had not gone very far after leaving two adversaries alive but immobile, and two others very much deceased lying around in the old house. He'd exited through a window for the second time in forty-eight hours but, having started to turn the tables, he decided that there might be more furniture to rotate if he hung around.

He stood still for a minute or two to allow his eyes to adjust to the dark and to try to get his bearings. Riley Bigg seemed to have access to any number of old piles out in the country, and this one wasn't much different from the house outside Gundagai. A bit more ramshackle, certainly, but a similar size. Pat had no clear idea where the house was but figured it couldn't be a million miles from Shepparton. The night was surprisingly silent for an Australian one, and he could hear no voices, not even Riley's. Why wasn't the lanky gangleader calling for help? Why had no one come running when they had heard the gunfire? Had Bigg after all been telling the truth when he had claimed there was only one person upstairs, the now lifeless Chinese gentleman? It hardly seemed likely, but the continuing quiet was making Pat twitchy.

He knew he couldn't just leave without getting some answers, so it looked as if he would have to retrace his steps, if not back through the window, then via a more dignified door somewhere. Although before he did, he would need to start planning ahead. So, keeping to the shadows in the unkempt garden, he started looking for a future exit strategy. A car, in other words. Again.

And a car he found, a sizeable black Audi with heavily tinted windows. Riley clearly kept a large stable of automobiles culled from the pages of "The Good Crime Boss's Guide to Suitable Motor Vehicles". The driver's side window was wound down to let in some air and slumped in the driver's seat was a man whom Pat did not recognise. He was amazed how many of Riley's cohorts he'd never met. Staff social events did not figure very high on the list of Bigg company benefits. The man, blond of hair and rather pockmarked of face, was snoring gently, so Pat edged closer, hoping that the snoring signified that he was asleep and not just a sufferer from enlarged adenoids. On the dashboard in front of him lay a half-eaten bar of chocolate and this seemed like a sufficiently good excuse for a hungry Pat to render the man slightly more unconscious than he already was. That outcome was achieved with the help of the butt of Chuckles' gun, and the chocolate was transferred partly into Pat's pocket and partly into his mouth. Just as he started chewing, he heard the crunch of footsteps on the drive behind him, so he slipped into the shadows formed by a small copse of the inevitable eucalypts. A few seconds later, he made out the unmistakeably bulky figure of Rambo approaching around a bend in the drive.

'Hey, Pizzaface,' Rambo called, not bothering to keep his voice down. 'I've got the beers, mate. Took a while. Grog shop was shut, and then it turns out the shop guy thought I ought to pay for them. I got some credit sorted.' And he laughed in a not-entirely-pleasant sort of way.

Pat couldn't help thinking that it might be a grand idea if Rambo and Chuckles were reunited before the night was out. But, not being that sort of man, despite the evidence of two dead bodies in the previous half hour, he decided he'd need a slightly better excuse than the theft of a few tinnies from the local store, so stayed hidden to await developments. Rambo approached the open window of the Audi.

'You're not fucking asleep, are you?' Rambo sounded aggrieved. 'I've just had to walk two bleeding kilometres to get these because you said you needed the fucking car to keep watch on the house.'

Rambo had clearly been easily persuaded by the acne-ridden man in the car that keeping watch was a sit-down job while going off to get liquid provender was not. Pat pursed his lips in silent respect.

'Jeez, you are too, the boss'll have yer guts,' said Rambo, leaning in the window and shaking the comatose Pizzaface by the shoulder. The shaking had an immediate effect that was obvious even to Rambo, given that the man in the car slumped sideways across the passenger seat. Pat decided that it was time to make his presence known.

'I don't think he's thirsty,' he remarked quietly from the cover of the darkness beneath the eucalypts.

When Pat spoke, Rambo was, unfortunately for him, still leaning in through the open car window. The sound of the voice coming unexpectedly out of the darkness behind him caused him to straighten up more quickly than he probably should have done, and the window frame turned out to be rather more solid than his skull. The cans of beer in his left hand crashed to the ground as Rambo clasped both hands to his head, which was now an even more virulent shade of red than it had been before. He spun round and staggered, tripped over a small rock that was one of many defining the edge of the driveway, and as he fell, cracked his skull for a second and more decisive time on another rock a couple of metres further along. He didn't move.

Pat looked at Rambo's prone form. 'That was surprisingly effective,' he murmured. He appeared to be getting quite good at laying out members of the opposition, both temporarily and permanently, and both by design and accident.

For the moment though, he wasn't sure if having both Rambo and Pizzaface out cold was necessarily a good thing. He needed some information from somebody after all, and if everyone was unconscious or dead his questioning techniques were likely to be severely stretched. On the other hand, if they were awake, they'd probably be inclined to make a lot of noise, which would not be a good thing. While he was pondering this conundrum, Rambo's body began to twitch slightly, and then started to hum. Pat took a step back. His first thought was that the thug was about to explode. As attractive as that might be, it dawned on him how unlikely it was. Still holding Chuckles' gun in readiness, he leaned towards Rambo and realised immediately that the hum was the vibration of a mobile phone. It was coming from one of Rambo's jacket pockets. The hum stopped, so Pat took a risk and plucked the phone out. He was about to check out the number that had been calling when the phone began to vibrate again. It was the voicemail kicking in. A prim female voice said: 'Hello, Mr Dawson. Juliet here, Napoleon's personal assistant. Please call me straight back.'

Pat did not know who Juliet was, or Napoleon for that matter, but it wasn't hard to make an educated guess. He half thought about returning the call, pretending to be Dawson himself, and asking where he was expected to be – although something about the tone of the voice persuaded Pat that any attempt at impersonating Dawson would be unsuccessful. For the time being, he decided that he would be better served by keeping his powder dry. He put the phone in his pocket.

His gut instinct was that he had to somehow find Dawson again. Dawson was the missing link between the half set of coordinates residing in the BfV safe in Cologne and what was presumably a second set somewhere. German Intelligence had run a complicated algorithm producing a 62% likelihood that the rest of the required information would turn up in the vicinity of where he was now. Sooner or later it would come to light, although no one was very sure how. It hadn't been sooner, and later was not currently looking too hopeful either, but what little chance there was of ultimate success lay with Dawson. Pat just knew it did.

Meanwhile, there was still no sound coming from the house. Pat couldn't understand it. He had left Bigg very much alive and conscious, and he was presumably aware that Rambo and Pizzaface were stationed on the front drive occupied with their own obscure version of keeping watch. But he hadn't shouted. Not once. Okay, certainly Bigg might have thought that Pat would be back to finish him off at the first cry for help but by now the gangly gangleader had had ample time to crawl to the door, open it and raise the alarm. But he hadn't.

Pat suddenly had a sinking feeling in the pit of his stomach. It wasn't the first he'd experienced lately, and it probably wouldn't be the last, but as these things go it was the sort of sinking feeling that hits the ocean floor and bumps resolutely along it without feeling the need to surface. Leaving Rambo and Pizzaface where they were and gripping the gun just a little more tightly than necessary, he broke into a run, crashed through the unlocked front door, and turned left towards the passage where he'd left Bigg at the foot of the stairs. The door to the cellar was still open, the Chinese gunslinger was still lying there, but of Riley Bigg there was no sign. Or rather there was one sign, a thin trail of small blood spots leading away from Pat and around a corner ahead.

___ In which Innes and Bates get
     on the case, and Elsa Bigg
     disappears

'So, let's think,' said Inspector Innes, sitting in his chair and idly swivelling from side to side. 'First off, Jeffers came in a car. We need to get out an APB on it, sharpish.'

Bates was standing by the door. 'You mean KALOF, sir. But yes, you're right. What car was it?'

Innes rolled his eyes. 'Great cops we are, aren't we? I don't know. Who saw him arrive? Check the CCTV.' He paused. 'Tell me we've got CCTV covering the car park.'

'Yes, of course we have. At least, I think so.' And she left the room.

Innes picked up the phone and asked for the number of the British Consulate in Melbourne. He was put through to the Deputy Consul, Piers de Havilland. Innes thought that possession of a name like that could only prove a help to any aspiring British Consul.

'Inspector Innes,' said de Havilland in a voice that matched his name. 'I fear this matter is desperately embarrassing for us but we are not standing still. We are contacting all known associates of Maurice Jeffers even as we speak. That being said, his network appears... somewhat slight. We are yet to ascertain where he was going fishing.'

'I doubt if fishing was on the agenda, don't you? Anyway, what I need to know first is the licence number of the car he was driving.'

'Ah, yes, of course, although we are not sure if it was one of the official vehicles. It might have been his own car.'

'Find out, would you? Should be easy enough to discover if any cars are unaccounted for. Oh, and Mr Havilland?' He deliberately left off the "de" to try to rile this smooth, smarmy English toff. 'Why am I speaking to you, and not the Consul himself?'

'Well, yes, I'm afraid to say that the Consul is unavailable at the moment, although he is on his way back today.'

'Why, where is he?'

'He's, um, gone fishing.'

Fuck me backwards, thought Innes as he put the phone down, before picking it up again and dialling the number of the Victoria State Police Commissioner. He was not looking forward to the conversation, and unfortunately the Commissioner was not away fishing so came to the phone promptly. However, the discussion turned out to involve rather more laughing at the incompetent Brits than any commenting on Innes' own level of competence in allowing Saul Dawson to leave his police station with Jeffers.

Bates came in. 'Bingo,' she said. 'Turns out we do have CCTV, and what's more it hasn't been vandalised again since it was last repaired. Our boys left in a white Ford Escape, so I've put the plate number out there and we'll see if we strike gold.'

'Ripper,' said Innes, and he relayed the conversation he'd just had with de Havilland.

'What now, sir?'

'Well, strictly speaking, Elaine, you'd better get back on traffic duty, I guess. I'll get the plain clothes boys to give me a hand.'

Elaine Bates tried not to let her face fall too far. She had been hoping this was the opportunity she'd been waiting for. She'd applied to the Criminal Investigation Branch twice in two years and was still awaiting the result of the second application. 'I'm available to help, sir,' she said. 'I've got nothing rostered for three days.'

'Really? What are you doing here then?'

'Just helping out, I guess. Got nothing on at home.'

Innes considered her for a while. 'Okay, you're hired. Come with me.'

'Where are we going?'

'First, we're going to get out of these uniforms and into something less conspicuous. After that, we're going to pay a call on Mrs Elsa Bigg. You might want to pick up a towel en route. She's a spitter.' He moved to a cupboard and took out a selection of civilian clothing, some of which he rejected. Having made his choice, he said, 'Bathroom', and disappeared out of the office and down the corridor. Bates followed him and stood waiting indecisively until Innes rejoined her, dressed in almost new jeans, Nike trainers and a dark blue showerproof top. He almost didn't look like a policeman at all.

'You can drive,' said Innes as they approached the unmarked, pale blue Mazda in the car park. 'It's got more oomph than looks likely and you being in traffic, you should be able to get a bit more out of it than me. If it proves necessary,' he added, grabbing hold of the strap above the passenger door as Bates left the car park rather more quickly than Innes had ever done before.

'Sorry, sir,' said Bates, slowing down. 'Shall we swing past mine so I can change too?'

'Yes, I'd have thought so. And you might as well call me Iain, as we're trying not to look like cops.'

'Iain Innes.' Bates tried not to smirk. 'Has a ring to it.'

'My Scottish ancestry haunts me.'

Innes waited in the car while Bates went in to change. His mobile rang and a gruff voice with a faint twinge of what Innes thought could be the English Midlands, asked, 'Inspector Innes?'

'That's right, who's this?'

'My name is Sir Royston Johns. I'm the British Consul in Melbourne. I understand you've been speaking to my deputy about...' and he paused. 'Is this line secure?'

'Pretty much, Sir Royston. As secure as any police line anyway.'

'Okay. Maurice Jeffers. I've had words with the Commissioner, and I'm assured they'll have him nabbed before long. He'll then be shipped to England. So, out of your hands, as you are no doubt aware. But anyway, what I called to say was thanks for your help. I doubt if young Piers thought to offer any. Forgetful like that, some of these younger fellas. Anyway, as I say, hugely embarrassing but we'll sort it. I don't imagine we'll speak again,' and he hung up.

Innes sat looking at his phone, thinking, until Bates appeared again dressed down to such an extent that Innes started to doubt his wisdom in inviting her along. Still, too late now. 'Just had a call from the Consul in Melbourne, warning us off,' he said.

'Oh,' said Bates, slumping slightly behind the wheel. 'So this is the shortest stint of plain clothes work in Victoria police history then? Shall I take you back to the station?'

'The station? We're not going to find Jeffers or Dawson there, are we? Nor the spitty Swedish lady. No, crack on, young Elaine. Mrs Bigg awaits us in Jerilderie.'

Unfortunately, nearly two hours later, they discovered that actually there was no Mrs Bigg awaiting them in Jerilderie. It appeared that an Inspector Innes had turned up the previous evening with a warrant to take her to Melbourne. This came as an unpleasant surprise to the real Innes, and a much worse surprise to the local sergeant who had signed the release form.

Still, anger made Iain Innes even more determined. So, although the sergeant wanted nothing more than to see the back of him, Innes settled down at a desk and started making phone calls. Elaine had an idea of her own and went in search of another telephone. She wasn't yet sure if this plain clothes lark was going to prove as exciting as she'd hoped, but she was certainly glad she wasn't the sergeant.

'Right,' said Innes, coming to find her after twenty minutes. 'Wagga Wagga.' Elaine put the phone down and looked at her watch. The afternoon was drawing on and Wagga Wagga was at least a further ninety minutes away. It didn't look likely that she was going to get home that night and Innes had said nothing about packing an overnight bag. Still, she wasn't a two-showers-a-day kind of girl.

She smiled at the Inspector. 'Have they found the house then, Iain?' She remembered to use his Christian name for the first time. It was a start.

'That they have. They've not uncovered anything yet, but then we don't really know what we're looking for. Hopefully they're a step up from the drongos running this place.'

'There'll be something there. And something is what I've got, too.' Her normally severe face broke into what may have been a small smile. 'I've been ringing car hire companies in Sydney, starting at the airport. Came up trumps on attempt number four.'

'What trumps would those be?' Innes found himself floundering a bit. Also, the historically positive nuance attached to the word trump had become considerably less positive in recent times, so he wasn't completely sure if Bates was the possessor of good news or bad.

'Saul Dawson didn't bring a car with him from England in his suitcase. He got to Gundagai somehow and the train doesn't go that far. So, a hire car. I've got the plate number and Gundagai police are on the hunt. They seemed quite keen to help, given the Riley Bigg connection. Meanwhile, Wagga Wagga's en route to Gundagai, isn't it?'

_____ In which Dawson thinks about the
lid of a teapot, and remembers
where he left his phone

Like Lucy, Dawson had been having trouble sleeping, partly because of the situation they were in and partly because he had to share the double bed with Martin. Somehow, he and Lucy had ended up covering all the watches themselves, two hours on, two hours off. Martin had not volunteered to help, and Lucy was convinced he would fall asleep on sentry duty anyway. A copious amount of beer was likely to have that effect. So Martin slept on all through the nights, and most of the time he snored, with a gentle, arrhythmic rumble. Martin had been quite put out that Lucy had refused to share what was left of the bed with him when it was Dawson's turn to keep watch, preferring instead to curl up in an armchair. She was small enough and bendy enough to do that. Dawson was quite pleased at this arrangement although, as he was madly in love with Rachel, he couldn't quite work out why it gave him so much satisfaction.

Dawson had another problem too, one which he had so far kept to himself. It concerned the teapot. He hadn't been entirely truthful when he had shot Martin down in flames for suggesting that he might have lugged it with him all the way to Australia. He hadn't of course. That would have been silly. He'd just brought the lid.

It was like this. Back at his flat in Stallford, what seemed like millennia ago, he had decided to make himself a proper cup of tea brewed in a proper teapot on the morning of his departure for Sydney. He had not experienced a proper cup of tea since he had left his mother's warm embrace back in Ealing. He had wondered how different it would taste from his usual method of swilling a teabag around in an old mug and slopping some milk on top. To prepare for this experiment, he had even gone so far as to purchase some proper high-quality loose tea leaves and a fresh pint of milk.

While wondering whether he was supposed to give the tea a stir in the pot, he'd managed to drop the lid. No damage had been done; it was still in one piece when he'd picked it up, but he'd noticed that inside the lid a small, perfectly circular crack had appeared in the china, running just inside the rim. Then he realised that the crack was not a crack after all. The circular section within it was now a fraction raised from the outer rim and further experimentation, eventually involving the donning of rubber gloves with a decent grip, proved that the central portion was in fact screwed into the rest of the lid. Having unscrewed it, he found a small scrap of paper inside with some numbers written on it. He had no idea what they meant, so had simply tossed the lid, safely tightened again with the piece of paper reinstalled in the cavity, into his suitcase and hurried out of the flat to the airport.

Now, here in Yackandandah, it was completely obvious that there was some importance attached to the numbers on the piece of paper. Unfortunately, he no longer had it. His suitcase, along with the Aardvark company phone, was locked in the boot of his hire car back in Gundagai. And then something clicked in his head. Actually, he had had the phone on him and it had rung while he was squashed between Rambo and Chuckles in the back of the car being driven to see Riley Bigg. Rambo had taken it and presumably he or, worse, Riley Bigg himself now had his official company telephone. Whichever way you looked at it, this could not be a good thing. He would have to tell Lucy, but she was sleeping peacefully in the armchair when he had arrived at this unsavoury conclusion, and he decided that sleep was probably more valuable to her at that moment. The information about the phone and, yes, he supposed the piece of paper with the numbers on it, could wait until morning. She would not be pleased, and Dawson found himself unhappy at that prospect.

__ In which Riley and Elsa Bigg
    are reunited, and Jarrod Lowe
    welcomes an imminent arrival

Few of Riley Bigg's employees looked as though they could impersonate a policeman. Jarrod Lowe, however, did not have to as he actually was one – although he was not the full inspector he claimed to be when he walked into Jerilderie Police Station, and certainly not an inspector named Innes. However, he was not going to let a little thing like that bother him and so, armed with a selection of useful documents from a collection he had painstakingly put together over time, he had found it straightforward to convince the local sergeant that he was there to relieve him of the onerous responsibility of looking after Elsa Bigg. The sergeant had hardly glanced at the official-looking paperwork placed on his desk, being secretly relieved that he no longer had to entertain the expectorating Swedish harpy.

Elsa was not happy. She was unused to being made a fool of, and until today had managed to steer clear of the police. She left that sort of thing to her husband, preferring to live on the proceeds of crime in the house in Wagga Wagga. There was also a pleasant villa that she had secretly acquired in Barbados, where she was likely to be headed shortly given recent developments. However, making her exit without Riley and without a bullet from one of Riley's associates might prove problematic. She believed that Riley would be sorry to see her go, but when Riley was sorry to see someone go, he couldn't bear the thought that they might return. So he made sure they didn't.

When they were safely away from Jerilderie, Elsa turned to Lowe. 'Thank you,' she said, remembering the good manners drummed into her during her strict Protestant upbringing long ago in Hudiksvall on the Gulf of Bothnia. 'Where are we going?'

'There's a house near Nathalia that your husband uses when necessary. He'll be there waiting for you.' He glanced across. 'He didn't sound too chipper when he called.'

Ninety minutes later, Lowe parked the Range Rover outside a double garage situated in a concealed dip to the rear of the Nathalia property and escorted Elsa up some steps and into the house through a darkened kitchen. Around a corner in the passageway beyond the kitchen, they came upon Riley Bigg, sitting up groggily against a wall with a concerned Bunny bending over him. Bunny had a red raw wound on his forehead but was still in better shape than his boss. He was in the process of loosening the belt binding Riley's thin wrists.

'Good,' said Riley, when he saw Lowe and Elsa. Riley gingerly brought his freed hands around in front of him and stretched his arms. 'We need to get out of here. Help me up and get me to the car.'

'What happened to Chang?' asked Lowe as he took one side of Riley Bigg's skeletal frame.

'Mutt Johnston happened. He's got away and, judging by the lack of activity from the front of the house, he's managed to get past that idiot, Rambo, as well, and... what's his name? Pizzaface?'

'Robbie,' grunted Bunny.

'Robbie. Morons, both of them. Your car's out the back clearly, so off we go.' He turned to Elsa, who was standing rather apprehensively to one side. 'We'll talk later. It might have helped your cause if you'd shown any degree of concern for your husband's well-being since you arrived.'

Elsa, pale skin notwithstanding, blanched. 'But of course I am concerned. Shocked, but...'

'Button it,' snapped a clearly recovering Bigg. 'Save it for the inquest.'

Elsa Bigg's first language was not English, but the word inquest was disquieting. She followed the three men meekly out of the house to the car. She was not, however, feeling particularly meek. She knew full well that she had to make a clean break of things but now was not the occasion. She was not going to get away from Jarrod and Bunny without a diversion of some kind so would have to bide her time.

'Where to, boss?' asked Lowe.

'We'll stop off at your place to clean up and sort out a few loose ends,' Riley replied. 'Then we're off to a little town called Yackandandah.'

Jarrod was clearly much brighter than most of the men on the Bigg payroll. 'Yackandandah? Folk music your thing, Riley?'

'Oh, I think we'll find the music to our liking,' Riley said, smiling to himself. He was feeling better already.

Given that it was getting well on into the night and they were driving along a narrow country road with few apparent indications of nearby civilisation, both Riley and Jarrod were immediately alerted when they spotted the glimmer of headlights approaching at some speed from behind them. Bunny was less interested. He was nursing a severe headache and an equally severe grievance with Mutt Johnston, who had inflicted on him serious bodily harm and huge embarrassment, as well as killing one of his closest friends, Chuckles. Chang he was less concerned about.

'Cops?' asked Riley, being fully aware that Jarrod was still in uniform himself under a nondescript fleece.

'Not a chance. It'll be our old pal Mutt, I'm thinking. We can probably take it that we've lost the services of Robbie and Rambo. Minor inconvenience.'

'What, Mutt showing up or losing those two clowns?'

'Both, although Mutt not knowing when to bow out just saves us the trouble of looking for him.'

Riley was aware that Jarrod's brain seemed to be in better working order than his own, which was probably understandable given what he'd been through that night. He was glad to have him here. There was a reason why he'd made him his second-in-command and anointed successor, after all.

'I'll just slow down a bit,' Jarrod murmured. 'We don't want to lose Mr Johnston again, do we?' Elsa Bigg, in the front seat next to Lowe, had the distinct feeling that her chance to say goodbye was approaching fast in the rear-view mirror.

_ In which Alan Flannery meets two
foreign gentlemen, and Rachel
Whyte has a nice cup of coffee

Alan Flannery was in his familiar carriage in his familiar train on his familiar route from Stallford to Waterloo trying to work out how to manoeuvre himself out of the increasingly difficult situation in which he found himself.

He was still unclear how he was going to transfer the Nazi diamonds from their current resting place somewhere near Yackandandah into his own possession. His original plan had been to use Dawson to find the diamonds, explain away his involvement in their discovery in some imaginative fashion, pass a reasonably satisfactory portion of them over to MI6 – presumably to either the Treasury or C's personal golf account – and then announce his retirement and enjoy a life of well-deserved luxury on the remainder of the proceeds. His extensive network of useful contacts included a completely reliable fence who would enable him to achieve that desirable end.

The Russian SVR's subsequent intrusion into this cosy plan had put a bloody great wrench into the works. It appeared it was not just the late unlamented MacGuffin about whom they possessed potentially incriminating information. Alan's unofficial liaison with the ex-Irishman tarred him with the same brush as far as Moscow was concerned. Alan had arrived home late on Thursday evening following the visit to Rachel's flat to discover a car in the drive containing two expressionless men with quiet voices whose names he never did find out. Their message was clear though. They expected Alan to recover the diamonds and to ensure that he did so, there would be an agent going by the faintly absurd nom de guerre of "Elbow" arriving in Yackandandah, poising as a member of a genuine folk group called Balaclava Lemon, to meet him and take possession of the cache when found. Alan was of course well aware that it was not beyond the capabilities of the Russians to sow fake news into worldwide search engines, but of more concern was that he had planned to keep as far away from Australia as possible in case anything went wrong and accusatory fingers started being pointed in his direction. The oblique reference the two men made about the decease of MacGuffin was enough, however, to convince Alan that his compliance, or at least perceived compliance, would probably be a good idea.

Beyond relieving him of the diamonds, should he find them, Alan did not know for sure what the Russian agent's instructions were or what his real name was. But looking at the non-smiling face in the small photo he was given, he doubted if "Elbow's" work experience with the Russian SVR would have had much to do with sitting behind a desk practising accountancy. Alan suspected that Dawson's presence in Yackandandah might not be the secret he had thought it was, and Lucy being there too meant that she was also in potential danger, although Alan was well aware that she possessed a sixth sense that would be the envy of cats everywhere, and would be unlikely to lie down quietly and let things proceed in the sort of way the Russians would like.

There was also Martin-Bloody-Evans to consider, of course. Alan had had experience of the Welshman's journalistic and alcoholic tendencies before, and he knew he would not be averse to asking the sort of second-rate questions that a Russian hitman might loathe to answer in a congenial manner.

Alan was on his way to the airport now to catch a flight to Melbourne but needed to stop off at the office en route to collect something. He hoped he would be able to get in and out before Juliet's arrival. Mysteriously, she rarely arrived at work before 10 o'clock on Mondays. He had never dared ask her where she went first, which probably didn't say a great deal for his managerial capabilities. He should certainly be long gone before Rachel appeared, as he had asked Juliet to pass on a message for her to pick up some unimportant documents from Vauxhall Cross.

—

Three coaches behind him, Rachel Whyte was also deep in thought. Alan's whole demeanour had changed since the discovery of the memory stick containing the frustratingly incomplete coordinates. Yes, she accepted that she had been thrust upon him but he had seemed to embrace her presence and the insights she could provide regarding Pat. He had been friendly, positive and amusing and then, suddenly, that had changed to an attitude only a step or two above curt and dismissive. It was clear that he no longer wanted her around and the change in his disposition could be traced back to only one thing, the coordinates, which he had claimed, laughably, not to recognise as such. That had clearly been a lie. He had known all along what they were and probably where they pointed to. In which case he possessed further information, which he had not shared. Not with her, anyway.

She wondered if she should cut and run. After all, she had a job to go back to. But if Alan Flannery wasn't trustworthy, that could have a knock-on effect on the safety of two of her friends. At least, Dawson was a friend, and Pat... well, Pat was an absolute bastard but she refused to think the worst of him until she had something more than the vague suspicions of some minor government-backed detective agency and a strangely unused fake solicitor's office containing an incomplete message on a memory stick stuck to the bottom of a chair. All right, maybe that was quite a lot to be going on with, but she still wanted to talk to her fleeting fiance. Probably after she'd hit him a couple of times first.

Rachel was not the sort of person to avoid a confrontation and she was determined that if Alan was in the office when she got there, she would have it out with him. She supposed that Juliet would be there to provide some sort of security, unless of course they were acting as a pair in whatever underhand thing was going on. She still hoped that Alan would be able to show her that he had been beavering away on something conducive to the greater good. Aardvark was after all part of the Secret Intelligence Service, however tenuously. But first, she had to pick some papers up from Vauxhall Cross for Juliet. She decided to walk the comparatively short distance from Waterloo to clear her head even though the morning was chilly and drizzly.

She didn't get to the Aardvark office until well past ten, and her hope of finding Alan there was dashed. The outer door was locked and she had not been given the code to open it. She was standing uncertainly outside getting wet when Juliet herself appeared, holding a large green umbrella.

'Here you are,' said Juliet, briskly stating the obvious. 'Come inside, you'll get wet.' Rachel was already wet, but she let that pass and followed Juliet through the door.

'Have you heard from Mr Flannery at all over the weekend, Miss Whyte?'

'No. Not since Friday. Why, is something up?'

'He has, for want of a better expression, gone off the radar. There are some influential people in the vicinity of Whitehall who are keen to have a word with him. I should not be telling you this, but I thought it best to include you.'

'Is it normal for an all-points alert to be sent out when Alan can't be contacted for a couple of days? It doesn't seem very long.'

Juliet pursed her lips at Rachel's use of his first name. 'I understand some disturbing information has come to light, and a conversation with a Government Minister may be imminent. A potentially uncomfortable conversation.'

'It wouldn't be about some geographical coordinates by any chance?'

Juliet, who had just been briefed about the coordinates indicating the wreck of the *Lusitania*, looked at Rachel long and hard before replying. 'I think you had better tell me what you know, or think you know, young lady.'

Rachel wasn't ready to talk just yet. 'I've only been around a few days, Juliet, so I really don't know who's who in this organisation yet. Specifically, you. Alan hired me, and the fact that he's possibly gone AWOL over a weekend doesn't give me cause not to trust him.'

'But you don't, all the same. Nor do you trust me, which is entirely understandable. If you wish, you can contact MI6 and ask for Jason Underwood, who is Head of Special Operations and my immediate superior officer. That may or may not clear your mind of any doubts you have.'

But Rachel was as convinced as she was ever likely to be, and if she was wrong she had several years, a few inches and a couple of stone on Juliet. So she laid bare her doubts about the coordinates found in Croydon, where they might point to, and how she was convinced that they had not been any sort of surprise to Alan. Juliet took in her stride the fact that these were nothing to do with the *Lusitania* after all, and merely nodded.

'That was not what I expected. Thank you. I think it fair to conclude that Antakya is not the place we should be looking. South-eastern Australia is undoubtedly the key to this mystery. That is where we shall find the pot of gold at the end of the rainbow. Trust me.'

'And what exactly *is* the pot of gold at the end of the rainbow?'

Juliet smiled tightly. 'Diamonds, Miss Whyte, and a great many of them if I'm not mistaken. Now, if you'll excuse me, I need to return to Vauxhall Cross. There are decisions that need to be made. You will have to forgive me but for the time being, I think you may stand down as it were. Go back to your travel agency. Or take a few days off. We will be in touch in due course. And remember, you have signed the Official Secrets Act.'

'What about Pat?' asked Rachel. 'I need to find him. He is my fiance after all.'

'Ah, yes, Mr Bootle. I believe we may have some ideas about who your fiance really is, although I'm not at liberty to disclose them. But I can say this. If we find the diamonds, then I suspect that Mr Bootle, not to mention Mr Dawson, will be close at hand. And possibly Mr Flannery too, if we have not managed to prevent him leaving the country.' And she gathered up her green umbrella and left the room.

Rachel made herself a cup of coffee and then, deep in thought, returned to Juliet's desk. Juliet, with an unexpected lack of efficiency, had not turned off her computer and it didn't take long for Rachel to find an interesting folder containing names and phone numbers. She scribbled down the one she was looking for and retraced her steps to Waterloo and then home. Once there, she stared uncertainly at the phone number in her hand for several minutes, then took a deep breath and dialled.

____ In which Valentin Prokofiev looks
in a hotel register, and Dawson,
Lucy and Martin meet a band

With a name like Valentin Prokofiev, he was always destined to be a musician of some kind, he mused as the coach neared the small town of Yackandandah. And a musician he was, amongst other things. An expert on the fiddle, he was also proficient on several other instruments, some of them musical. He settled down as comfortably as possible into his seat and shut his eyes. The four other members of Balaclava Lemon were chattering inanely amongst themselves. It was usually that way. Valentin was used to it now and put up with it. He was essentially a very patient man.

The folk group had been happy to take his money, much needed income in an uncertain profession, and accept his expertise as an improvement on the fiddle player who had mysteriously disappeared three weeks ago. True, they would also breathe a collective sigh of relief when he left them again, as promised, after the folk festival. He was uncomfortable to be around, and they were all happy not to prompt further discomfort. Best to put up and shut up.

Valentin Prokofiev was not the name they knew him by. He had turned up the day after they had received Thomas's note saying he was off to find himself. The quiet man with the thousand-yard stare and the Eastern European accent had played a few tunes, much more than passably well, had confirmed his availability to help fulfil the band's obligation to appear at Yack, and had announced himself as simply "Elbow". Valentin was privately quite proud of the joke contained within this alias, especially with English not being his native tongue.

Balaclava Lemon had three rooms booked in The Sun Hotel. The four boys had been due to double-up in two of them, leaving their singer, Alice, to hunker down by herself. It was, however, tacitly understood that it would be Elbow who now had the single room.

Having booked themselves in, the four original band members ventured straight out to announce their arrival to the festival organisers and check out rehearsal facilities. Elbow declined to join them, which they were quite glad about. Halfway down the stairs, they met three people coming up, a very pretty blonde girl and two men, neither of whom, Tony the drummer remarked, were, in his opinion, remotely in her league.

Valentin had his own agenda to pursue. He was adept at the art of hiding in full sight and strolled openly into the empty back office, found the guest register and immediately turned up the name Dawson together with a room number which was only three doors from his own. He had been prepared to spend the rest of the day trawling through other hotels' registers in similar vein, followed by campsites and guesthouses, but none of that had been necessary. The fly was in the web. He retired to his room.

—

There was, however, something he was unaware of. The fly, together with a couple of his mates, was on the lookout for the arrival in Yackandandah of a spider, a spider connected to Balaclava Lemon. And at that moment, three doors along from Valentin's room, the fly was jumping to his feet. 'That was them!'

'Who was them?' asked Martin, spilling beer from the bottle he was opening.

Lucy, however, was on it. 'Bloody hell, yes,' she said. 'On the stairs. Those four guys. Two of them were wearing Balaclava Lemon T-shirts.' The fact had passed her by at the time as she was backed up against the wall on the half-landing to allow the four slightly unkempt thirty-somethings down the stairs. She found herself irritated at her lack of professionalism.

'They could just be fans,' said Martin, who had the feeling that he might not have time to finish his beer before they were off again.

'Fans be buggered,' said Lucy with certainty. 'That was the band. Let's go. We might get this sorted a day early.' She and an enlivened Dawson were already halfway out the door before Martin, with a sigh, drained his beer and followed.

They didn't have to go far. The four band members were climbing the stairs towards them, returning to collect their instruments, having been allocated a rehearsal room that they could use for an hour. They had been debating whether to knock on Elbow's door to see if he wished to join them. The consensus was that they wouldn't bother. They could manage fine without him and, frankly, he was a good enough player to not need to practise.

Lucy dived straight in. 'Are you guys Balaclava Lemon?' she asked as they came face to face.

Tony broke into a smile. 'Are you a fan, gorgeous? D'you want a selfie?'

Lucy rolled her eyes and turned to Alice, a curly redhead with big round glasses and several scarves. She suddenly realised she hadn't really worked out how to broach the question but went for it anyway. 'Not a fan really, I'm afraid, but you're certainly on our list.' Whatever that meant. 'We think you might have something for us. Some information possibly?' Blank looks all round. She indicated Dawson. 'This is Saul Dawson?' Dawson wasn't sure he appreciated having his name bandied around to total strangers in the current circumstances but stayed silent.

'I'm sorry,' said Alice, 'but I really don't think we know what you're talking about.' She turned to the rest of the group. 'Does the name Saul Dawson ring any bells?' They shook their heads. 'No disrespect, Mr Dawson, but we've never heard of you. Are you supposed to be famous?'

'I thought we were supposed to be famous,' grunted Tony.

'That was the plan anyway.' Everybody ignored him.

'What was it we're supposed to have for you?' asked Alice.

But, of course, neither Lucy nor Dawson nor, for that matter, Martin, who was already at the foot of the stairs looking longingly towards the bar, knew. A clue? Directions to some place, time or further person unknown?

The one person who could help them, although not necessarily in the way they were hoping, was Valentin Prokofiev who, with his room door in the corridor above them open the merest crack, was by now listening to the conversation on the stairs and weighing up his options. His job was to locate Dawson, get the required information from him, dispose of him and make good his departure, ideally after the band's three performances at the festival so as not to arouse suspicion. But he was confused by what he was hearing. It sounded very much as though Dawson and the girl he was inconveniently with, were after something from him, or from Balaclava Lemon as a whole. And it was surely only a matter of seconds before Alice, who was the brains of the band, arrived at that same conclusion.

'Mind you,' said Alice, 'this isn't all of us.' And there it was. 'We've got a fiddler too, but he's in his room, I think.'

'A fiddler?' enquired Lucy.

'Yes, his name's Elbow,' said Tony. 'Get it? "The Fiddler's Elbow"?'

Although Lucy's first from Cambridge was in Modern Languages, not in awful puns, she got it. 'So, I'm thinking probably not the name he was born with?' This was altogether more promising. 'What's his real name?' The band members shrugged in unison. 'Don't tell me, he's not been with you long.'

'That's right, he's just helping us out,' said Alice thoughtfully. 'Our other fiddler did a sort of runner. I think you probably need to talk to him.'

Valentin made up his mind and decided to make an appearance.

___ In which Domingo Marquez answers
    the call, and he and Jeffers
    suffer a major falling out

Domingo Marquez had always known that if he bided his time, his time would come and he could return to Mexico considerably richer than he currently was. He had tied his colours to Maurice Jeffers' thicker-than-usual mast after discovering during a routine search of the bedroom he'd once shared with the British diplomat, some papers which he could not read. This was hardly surprising because they were written in Russian. However, he was sharp enough to take photos of the papers and send the images to someone he knew who was conversant with foreign scripts.

Yes, Russian, had come the reply, along with a translation that appeared to provide the sort of information about certain Australian federal and scientific establishments that a Deputy Consul of a foreign power, if Great Britain could be legitimately described as such, might have trouble explaining away.

Domingo had stored the information away for future use, unsure if it would be enough to blackmail his lover. And so, he had continued to come when called, and to share his bed with a physical specimen he loathed to touch, in case something more substantive came his way. He was sure it would, and it had. By means known only to himself he had managed to discover the real purpose behind the "fishing trip" and he was, therefore, only too happy to come running when Jeffers called, despite the lateness of the hour. This time, he felt that his payday was looming encouragingly large.

—

Jeffers managed to force his bulk into Domingo's Mini Cooper and instructed him to head for Yackandandah. It was only after they had set off that it occurred to Jeffers that taking the Mexican along with him to recover Dawson, his dignity and the diamonds, if not his prospects of any sort of continued good health, may not have been the perfect plan. He should have ordered him out of the car in Broadford and gone alone. It was not, however, too late. Dawson had, of course, stolen his gun, but he was aware that Domingo kept a small ladies' revolver in the glove compartment which, while a fairly useless weapon over more than a handful of paces, would probably suffice in the present circumstances. He had had enough of the slight, rather insipid Mexican in any case.

Driving along the relatively busy M31 was not the ideal place to undertake anything dramatic, so he quietly bided his time. Eventually, they reached the town of Wangaratta and turned on to a minor road signposted Beechworth. The road was suddenly empty, the trees started encroaching on either side and Jeffers opened the glove compartment. He had to breathe in to do so, and having located the small pistol he found it was not an easy matter to wrap his chubby forefinger around the trigger. Up to this point, Domingo had had his eyes on the road and his thoughts on scenarios that might involve large amounts of cash transferring itself into his possession, but he suddenly became aware of the movement and grunts coming from the seat beside him. He turned his head just as Jeffers finally succeeded in getting to grips with the gun and found the barrel starting to point towards him. To say he was surprised and alarmed rather understates the case, and the look on Jeffers' fat face suggested that the relationship would be coming to an end very shortly and very finally.

Domingo, understandably upset at this turn of events, removed a manicured left hand from the steering wheel and attempted to bat the gun away. Unfortunately, he had forgotten that his right hand had been hanging out of the driver's window, tapping the chorus to *Y Viva Espana* on the outside of the door. Even more unfortunately for both of them, the Mini was at that point traversing a bridge over one of the many gorges that criss-cross south-eastern Australia. The car swerved violently as it hit a pothole in the road surface, bounced into the left-hand fence of the bridge, shot back across the highway, and plunged through the poorly maintained fence on the other side before twisting and plummeting into the rocky river twenty metres below. There was just enough time as they fell for Jeffers to let off a shot, which found Domingo's forehead. This turned out to be a complete waste of ammunition as the Mexican's death was followed only a second or so later by the demise of the fully-rounded English diplomat and unsuccessful traitor, as both car and Jeffers hit rock bottom.

___ In which Innes and Bates open a
    suitcase, and Inspector Davies
    is very helpful

Iain Innes and Elaine Bates had reached Wagga Wagga too late the previous evening to do anything other than book into a motel for the night. Elaine had discovered that while she may be short of a toothbrush, the inspector seemed somehow to have come fully equipped. Live and learn, she thought. The local police suggested they meet them at the Bigg house at 10.00 the next morning, but not to expect much in the way of results.

'Ten o'clock!' snorted Innes in disgust. 'That's nearly bloody lunchtime.' But the local sergeant had been steadfast, so ten o'clock it was, and they soon discovered that any expectation of even poor results was rather on the optimistic side. Certainly, nothing had been uncovered that would give a clue as to where Saul Dawson, or indeed Riley Bigg, might be. As they were standing morosely around in the Scandinavian minimalism of the open-plan living area, Elaine's phone rang and she moved into the entrance hall to answer it. She was back within a couple of minutes.

'They've found the car, sir. And Dawson appears to have left a suitcase in it. I've told them we're on our way.'

'I'm not sure that's really your call,' said Innes. 'However, it's a much better lead than this place. No offence,' he added to the local sergeant, who nodded and said that he and his men would carry on searching. There was quite a bit more to search, he added. The Bigg house was a big house, he suggested with a smirk. Innes ignored him and went outside to join Bates, who had already started the car.

Gundagai was only an hour up the road, and they had reached the outskirts when it was the turn of Innes' phone to ring. He was surprised to hear the overly-smooth tones of

Piers de Havilland. The restrained plumminess of the voice contained distinctly triumphant undertones.

'Inspector Innes, I believe we may have found Maurice Jeffers.'

'Really?' answered Innes. He was riled by the implication that the British Consulate had achieved what the police had not, while at the same time was grateful to be told, given that he was not supposed to be pursuing the case. 'You've been out in the company Rolls looking, then?'

'That is slightly uncalled for, Inspector. I merely thought that you might not be informed by any other source following your conversation with Sir Royston.'

Innes swallowed, and replied rather more contritely. 'You're right, Mr de Havilland. I'm sorry. Is he in custody somewhere?' He was wondering if he could afford the time to barge in on the interview process before the State Commissioner sent the men in dark suits.

'Not exactly in custody, no. He appears to have had a road accident. I'm afraid he is, er, deceased. Together with another gentleman of possibly Spanish extraction whom, I'm told, may be his lover.'

'Damn and blast. How did it happen, do you know? And where?'

'I understand they drove off a bridge sometime yesterday. The police believe there were no other vehicles involved. They were on a C road a few miles east of Wangaratta. From the tyre marks, it appears they were heading in an easterly direction.'

'Thank you, Mr de Havilland. You've been very helpful. I hope you don't get into trouble for telling me this. Presumably the Consul knows about Jeffers' death?'

'I couldn't possibly say, Inspector. Sir Royston is not presently speaking to me. Still, no doubt the Police Commissioner will apprise him of the situation in due course. Good day to you.'

They were turning into the car park of Gundagai police station by now. There was a row of open car ports in front of them, and in one was a dusty white Holden which had "hire car" written all over it. On the doors anyway: Claremont Hire. It was presumably Saul Dawson's car, and the bored-looking constable sheltering from the noon sun next to it merely emphasised the fact. As they were getting out of their own car, a voice called to them from the door of the police station.

'Over here, guys, come in out of the sun. I've got the suitcase and a couple of beers for you.' A tall, broad-shouldered man with grizzled grey hair was smiling at them.

'Beer?' murmured Elaine. 'On duty?'

But Innes was grinning back at the man in the doorway. 'Well, I'll be buggered,' he said, shaking him warmly by the hand. 'Joe Davies, haven't seen you since college. You didn't tell me you'd been talking to Joe,' he added accusingly to Elaine.

'Don't have a go at her,' said Davies. 'Thought I'd keep it a surprise. I only came down from the Gold Coast a couple of weeks back.' They moved indoors and into a large, comfortable rest room with three bottles of iced light beer open on the low table in the middle. 'This is all very exciting. I take it that the car and this suitcase,' he pointed at a plain, medium-sized black case on the floor, 'are closely connected to the house outside town that's currently tying up half my boys. So that got me interested, Elaine's call's got me more interested. And when I then get a fierce instruction from some jumped-up arse in the Commissioner's office telling me to let him know if you show up, and not to talk to you, well, interest doesn't really cover it. What's going down, Iain?'

'You haven't changed, have you?' smiled Innes. 'I take it the Commissioner's men aren't about to show up.'

'What they don't know, won't hurt them.' Innes briefly ran through what he and Bates knew, and Davies ticked items off on his fingers. 'So, one, our old pal, Riley Bigg and two, some Brit traitor who may be a Russsky, God help us, are on the trail of this Englishman, Dawson, who may not know which way is up, because they clearly think he has something of value.

And the only thing that speaks valuable to Riley is hard cash or something that can be turned into hard cash. You had this Dawson fella in your grubby mitts but the traitor ran off with him, the traitor's now dead and you've lost Dawson. But you don't know if Riley's found him. That about it?'

'That's about it,' admitted Innes. 'Have you come across anything in the case?'

'Haven't looked. Thought I'd leave that to you. Shall we?'

The three of them spent an hour searching the unremarkable suitcase, which was full of the unremarkable clothes of an unremarkable man who hadn't quite known what to pack for an Australian summer. 'Three sweaters?' said Elaine at one point, shaking her fierce head in wonderment.

'Only two pairs of boxers though,' grunted Innes. 'Got packed in a hurry, do we think?' But the lack of underwear was nearly the most unexpected thing they had found. Nearly, but not quite. Wrapped up in an old Def Leppard T-shirt was a lid. 'What's that?' asked Innes as Elaine held it up.

'Well, it looks like the lid off a coffee pot. Teapot maybe.'

'Where's the pot it's from?'

'Not here. I think we'd have noticed.'

'What is that, bone china?'

'Porcelain, more like. Bit heavy to be china,' Elaine replied. 'It's odd, isn't it? Why bring it to Australia?'

'I don't know. Maybe he acquired it here. Maybe it matches a lidless teapot back home. Pass it over.' She did, and Innes fiddled with it, but failed to spot that the inside could be unscrewed. He put it in his pocket. 'We'll hang on to it. It may be nothing, but it's the only nothing we've found.' Innes opened another beer. 'I reckon whatever young Dawson knows, he doesn't know he knows it.'

'He wasn't searched when you picked him up?' asked Davies, keeping his voice as level and non-accusatory as he could.

'We just took his passport,' said Bates. 'Jeffers turning up mucked up the normal course of events.'

'Don't try and defend me, Elaine,' said Innes. 'My responsibility, my fault. What now? Any ideas?'

Before Elaine or Davies could answer, there was a knock at the door and a young uniformed officer still looking forward to his first shave poked his head into the room.

'Call for you, sir,' he said to Davies, who excused himself and went out. Elaine picked the case up and shook it, but nothing fell out.

Davies came back in with a big smile on his face. He had news.

'I have news,' he said. 'Pays to have friends in high places, or in this case, low places, such as at the bottom of the creek where your fat treacherous diplomat cashed in his chips. The Wangaratta cops don't like being told what to do by the State boys, like you I guess, Iain, so they thought they'd give me a quick call before they got invaded. They've given what remains of the Mini a pretty thorough going-over and it seems that Jeffers' Mex pal keeps a locked steel case hidden next to the spare wheel. Car didn't explode when it hit, so they were able to open up the case and it was full of documents, which Marquez may have been planning to use to blackmail Jeffers. One of particular interest, written in Russian, contained one word that leapt out at them.' He grinned.

'Well?' barked Elaine Bates, rather forgetting herself.

'Yackandandah!' announced Davies with a flourish and, walking over to the map of Victoria, which covered most of one wall, he pointed it out. 'Here.' His finger travelled a couple of inches left on the map. 'And here's where they crashed. Fifty-k west. They'd have been there in under an hour. Unless I'm a purple-arsed wombat, it's all going down in Yack, so I guess that's where you'll be going too.'

Innes looked at Bates and nodded. 'I think you're right, Joe. We'd better be off. Thanks for your help.'

'No worries,' said Davies.

'And for the beer,' said Elaine politely, but Davies called after them as they hurried out of the police station.

'Guys, wait up, I've just remembered something.' They turned back to him. 'There's a big music festival starting in Yack next week.'

'Why is that relevant?' asked Innes. At the same time, he felt it could be. If Yackandandah was a backwater for fifty-one weeks in the year, could it be a coincidence if they, and everyone else who might be involved in this as yet unidentified shenanigan, were turning up there at the start of the single week when it got busy? Innes didn't often believe in coincidence, and he didn't believe in this one.

'Apart from anything else, you're going to find it hard to get a bed for the night,' said Davies. 'Look, it's quite a way up the road. It'll be getting late when you get there. And I'm guessing you're in need of a meal. My suggestion is that you kip down at mine for the night. It'd be nice to catch up properly and I doubt if your bird is going to be straying far.'

Innes put his hand in his pocket when they got to Davies' bungalow and felt the teapot lid. That its existence was unconnected to whatever was going to be happening in Yackandandah was something else he didn't believe.

__ In which Pat Bootle gives chase,
and he and Elsa help each other
out

Pat gripped the gun even more tightly and turned to the door that led to the cellar, where he found what he had expected to find. The body of Chuckles was still where he had left it but there was no Bunny next to it. Both he and Bigg had flown the nest while Pat had been hobnobbing with Rambo and Pizzaface. Pat found himself wondering whether his natural instinct to let sleeping dogs lie had been a bit too generous.

He was still in the cellar when he heard the sound of an engine. He bounded back up the stairs, swerved around a couple of corners and emerged into the kitchen. He could see the headlights of a vehicle through the window.

Pat realised he could not afford to lose that car. Bigg was in it and Bigg was the only lead he had. He reversed his tracks through the house at a dead run, flung open the front door and made straight for the big black Audi. The driver was now awake, after a fashion, and was just emerging groggily from the car. That saves a bit of time, thought Pat, relieved that he wouldn't have to yank him from the vehicle by a pockmarked ear. Pizzaface's return to consciousness was short-lived as Pat thumped the gun against the man's left temple before he had time to realise that Pat was there. The thug toppled to the ground. He was having a bad day, but not as bad a day as he could have been having if Pat was a little more bloodthirsty.

Pat leapt into the driver's seat, turned the key, shoved the automatic gear change into "drive" and hurled the wheel hard round to the right, just missing two of the small boulders that dotted the side of the drive but not, unfortunately, Rambo's outstretched right leg. There was a small noise halfway between a crunch and a squelch as the wheel ran over the leg. 'Whoops,' said Pat.

At the bottom of the drive, instinct told him that left was the way to go, so he flung the car in that direction and set off in hopeful, but not confident, pursuit of Riley Bigg, realising as he did so that he had no idea what make or colour of vehicle he was chasing. In the dark.

As he drove, he thought back. If Pat had one major failing, it was that he had no head for remembering numbers, be they telephone numbers, pin numbers or indeed geographical coordinates. When shown the coordinates kept under lock and key in headquarters in Cologne, he had not dared admit that he would certainly forget them in a few minutes. So he'd made a quick trip to the toilet and scribbled them on a small piece of paper which he had placed in the heel of his right shoe. The scrap of paper had stayed in his shoe ever since, only being removed on one occasion, to be copied on to the memory stick which had eventually ended up stuck to the bottom of a chair in the offices of Franklin, Boasman and Bootle.

Now, bucketing along the narrow, rutted lane, he realised the urgent need to bring his mind back into focus. Just as well, because it took only a couple of minutes to confirm that turning left had been the correct decision. The bends in the lane came thick and fast, but as it straightened out, he caught a flash of taillights ahead. At that time of night, it was too much of a coincidence for it not to be the car he was chasing and as if to endorse the fact, he noted that the vehicle in front was slowing. 'They're expecting me,' he murmured.

Having thus caught up with what he momentarily and somewhat laughably thought of as his prey, Pat had no idea what his next step would be. He knew there were at least three people in the car ahead and could only hope that it was no more than three and that two of them, Riley and Bunny, were still less than compos mentis.

Needing to gain the upper hand before the opportunity was taken away from him by events outside his control, and almost without making a conscious decision, he slammed his right foot still harder to the floor and rammed the back of the big 4x4 with shuddering force. Such force, in fact, that the airbag in the steering wheel of the Audi dramatically inflated, thrusting him hard back in his seat. In the nanosecond before that, he caught a glimpse inside the car he had hit. Only a glimpse, but enough for him to realise there were four, not three, occupants. 'Bother,' he muttered under his breath, as the two vehicles came together in a forceful marriage of twisted metal.

Riley Bigg's Range Rover was a hefty piece of machinery but somehow the smaller Audi, perhaps imbued with extra power by the force of Pat's determination, or possibly just catching the 4x4 on the wrong side of a bit of steep camber, managed to shove it off the road and into some trees. One tree in particular, which brought it to a shuddering halt.

Elsa Bigg, having awaited her opportunity, had thrust open her door and rolled rather than jumped out half a second before the collision of Range Rover and eucalypt. Jarrod Lowe managed to fling himself backwards and across the bony torso of Riley. Bunny was unsure what was going on and was quite fortunate to be propelled into the back of the driver's seat rather than anything harder. Even so, the collision was enough to return him to a state of unconsciousness and he slumped back against the door beside him just as the Range Rover's severely damaged engine gave up its unequal struggle with the tree and coughed itself to silence.

Pat, meanwhile, had disentangled himself from the now deflated air bag and, opening the door and using it as a shield against possible retaliatory gunfire, stepped warily out into the darkness. Both engines had stalled, and the silence was only broken by the squeaks and chattering of some local wildlife expressing their outrage at the disturbance. Holding Chuckles' gun in his left hand, he decided to continue mining his current seam of intrepidity and yanked open the right-side rear passenger door of the Range Rover, pistol to the fore.

Understandably, his eyes were looking towards where danger might be expected to lurk. Not towards the footwell. As he opened the door, the full comatose sixteen stone of Bunny fell into him at knee height, sending him sprawling backwards. Jarrod, the only one of the remaining occupants of the Land Rover who still possessed fully functioning brain power, had scrambled his own gun from its underarm holster and loosed off two shots at where Pat's head had been a half second before. The bullets passed narrowly over Pat as he sprawled backwards, dislodging his gun as his elbow hit the ground. Jarrod heaved himself awkwardly off the crumpled, thoroughly befuddled figure of Riley Bigg to try and get another finishing shot off at the defenceless Pat.

Jarrod failed to hear the door behind him open and only knew things were seriously amiss when he felt, with considerable surprise, something extremely sharp enter his neck under the jawline. Dropping his gun and falling back across his boss, damaging the latter still further in the process, he managed to clamp his hand to his neck, find the handle of the small knife which protruded from it, and pull it sharply out with a cry of anguish. As he did, he caught a glimpse of the face of Elsa Bigg reversing back out of the door. Of more pressing concern than the vexing question of why Elsa had stabbed him were the copious amounts of blood beginning to spurt from the wound. Jarrod was renowned for his creativity, however, and using the knife that had caused the damage, he ripped two large oblongs from the front of his shirt, scrunched one into a pad which he thrust into the gash, and used the second piece to hold it in place, tying it tightly but not too tightly around his neck.

He became aware of the silence being broken by the sounds of the Audi's engine unenthusiastically restarting and the ripping noise of the two cars being pulled apart. It was too late to do anything about it in his now dizzy state, so he reached for his phone and fell back on to the seat.

Pat knew that his bull-in-a-china-shop approach had not gone as well as it could have, but at the same time had probably gone better than it would have without Bunny's unwitting intervention. While he was unsure what the commotion coming from the back seat of the Range Rover signified, he was clear he needed to retreat and take stock. He had no idea where his gun had landed in the dark but he was sure it would be a bad idea to try looking for it. He scrambled back to the Audi, climbed in and, after a couple of failed attempts, gunned the engine and put the stick in "reverse". At that moment the passenger door opened, and the slightly dishevelled figure of Elsa Bigg hurled itself in.

'Do not sit there gawping, you idiot, Mutt,' she muttered. 'Get us out of here!' Pat didn't need a second invitation.

He managed to reverse the Audi back on to the road without doing any fundamental damage to its undercarriage. There was only one working headlight, but it was enough. He was about to turn to the right when Elsa grabbed him by the arm and hissed in his ear.

'The other way, you fool, do not go back to the house. What are you thinking?'

'I'm thinking: what the hell am I doing driving you away from your husband when I've just spent so much effort meeting up with him again?' Nevertheless, he pointed the car in the direction she demanded. After all, it was likely that Pizzaface and Rambo were both awake by now, although the latter probably wouldn't be capable of running them down if it came to a foot race. But they were certainly both still armed, while he no longer was. 'So, lady, shouldn't you be tending lovingly to your husband instead of hightailing it away as fast you can?'

'My husband considers our marriage to be over. And he probably will not be thinking about a divorce.'

Pat thought. 'I suppose I owe you my life. What did you do back there?'

'And I owe you mine. Thank you for so stupidly but cleverly crashing into our car. And I did nothing much. I stabbed Lowe in the neck, but I think he is still alive, unfortunately.'

'You don't take prisoners, do you?'

She ignored him. 'Lowe has a telephone and already – how you say? – the net will be closing in. The main road is five kilometres away. We must get to it before help arrives. Put your foot down.'

He did, as much as he could on the increasingly potholed lane, and they reached a wider strip of smooth black tarmac a few minutes later without meeting anybody coming the opposite way.

'Turn right,' instructed Elsa. By now, dawn was on its way and the sky was lightening. Pat was thus able to tell that turning right would be in a roughly easterly direction, but beyond that he had no idea where they were. He still had what he presumed to be Dawson's phone, taken from Rambo's jacket, and if he could shake off the irascible Mrs Bigg, he could use it to pinpoint his position and see if it offered any clues as to where he should be going. As if reading his thoughts, Elsa said, 'I have a bolthole that Riley is not aware of. It is only an hour's drive away. You can drop me there and then go on to Yackandandah.' She glanced at him with a small smile on her thin lips.

'Yackandandah?' Pat was completely nonplussed. He had never heard the name before. 'Where the hell's Yackandandah? And why would I be going there?'

Elsa smiled grimly. 'I do not know what is there, but I know that that is where everybody is going, Riley included. So, I am thinking that you would not want to be left out. We are even now, yes?'

'Yes, I think we probably are.' Shortly after full daylight they crossed the state border into New South Wales and not long after that they reached yet another small dusty township called Berrigan.

'Stop here,' said Elsa a couple of minutes later, as they arrived at what may have been the town centre although it was difficult to tell, so bland was it. 'Good luck, Mutt Johnston Bootle. You will need it, I think.'

'You too, Mrs Bigg. I hope you avoid your husband.'

She laughed as she got out of the car. 'He will be looking for you first and me after. It is always money first with Riley. I will be long gone before he gets back to me.'

'Yackandandah, here I come,' murmured Pat to himself as he drove off.

___ In which Alan Flannery makes a
    small detour, and Laurie McGee
    goes for a drive

Alan Flannery was on his way to catch a plane, but not from Heathrow or Gatwick. Instead, he caught a slow, quiet suburban train to Chertsey and then took a taxi to a small private airfield near Chobham manned by a lonely ex-forces flying instructor who was one of the several people who owed him a favour. He was not too enthusiastic about ferrying Alan across the channel in poor visibility, but he did. Once in France, it was only another short train ride to Charles de Gaulle Airport, and Alan was off to whatever fate had in store for him on the other side of the world.

He was angry and vengeful before he left, but that was nothing to his mood when he eventually arrived at a wet and blustery Melbourne. He looked again at the small photograph of the Russian musician known only to him as Elbow that he had obtained from his unwelcome evening visitors.

___

Back at MI6, Jason Underwood realised that his bird had flown before he had been able to put a block on the ports and airports. Reluctantly he contacted his Australian counterparts to beg their help in collecting Flannery from whichever airport he turned up at. They were unenthusiastic. Which airport? they asked. He didn't know. When was he arriving? Jason couldn't help as he had no flight number or airline to give them. All right, they said at last, audibly huffing down the line. We'll post a man at Sydney Airport for the next forty-eight hours. Yes, we're very short staffed, they said. Best we can do.

Juliet was being more useful, however. While all this was going on she phoned and spoke to Laurie McGee.

'Who?' asked Jason.

'Laurie is our man in the Antipodes,' explained Juliet.

'You don't have a man in the – er – in Australia. I've seen the payroll.'

'One of Mr Flannery's private arrangements. He has several.'

'Had. So why would this McGee turn against him?'

'Oh, didn't I mention?' Juliet smiled. 'Laurie is my cousin. Mr Flannery needed some occasional assistance in Australia, so I thought it might be useful if I suggested Laurie. Blood is, after all, thicker than water.'

—

In Melbourne, Flannery was searching for the car rental office at the airport when a familiar voice, if not face, called out to him.

'Hi there, cobber, need a lift?'

As far as Alan was aware, Laurie McGee was the only Australian outside the pages of a book who actually used the word "cobber". He turned towards the voice with a smile, but he wasn't smiling inside. Laurie's appearance was an unwelcome intrusion. He didn't know that Laurie was Juliet's cousin, but he could smell her involvement, which certainly meant that the wolves of MI6 had tracked him down.

'Hello, Laurie. Bit off your beaten track, aren't you?' He was considering how he could rid himself of the big, bluff New South Welshman. Violence would probably not be successful given the differences in age, size and fitness, and Alan would not possess a weapon of any kind until he visited a little man he knew who worked out of a small building tucked away in the back streets of Carlton.

For now, he would have to be patient.

'Car's this way,' said Laurie, ignoring Alan's question and grabbing his bag. Alan followed him into the lift to the car park, but an opportunity to extricate himself arrived sooner than he had expected. Laurie had exited the lift first and as Alan started to follow, a group of three tall and not noticeably narrow men pushed into the compartment, arguing amongst themselves. Apparently by accident, they forced him back inside, one of them closing the doors while still quarrelling with his colleagues.

The lift started back down, and Alan permitted himself a small grin at the fortuitous intervention of the three men. They continued their argument for two floors but then stopped abruptly and looked at Alan. The smallest one, who was still well over six feet, pushed the button to open the door.

'G'day, Mr Flannery,' he said in a jovial voice. 'Hope you had a pleasant flight.'

Alan was dumbstruck. Who the fuck were these guys? They did not look especially like policemen but then, who did these days? The thought that they might be connected to the Australian underworld did not occur to him. He had never heard of Riley Bigg, but he was about to.

'My name's Demetriou. Riley's looking forward to meeting you,' continued the small, not-so-small man. They ushered him out of the lift, close enough for Alan to feel something hard pressing persuasively into the small of his back. He was aware that pleading innocence or mistaken identity was unlikely to work but he tried anyway.

'My name's not Flannery,' he started, but even he could recognise the lack of conviction in his voice.

'Yes, it is,' contradicted Demetriou, who was obviously in charge. They arrived at a black Toyota Land Cruiser with darkened windows, and Alan got in. He didn't feel he had much choice.

'Who's Riley?' he ventured.

—

Two floors above, Laurie had quickly realised he was alone. He was not the panicky type and although he felt no particular loyalty to Alan Flannery, he did to his cousin. Besides, he possessed enough personal pride to not just shrug his shoulders and go on home.

Juliet had asked for Flannery to be escorted to the British Consulate in Melbourne. She had omitted to explain just how little enthusiasm Alan might have for this arrangement. However, Laurie's amiable exterior hid a keen brain and a past with more knots in it than a set of rigging, so he did not waste time on recriminations but got into his car, rapidly exited the airport, parked up outside and settled down to wait. He doubted if Alan Flannery, having taken so much trouble to get to Melbourne, would be flying out again, and would therefore soon turn up.

He was right. His eyes passed over no more than twenty vehicles before alighting on a heavily laden black Land Cruiser that seemed to be in a hurry. He had chosen his vantage point well and had a clear view through the windscreen of the car before it swung right on the highway. There were four men inside, the smallest of whom was the still bulky figure of Flannery, hunched on the back seat.

'Probably not pals of his,' Laurie muttered to himself. He started the engine, pulled into the traffic and pressed a button on the hands-free phone. Juliet answered. 'Got him, lost him, found him again. He's with three guys who don't look like friends of the family. Messed up a bit, but leave it with me. This could turn out to be fun.'

—

Riley Bigg had spent the remainder of the weekend recuperating at Jarrod Lowe's inconspicuous bungalow in Shepparton. He couldn't help noticing that one way or another he'd been losing a few too many employees. He was now two down in a permanent sort of way, and Rambo was inconveniently out of action for a few weeks too. He would deal with him and Robbie in due course. Riley rather liked to incubate grudges until they were nice and warm, and the same applied to Elsa but even more so. She could certainly wait. She would turn up in Barbados at the villa she didn't know he knew about sooner or later and he could combine a reunion with a holiday once the present business was completed. The thought made him smile. But for now, Yackandandah and the diamonds were his pressing concern.

Riley took stock of his remaining personnel. The three idiots who had allowed Dawson to escape into the hands of the Shepparton police could be spared to collect the unanticipated Mr Flannery from the airport. Riley had been surprised to hear that Flannery was on his way to Australia, but now he could ask him politely to lead him straight to the spot marked X.

'Ready to go, boss.' Jarrod stuck an expressionless face through the doorway and disappeared again. He was already in the driver's seat of the rented Swagman Motorhome when Riley emerged from the house. A patched-up Bunny was in the seat behind him. Riley hauled himself up into the passenger seat and waved a thin arm. 'Wagons roll,' he said. He was feeling a lot more cheerful.

———

It soon became apparent to Laurie McGee that this was not to be a short trip. He followed the Land Cruiser on to the M31 and settled back with a mixture of resignation and excitement as the small convoy sped north. He would have liked to be more in the loop about what was going on, but then again it was ten years since he'd given up this sort of life and he rather missed it. He grinned to himself.

___ In which Pat meets a Dog, and has
dinner with a policeman

Having left Elsa, Pat Bootle considered it inadvisable to be driving around in Riley Bigg's Audi for longer than absolutely necessary. The damage to the front of the car made it easy to spot, especially on the relatively empty roads of this part of south-eastern Australia. First, though, he needed to discover which part of south-eastern Australia he was actually in. He fished out Dawson's phone, but the battery was dead.

Instinct told him to carry on eastwards, to put as much distance as possible between him and any pursuing pack, and it wasn't long before a signpost told him that he was heading towards the major town of Albury, 120 kilometres away. However, he was as sure as he could be that driving Bigg's Audi into Albury would be to invite more trouble than was necessary. Probably fatal kind of trouble.

He needed, therefore, to divest himself of the car and find alternative means of transport. There were plenty of places where he could dump the Audi out of sight, and he could always try hitchhiking, although he suspected that a lone, rather dishevelled man of his stature was unlikely to be an inviting travelling companion.

So he drove on. Half an hour later he almost missed the sign to Rennie, which was partly hidden in a clump of bushes and pointed down a minor road to the right. He doubted if Rennie boasted a car hire business but something on the sign caught his eye. What he had spotted was the common Australian icon for a railway. Rennie had a station! And it was only a couple of kilometres away. He turned into the narrow lane. Five slow minutes later, he saw a well-hidden track on his left, heading into some thick woodland. He drove a short way down it and pulled into a gap in the trees, manoeuvring the reluctant Audi well off the track. The engine finally expired of its own accord as he crashed crazily through a small stream. 'Okay,' he murmured. 'This'll do.'

Extricating himself from the car, Pat worked his way back to the lane and turned left towards Rennie and its railway station. He hoped the town, however small, might provide refreshment as well as onward transportation. The sun was well past the yardarm by now, although still intensely hot, and he was hungry and thirsty.

Rennie, when he reached it, was not promising. He passed some towering grain silos and a couple of ramshackle bungalows set back from the road, but the building proclaiming itself to be a hotel clearly had not been for several years, except maybe for rats and possums. The station, when he found it, comprised a lone boardwalk platform but no building or shade of any description. The single-track line disappeared emptily in both directions, shimmering in the heat. Of people, there was no sign. He could have been the only person in the settlement.

That, however, seemed unlikely. Beyond the tracks, he spotted a rusty-looking tin roof peeking above the trees. Looking unnecessarily left and right, he heaved himself down from the platform and crossed over the line, through the trees and up to the shack. He knocked on the door, and from inside a dog started barking. Quite a large dog by the sound of it. Pat did not like dogs, and dogs did not like him.

The door opened and a thin, wizened man with straggly hair loosely tied in a ponytail peered out at him. He looked about seventy, but was probably younger. 'Yeah?' said the man, in an unwelcoming fashion.

'Good afternoon,' Pat began. 'I wonder if you could help me? Do you know when the next train's due?'

The man replied with a hoarse cackle. After a few seconds wheezing, he turned and called back to someone inside the house. 'Hey, Jed! Guy here wants to know when the next train's coming.' He made it sound like the funniest thing he'd ever heard.

He was joined at the door by a younger man, who could have been his son and was a good foot and a half taller, and about as bulky as the older man was skinny. He was holding a fierce-looking, but mercifully silent, German Shepherd tightly on a short leash. The dog looked unimpressed by this arrangement and stood eying Pat with an unpromising glint in its eye. 'Train?' said the younger man, who was presumably Jed. The word appeared almost unfamiliar to him. 'You ain't catching no train here, mister.'

'Not unless you're a sack of grain,' chipped in the older man. 'And not for a month or more, even then.'

'He's a sack of somethin', that's for sure,' said Jed in an altogether more menacing tone. 'Somethin' don't add up, Pa. Why's he turned up here? D'ya think we should get old Mick down to check him out?'

Pat had the feeling he'd fallen into a Wild West B-Movie. He decided to take back some control of the conversation. 'So, no trains then. Buses? Taxis?'

'Yeah, Mick'll know what to do with him,' said Pa, ignoring Pat. 'I'll go find him.'

'You, git in here,' demanded Jed, allowing a foot or so of the dog's leash to slide through his fingers.

'You've been very helpful,' said Pat in the least sarcastic tone he could manage, turning away as he spoke. He'd only taken a couple of steps, however, when he was thrown to the ground on his face and a low growling in his ear told him that he had a German Shepherd on his back.

'You ain't goin' nowhere,' said Jed, moving round into Pat's field of vision. An elderly but doubtless trustworthy shotgun had appeared in his hands, as if by magic. Meanwhile, the old man had disappeared behind the shack, but he soon reappeared driving a battered red Ute with about 20% of its exhaust fitment intact. He drove off in a cloud of dust down an almost imperceptible path running alongside the railway line.

'Here, Dog!' commanded Jed, and the German Shepherd obediently dismounted from Pat's back and went to stand next to his master, all the while looking for an excuse to return. Pat got to his feet and brushed himself down. 'Inside,' said Jed and, lacking any obvious alternative, Pat entered the shack. To call it run-down would be an understatement, but at least one of its rooms had a lock and Jed ushered him in with the shotgun and secured the door behind him. There were some surprisingly sturdy bars on the window, and the walls were considerably more solid from the inside than they had looked from outside, so he thought he may not be the first person to find himself imprisoned in the room. However, the good news was that it was a storeroom of some kind and in amongst various boxes of indeterminate tat, Pat discovered a crate of Coca-Cola. He made his way quickly through two cans, which made him feel considerably better.

Sometime later, Pat heard the Ute returning, followed by muffled voices, but no one came to let him out and gradually the sky outside his barred window darkened as night closed in. He made himself as comfortable as he could and fell asleep. He was exhausted. Tomorrow was another day and Pat knew he would be better able to work out a plan of action after a few hours' sleep.

He was woken by the sound of a car engine, a much quieter engine than Pa's Ute's. Sunshine was streaming through the grimy window between the bars. This could be "Mick", he decided, who "would know what to do." Hopefully it would not involve the use of the shotgun.

It didn't. There was the sound of raised voices, the door to the storeroom was unlocked, and a weary-looking middle-aged man with a deep tan and wearing at least part of a scruffy but unmistakeable police uniform entered. Jed and Pa were skulking in the half-light behind him. There was no sign of either Dog or the shotgun.

'I've told you fellas before, you can't go around kidnapping passers-by,' said Mick the policeman exasperatedly, pushing his wide-brimmed hat further back on his head and mopping his brow. He half shoved Pat out of the room before him, through the open front door and into an old Land Rover, which may or may not have possessed police insignia under the thick layer of dust. Jed and Pa did not come out to wave them off as they bucketed down the overgrown path alongside the railway.

'Aren't you going to arrest them?' asked Pat, twisting in his seat. Mick, who had removed his hat to reveal a shiny baldpate, grunted.

'Nowhere to put 'em if I did. How'd you end up here, anyway? You probably put the wind up 'em. They didn't mean any harm. Old Jim came and told me, didn't he?'

Pat had to admit that genuine kidnappers rarely called the police except to make ransom demands. 'I was trying to catch a train.'

'From Rennie? Passenger line's been closed for years. Just grain wagons in season these days. Again, fella, how did you get here? You didn't walk all the way out here.'

Pat could have pointed out that Rennie was not actually very far off the beaten track; the fact that it seemed to inhabit a different, earlier, century was another matter altogether. Also, he did not want to reveal that he'd dumped Riley Bigg's Audi in some local bushes. Mick may have been an unlikely looking copper, but a copper he nevertheless was, and Pat supposed that he would almost certainly want to go and have a look at the car. And that would give rise to an undoubtedly difficult line of questioning. He tried, therefore, to move things on a bit.

'I'm trying to get to Albury.'

'Albury?' Mick turned to him with raised eyebrows. 'Trains don't go to Albury, even when there were any.'

'My mistake. Can you get me there?'

'I'm not a bloody taxi, mate. Nope. I'll take you to my place. I got too much work on to do anything else.'

Pat bit his tongue again. Mick didn't seem particularly

overworked but perhaps sheep rustling was rife in the area. 'Okay,' he conceded. 'And where's your place?'

'Mulwala. It's not far.'

Half an hour of uncomfortable travel later, they drove into the outskirts of a town bigger than Pat was expecting. It looked altogether more promising than Rennie.

'Can I get a train here?' asked Pat. 'Or a bus?' he added as they passed what was unmistakeably a bus stop.

'Yep. You could. Bus anyway. Be one along on Monday.'

'Monday?'

'No call for buses on weekends. You hungry, fella?' Mick asked, changing the subject. 'I'm due my lunch. Join me.'

They pulled up beside an almost empty, neon-lit diner and ate in near silence for a while. Pat spent the time between mouthfuls running through in his mind the answers to questions that never came. Finally, Mick drained his cup of tea, mopped his face with a copious napkin and said, 'Food's on you, fella. There's a half-decent motel couple of hundred metres up that way.' He nodded towards the window. 'Good luck, son,' he added mysteriously, plonked his hat back on his bald head and ambled out into the sunshine.

___ In which Lucy speaks a foreign
    language, and a hotel bedroom
    becomes extremely crowded

'Good afternoon,' said Valentin Prokofiev, appearing suddenly on the landing above the group. Six pairs of eyes turned to look up at the lithe man with the disconcertingly piercing gaze who was now slowly descending the stairs towards them.

'Oh, hi, Elbow,' said Tony, trying to smile but failing. 'This is Elbow, guys,' he added superfluously to Lucy and Dawson.

Lucy was eyeing the stranger thoughtfully. Meanwhile, at the foot of the staircase, Martin had also noted the new arrival and had decided that he would be better off waiting for Dawson and Lucy in the bar.

An uncomfortable pause was developing when Lucy unexpectedly said, '*Zdravstvujte.*'

Dawson said, 'Wha...?' and the four band members looked confused.

Elbow allowed a small smile to play about his lips as Lucy continued, '*Itak, chto delayet russkiy, igraya s nebol'shoy avstraliyskoy folk-gruppoy?*'

'What did you say?' asked Dawson.

'I was asking our friend here what a Russian is doing playing with a minor Australian folk group.'

'Minor?' squawked Tony, but everyone ignored him.

Prokofiev smiled again and answered in English. 'What makes you think I am Russian, little lady?'

'I don't think, I know. And now you've said a bit more, I'm guessing from, oh, let's see, Yekaterinburg perhaps, somewhere round there anyway.'

'Impressive,' said Prokofiev with a nod. 'What is your name?'

'Smith,' said Lucy with a degree of accuracy. 'What's yours?'

'It is Elbow, as you know.'

'Except that's not true, is it? And you're not just here to

make merry with your fiddle. Don't know someone by the name of Jeffers, do you?'

It was as though the two of them were alone, Dawson and the band merely shadowy extras in the unfolding drama. But with a shake of the head, Prokofiev broke the spell.

He turned his pale blue eyes to Dawson. 'You, I am thinking, are Mr Dawson.'

'Who knows?' shrugged Dawson. Prokofiev's eyes narrowed and he opened his thin jacket just enough to reveal a pistol in a shoulder holster.

'Oh, look,' said Dawson. 'Some other bugger with a gun. We haven't seen enough of those, have we?' No one seemed particularly surprised at the appearance of a firearm. There was a kind of collective shrug as Prokofiev plucked the gun from its holster and waved it persuasively to usher the small group upstairs. Despite their outward sangfroid, there seemed little alternative. It wouldn't do the quality of Balaclava Lemon's performances at the folk festival much good if some of them turned up dead. Even Lucy figured that now was not the time to dispute the invitation.

Prokofiev's room turned out to be a tight fit for seven people, so the Russian pointed to the en-suite bathroom and said to the four band members, 'You people, go in there. You too, lady, I will come to you later,' he added to Lucy.

'No thanks,' Lucy replied. 'Whatever you have to say to Saul, you can say to me.'

'As you please. Although there will not be much – what is it? –"saying."' He raised his voice to the Balaclava Lemons, who had yet to move. 'Inside! Now.' They filed into the bathroom and Prokofiev turned the key in the lock and dropped it in his pocket.

'That's convenient,' remarked Dawson, who had exchanged glances with Lucy while this was going on. 'Most hotel bathrooms only lock from the inside.'

'Yes,' said Prokofiev. 'Old hotel. I choose well.' His eyes were focused on Dawson, who had shifted slightly to his left while Lucy had unobtrusively moved two paces in the opposite direction. Suddenly she dived towards the floor and hurled her full eight stone at Prokofiev's knees. At the same time, Dawson, partly out of a sense of self-preservation and partly to support Lucy's courageous attack, twisted back to his right and leapt with a silent prayer towards the Russian's gun hand. Even an assassin of Prokofiev's experience struggled with the impossible task of training his weapon on both of his assailants and instead of hitting on one target, dithered for the fraction of a second it took for both Lucy and Dawson to crash into him. Somehow, he managed to retain his grip on his gun as he fell under their combined weight, landing heavily on the girl and letting off a shot at Dawson. It missed, but only by a hairsbreadth.

—

On Tuesday morning, Yackandandah was a blur of activity, and Innes and Bates noted that another hot day was in prospect. The town's normal population of under a thousand had already more than doubled and every passing hour saw streams of folk enthusiasts continuing to arrive. Not only were the few local hotels and guest houses full to brimming, the many campsites in the area were too.

Despite the crowds, Innes was surprised they had yet to spot Dawson. Not even showing the enlarged copy of his passport photo to literally hundreds of people had elicited any glimmer of recognition. He and Bates were listening out for an English accent but had yet to hear one. Innes stared at Dawson's likeness for the umpteenth time and shook his head in exasperation. The bland, totally unmemorable face stared back at him.

'It would help if he stood out a bit more,' said Elaine, looking over his shoulder. 'I bet half the people we've spoken to actually have seen him. They just haven't noticed him.'

'Time for a drink, young Bates,' decided Innes. They were standing in a welcome patch of shade outside a pub called The Sun. They looked up at the faded facia board. 'Don't think we've been in here yet. We can kill two birds with one stone.'

They went inside and ordered two beers. Innes laid the photo of Dawson on the bar counter. 'Have you seen this fella by any chance?' he asked. The bar was busy and the young barman a bit frazzled, but he glanced down briefly.

'Nah, mate, don't think so.' He started to move away, but stopped and came back. 'Wait a sec, let's have another look. Yeah, actually, I do know him. He's staying here. With a blonde chick and, hang on a mo, yep, that bloke there.'

Martin Evans, quietly drinking his second beer at a nearby table, had his back to the bar, but some sort of journalistic instinct made him aware of several pairs of eyes boring into him. He turned his head slowly and saw a middle-aged man and a young woman looking at him. The same journalistic instinct immediately identified them as police. He didn't know whether to be relieved or worried. The woman walked over, flashed a badge in his face and said, 'Police,' thus confirming his instinct. She replaced the badge with the photo of a serious looking Dawson. 'Do you know this man, sir?' She looked and sounded slightly scary, but Martin was becoming used to small, slightly scary females. This one was less blonde and more fierce-looking than Lucy but obviously came from the same mould.

'Erm,' he said, glancing from the policewoman to her older, male colleague who was now standing on his other side looking down at him.

The man sat down. He had a bottle of beer in his hand and a friendly look on his tanned, lined face – or at least a friendlier look than his companion. 'My name's Inspector Innes,' he began. 'You're a friend of Saul Dawson, I believe. We need to find him urgently. We believe he might be in some danger.'

He paused. 'Which of course means that you may be too, Mr...?'

'Evans,' said Martin, 'Martin Evans.' Involuntarily he glanced upwards.

Innes didn't miss the glance. 'Upstairs, is he? Let's go. You can leave the beer.'

The landing halfway up the stairs was empty.

'I left them all here,' said Martin. 'Less than ten minutes ago. I don't know where they've gone.'

'All?' enquired Elaine. 'Who else are we talking about?'

'Oh, you know, Greta – Lucy rather – and the erm... band.'

'Any chance of expanding on that, Mr Evans?' asked Innes. It sounded like a lot of unexpected people muddying the waters. The only person he was interested in was Dawson. If he'd left the hotel, they'd not be much better off than they were before.

'Who are Greta and Lucy?' asked Elaine, more specifically. 'And which band?'

'They're called Balaclava Lemon. We got a message in code that suggested we needed to meet up with them. That's to say, Greta, sorry, Lucy got a message. In code. But they didn't seem to know what we were talking about. Then Elbow turned up, so I thought I'd head for the bar.' Martin was aware he was not making any sense. He didn't need to see the blank expressions on their faces to confirm that.

'The only question as far as I'm concerned is where Mr Dawson's got to, either alone or with all these other people. We can sort out who they all are in due course,' said Innes.

But Elaine had been picking through the bones of what Martin had just said. 'A message in code?' she queried. 'What about?'

'Wish I knew. I was hoping to get a story out of this, but I'm not sure if I've got anything to hang a hat on. Not yet anyway.'

'And you thought you were more likely to get a story sitting in a bar by yourself drinking beer while goodness knows what was going on up here?' asked Innes sardonically. 'Where's your room, Mr Evans? Hopefully they've all gone there.' He glanced at Bates. 'Pop down and find out if this band, Balaclava Whatsit, are staying here too, and get their room number, will you, Elaine?'

As Elaine started to descend the stairs again, the unmistakeable sound of a gunshot rang out from above them. The officers looked at each other and as one, took the stairs two at a time with Martin trailing behind them.

—

The echo of Prokofiev's shot had just died away when the door crashed open and Innes and Bates burst into the room, the former pulling out his own firearm as he did so.

Innes was quick on the uptake. 'Mr Dawson, move to one side. You,' to Prokofiev, 'stay where you are and drop your weapon.'

'I'd really rather he didn't stay where he is,' wheezed Lucy from underneath the Russian. 'If it's not too much trouble.'

Prokofiev tried to take advantage of this slight diversion by swinging his gun up towards Innes, who had advanced until he was standing almost on top of him. Dawson had retreated until the back of his knees came into contact with the bed, on to which he toppled in a rather ungainly fashion. Lucy, aware of Prokofiev's movement but with only one free arm, attempted to swat away the Russian's weapon before it pointed at Innes. The back of her hand impacted with Elbow's elbow, but at the same time he managed to swing a leg at Innes' ankles. The inspector went down in a heap, and as he did so, his gun slid across the polished wooden floor towards the bed and Dawson.

Dawson was quick to react. He rolled off the bed, plucked Innes's gun from the floor as he landed and, hoping that he'd taken in Pat's lesson from a couple of days ago on the effective use of firearms, aimed it roughly in Prokofiev's direction as he was scrambling to his feet and, more in hope than expectation, pulled the trigger.

There was an echoing silence as the sound of the shot trailed away.

Elaine Bates was still by the door, her mouth open as she took in the scene in front of her.

Innes was on the floor in front of the bathroom door, trying to hoist himself to his feet.

Prokofiev was on his knees, looking down stupefied at a steadily growing pool of blood on the front of his pale blue shirt below his left shoulder.

Dawson had dropped Innes's weapon with a heavy clunk. His own expression was not much less stupefied than the Russian's.

Lucy, in a slightly muffled voice from behind Prokofiev, and looking quizzically at a small graze that had appeared on her left forearm, said, 'I'd rather it hadn't come as close to me as that but, all things considered, that was a pretty good shot.'

___ In which Pat continues to
    experience travel delays, and
    Rachel gets a surprise

Monday morning found Pat crammed into the back of a bus on his way at last to Albury, having spent Sunday in enforced idleness. It had at least given him time to think, although he had come up with no further answers. Perhaps those lay in Yackandandah, if and when he ever got there. Or perhaps it would all be over, whatever "it" was, and he would be free to return to Cologne with his tail tucked even more firmly between his legs.

When he eventually got to Albury, he discovered there was an onward bus to Yackandandah that left twice daily. Unfortunately, he'd missed them both, but his original plan had been to hire a car and that again seemed the best option. Unbelievably, there were no cars to be had that afternoon and by the time he gave up trying to find one, it was dusk. He put a deposit down on a Honda for eight the next morning and booked himself in for dinner and a bed. Remembering Dawson's phone, he bought a charger and left it powering itself up while he went down to eat.

The phone was ringing when he returned to his room. He rushed across and answered it without thinking. 'Hello, who's this?'

'Dawson?' came a voice down the line, a very familiar voice. Pat paused in indecision about how to answer or whether to switch the phone off and chuck it out the window. 'Is that you, Dawson? It's not, is it? Speak to me.'

Pat had no idea why Rachel was phoning Dawson on what must be some sort of official phone, so after a further short bout of dithering, he decided there was only one way to find out.

'Hello, Rachel,' he said brightly. 'How nice to hear from you.'

'What the fuck!' exploded Rachel, loud and clear from 12,000 miles away. Pat felt he could forgive her the explosion in the circumstances. 'Pat? Is that you, you complete and utter bastard? Where's Dawson? What have you done with him?'

'I don't know where he is, as it happens. I did, a day or two back, but our paths seem to have diverged. I'm doing my best to find him again. And I must say, I'm a bit disappointed that you seem more interested in him than your fiance.'

'Fiance be fucked. What's going on? And who the hell are you anyway?'

'Does this phone I'm using belong to British Intelligence, by the way?'

'What? I don't know. Probably. Don't you know?'

Pat was beginning to realise that there was more than a hint of the blind leading the blind about the conversation and so, not worrying too much about whether or not anyone might be listening in, he ran through as much of what had been going on as he could. Including his own backstory. It seemed only fair.

'So you're a German,' said Rachel. 'That would have been nice to know.'

'Do you disapprove of Germans?'

'Only one – apart from dictators with little moustaches.'

'I think Dawson is in a place called Yackandandah. I aim to be there tomorrow. I suspect lots of other people will turn up as well, including Riley Bigg.'

'Yes, this Bigg character. No one here has mentioned him. I don't think MI6 are aware of him.'

'Since you suddenly appear to be working for British Intelligence, unlikely as that seems, you presumably know about the diamonds we're all nearly killing ourselves to find. No one's told you where they are, have they?'

'I don't think anyone here knows more than you do. Should I be discussing this with you if you're a representative of a foreign power?'

'I think we're probably allies. By all means report back to

your superiors about me and this conversation. I'm doing my best to retrieve the diamonds for Germany, of course, but I'll try to keep an eye out for Dawson's safety. We got quite close for a while. Wish me luck. Oh, and Rachel?'

'Yes?'

'Is the engagement still on?'

'What do you think?' But she rang off before he could answer the question.

—

Pat rolled into Yackandandah mid-morning the next day, Tuesday, and parked up. The small town was full to bursting point. He was sure that Riley Bigg or some of his associates would be there soon, if not already. It was imperative that he found Dawson before they did. But where was he?

He was just debating where to begin his search when he heard the unmistakeable sound of a gunshot. One or two people looked around in a puzzled fashion, but the bang had been so muffled and so overwhelmed by the noise of the crowd that most people simply ignored it. Then a second shot rang out. Pat set off towards the building where he was sure it had come from, a pub, that a fading sign above the lintel informed him was called The Sun Hotel.

Two police cars, sirens blaring, beat him to it. He was not allowed entry into The Sun, and he and the rest of the crowd were quickly pushed back behind a hastily unwound incident tape. He started towards the rear of the building but had not got very far when two policemen came out of the hotel in charge of a securely handcuffed slim, pale man with angry blue eyes and blood on his shirt, who was quickly ushered into a squad car and driven away. Pat had no idea who the man was, but he had no doubt that if he could gain entry to the building, he would find Dawson, possibly dead, which might not go down well with Rachel.

__ In which Lucy breaks something,
    and two pieces of a puzzle come
    together

Martin had opted not to burst into the bedroom with Innes and Bates, deciding that standing guard in the corridor might be more useful on health and safety grounds. A scattering of guests together with the young barman, who seemed to be temporarily in charge of the hotel, had started to appear when they heard the gunshot. The second shot had not noticeably increased Martin's levels of courage, so he was relieved when he heard sirens approaching. Martin preferred not to think about who might have been on the receiving end of the shooting inside the room, but he could still hear voices and at least no one was screaming.

The first thing the police did on arrival was to remove all the onlookers, including Martin, down to the bar on the ground floor, where the barman was trying to emphasise his managerial status to a policewoman. Martin was beginning to realise that the story he had come to Australia to write was going on over his head.

—

Meanwhile, upstairs, with Prokofiev arrested and taken away, and Balaclava Lemon released from the bathroom and escorted to the local police station, there was just Dawson, Lucy, Innes and Bates left in the bedroom.

'I believe this may belong to you.' Innes fished the still intact teapot lid out of his jacket pocket.

'Yes,' said Dawson, 'it does. Have you opened it?'

'Opened it? I don't follow.'

'There's some sort of code inside, but I don't know what it means. It's why I lugged it all the way out here in the first place. Here, I'll show you.'

Innes handed the lid over and Dawson fiddled with it for a while without success. The crack in the porcelain was hardly noticeable and there was nothing for him to get a grip on. Lucy was looking over his shoulder and saw what he was trying to do. She reached across, grabbed the lid from him and, without so much as a by-your-leave, hurled it against the wall, where it smashed into several pieces and dropped to the floor. A small fragment of paper drifted down in its wake. Lucy walked across and plucked the paper out of the air before it hit the ground.

'Is this what you're after?' she asked casually.

'Bit unnecessary,' grumbled Dawson. 'That teapot could have been valuable.'

'Not as valuable as this, I suspect,' said Lucy, reading the numbers on the paper. '**146.47172**. Any ideas anyone?'

'It's obvious, isn't it?' came a quiet voice from the door.

The four occupants of the room spun around as one. They saw a very large, somewhat sweaty and bedraggled man standing there with a weary expression on his face. He was a complete stranger to three of them and Innes had started to move forward to usher the newcomer out of the room when Dawson said brightly, 'You made it then? I wasn't sure you were going to.'

'Hello, Dawson. And Dawson's friends. I'm quite hard to kill apparently. Not for want of people trying.'

'Inspector Innes, Victoria State Police. Mind telling me who you are, sir? No, wait a second. This is your colleague from the car that was run off the road by Bigg's thugs, isn't it, Mr Dawson?'

'Allow me to introduce Mr Patrick Bootle,' replied Dawson. 'Rival in love, saver of lives and, at a guess, the official representative of the rightful owners of the booty we're all after.'

'Rightful owners?' queried Elaine. 'How's that?'

'Excellent guess, Dawson. Yes, it's true. I am working on

behalf of the German government to recover the "booty", as you call it, which is unarguably ours. And I think that between us we may now have the complete picture of where it might be.'

'Wait a minute,' said Dawson. 'What is this booty? You sound as if you know.'

'Ah, yes, of course, the innocent donkey has no idea why everyone is after him.'

'I think you mean mule,' said Innes.

'I know what I mean. And also I mean diamonds. Nazi diamonds to be exact.'

Everyone stared at him, then Innes asked, 'Do you have ID?'

'Unfortunately, none that will confirm my bona fides. However, that is beside the point. You have a geographical coordinate in your hand, young lady, which when combined with the one I have, well, X marks the spot as they say.' He sat down on the edge of the bed and for some reason not immediately apparent began to remove a shoe.

After a good deal of peering and poking away inside the shoe, Pat was able to extract another small piece of paper, which he passed to Innes. '**S 36.19827**,' read the inspector out loud. 'I see what you mean. So, what you've got there, Lucy, is the east coordinate. I'm guessing we're not a million miles away from where they cross. We need to find out where that is, and a hotel room is probably not the place to do it.'

They retired to the one-room local police station, where there was a laptop sitting unattended on a small table in the corner.

'Now then,' Innes began, but he was interrupted by Pat.

'Before we go any further, Inspector, what exactly is the Australian police's involvement in all this? It's bad enough that I've got British Intelligence queering my pitch, but I'm not sure that my bosses back home would take too kindly to me sharing all this with the local coppers.'

'I'm afraid you have no choice. But you're right. I'm a bit

off-piste here, truth be told. Elaine and I went out on a limb to try to track down Mr Dawson before any more harm came to him from either the Russians or your old friend Riley Bigg. It's Bigg I'm after and if I get him, trust me, the diamonds will never have existed as far as I'm concerned.'

News of any Russian involvement came as a surprise to Pat, but he was beginning to catch on to the unexpected much more quickly now. 'Ah, yes, the gentleman seen leaving the hotel in cuffs, I presume. Was he responsible for the shooting?'

'Not entirely,' said Dawson with a smidgen of pride.

'Saul shot him,' explained Lucy with rather more than a smidgen of pride.

'I felt I owed Mr Dawson my assistance,' continued Innes, 'after I inadvertently let the Russians take him away from my police station.'

'Yes, that was quite careless,' said Dawson. 'Do we know what happened to Mr Jeffers, by the way? Or is he still wandering around in the undergrowth where I left him?'

'Oh, no,' remarked Elaine. 'He's dead. Fell into a gorge. Talking of careless.'

'Anyway,' said Innes. 'Back to business, folks. Are you happy to continue, Mr Bootle?'

'Indeed. Frankly, it's nice to have some friendly company. One more thing though. Unfortunately, we can still expect Bigg to turn up at any time. He's got half the clue and I didn't manage to kill him off, I'm afraid.'

During this conversation, Lucy had gone across to the laptop in the corner. Somehow, she had also managed to take control of the two pieces of paper containing the coordinates.

'What does anyone know about a place called Karr's Reef Mine?' she called out. The others stopped talking and moved over to join her.

'I've heard of it, why?' asked Innes.

'Because it's where the coordinates cross.' She was still tapping away at the keyboard. 'It's only six or seven kilometres from here, but I'm not sure if we've got a suitable vehicle between us. We definitely need a 4x4 according to this.'

'Not a problem,' said Innes, smiling. 'I'm a policeman, and this place is crawling with four-wheel drives.'

___ In which Laurie McGee stays
    awake, and Alan Flannery is
    introduced to Bunny

Laurie McGee trailed the Toyota northwards until afternoon turned into evening and the light faded. He had no idea where they were headed. He debated calling Juliet to see if she had any ideas, but he had no hands-free phone and the opportunity did not present itself. So he settled back in his seat, turned up the radio and carried on with the pursuit.

It was past 9 o'clock when the small convoy rolled into the town of Wangaratta and the Land Cruiser pulled into a car park and stopped next to an overlarge Swagman motorhome. Laurie parked up around a concealed corner and doubled back on foot. He was in time to see the door of the motorhome close as the occupants of the Toyota filed in. He retired to the shadows and, not willing to risk making a call, texted his cousin and waited for the response. He did not have long to wait. Juliet was always efficient. She was also economical with words, despite her phone's bill payer being the UK Government. "Diamonds. Yackandandah. We think." Laurie knew of Yackandandah and was aware that there was a folk festival about to kick off. Could that be relevant? He didn't see how.

Even with the revolver he habitually kept strapped beneath the seat of his car, he was not about to charge in without being mob-handed, when the motorhome clearly contained a genuine mob. He was starting to get tired, but his loyalty to his cousin was absolute and he was well used to living rough in the outback, so he slunk further back into the bushes and prepared to see out the vigil for as long as it took.

It took until the first vestiges of light appeared and the local corella population was starting its early morning round of greeting calls. The door of the motorhome opened, and a large man got into the Toyota and drove off. The engine of the motorhome started up almost immediately, so Laurie moved unobtrusively back to his own car and prepared to continue the chase, hoping that Alan Flannery had survived the night. They drove off and turned eastwards on to a minor road signposted Beechworth. 'And Yackandandah,' whispered Laurie. 'Well done, cuz.'

—

Alan Flannery spent the journey musing on how far wrong things had gone. This was exactly the sort of scenario he had been so keen to avoid in the first place. He still had no clear idea where they were taking him, but it looked like he was due to meet the gentleman by the name of Riley Bigg. This Bigg character clearly was nothing to do with the Russians, and going purely on the Australian accents and general unpleasant demeanour of the men around him, Alan came to the conclusion that he was in the hands of some sort of criminal fraternity who, God knows how, had got hold of at least part of the information regarding the diamonds. He was beginning to wish he'd never taken the bloody call from MacGuffin in the first place.

Eventually, they stopped in a car park and Alan was ushered closely across to what appeared to be some sort of Winnebago parked alongside.

'Good of you to join us, Mr Flannery.' The sudden burst of light as Alan was thrust into the cavernous interior momentarily blinded him, and it took him a few seconds to locate the source of the smug Aussie twang. 'We're hoping you can help us.'

'I don't know what you're taking about,' blustered Alan, looking around him and seeing three men in addition to the three who had driven him here. 'Who the hell are you?'

The thin, bald, immaculately dressed man lounging at the

far end of the cabin smiled. 'You really have no idea, do you? Playing your little games from your little office in London, thinking you're God Almighty, using people like pawns, not getting your hands dirty. Well, your hands are dirty now. We want the diamonds, Mr Flannery, and you are going to tell us where they are.'

Alan tried one last time. 'Diamonds?' he squawked. 'What diamonds?'

'Oh dear,' sighed the man who Alan presumed must be Riley Bigg. 'Wrong answer. Bunny?'

One of the men heaved himself off the padded bench to Alan's left. His face, with its missing ear and vivid scar, did not fill Alan with confidence, nor did the force with which he yanked Alan's arms up between his shoulder blades. 'Bunny's been through a lot lately,' Bigg continued calmly as Alan yelled in pain. 'I'm afraid he's looking for something to work off his frustrations.'

___ In which a gathering takes place
at Karr's Reef, and Dawson falls
down a mine

Karr's Reef, when they eventually got there after much low-gear struggling over rutted forest tracks, was not what Dawson was expecting. They were standing in a clearing in the woods, 100 metres from where they had been forced to abandon Innes's purloined four-wheel drive. Ahead of them was a locked iron gate set into a steep bank, while scattered around were several pieces of rusting machinery, only some of which had a clear purpose. A set of equally rusty railway lines led from the gated entrance to the mine and disappeared into the overgrown forest behind them. Three old mining wagons stood chained together halfway along the tracks, held in place by wooden chocks under the wheels.

'This place looks like a film set,' remarked Dawson. 'I was imagining something a bit smarter.'

'I believe they have sometimes used it for films,' said Innes. 'And they occasionally run guided tours. Not quite sure why. There's not a lot to see.'

'Why would anyone hide a pile of diamonds in a tourist venue?'

'It probably wasn't then,' said Elaine. 'Presumably they've been here since the war, or soon after anyway.'

'Lucky they haven't been found.'

'We don't know they haven't been found,' Lucy pointed out.

'That's true.' Innes nodded as he spoke. 'Still, we're here now, folks. Don't suppose any of you wants to turn around without having a look-see.'

'Certainly not,' said Dawson. 'I haven't put up with all these people trying to bump me off for the last week just to give up now. In any case, surely we'd have heard if they had been found.'

'Who's we?'

'Clearly no one's told the respective espionage agencies of Britain or Russia for a start.'

'Or Germany,' said Pat. 'Unless I'm being kept even more in the dark than I thought I was.'

'Or Riley Bigg. Wouldn't it be a good idea if we stopped standing around chewing the fat and got looking before he turns up with a gang of his mates?' Lucy sounded a touch exasperated.

'I'm afraid that particular roo has hopped off, young lady. Everybody, put your hands in the air nice and slow, or my friends here might have to thin the crowd a bit. Starting with you, Mr Dawson.' They all spun round at the sound of the Australian drawl. Riley Bigg, with a broad-brimmed cream hat covering his bald head and putting his thin face in deep shade, was standing ten metres away flanked by Bunny and a heavily-bandaged Jarrod Lowe. Both of them were equipped with the sort of heavy-duty armament that brooked no opposition. Three more men stood away to one side, one of whom was extremely familiar to Dawson and Lucy, if not to the two police officers.

'Come to finish us off and take your ill-gotten goods, have you, "Napoleon"?' Lucy asked witheringly, entirely failing to keep the sarcasm out of her voice.

Alan, with a mouth missing most of its teeth, stayed silent, but Riley Bigg, raising his eyebrows in surprise, said, 'Oh, no, young lady, you've got the wrong end of the stick. Mr Flannery, realising the error of his ways, has kindly agreed that the diamonds should stay here in Australia. Before we go any further, perhaps you'd all like to introduce yourselves. Not you, Mr Dawson, nor you, of course, Mutt, but the rest of you. I think we'd all like to know who we're about to say goodbye to.'

'My name's Inspector Innes, Victoria State Police, so if you gentlemen would just like to lay your firearms on the ground and take a few steps back, we...'

He was interrupted by Riley Bigg's laughter. 'Oh, looky here, fellas, a brave copper. This is just too exciting for words.' The smile disappeared instantly from his face and he nodded at Bunny, who raised his gun in Innes's direction. However, the shot that rang through the clearing did not come from Bunny, who didn't see and hardly felt the bullet that finally ended his recent suffering. He slumped to the floor, and there was a second or two's stunned silence before anyone moved.

The first person to realise what was happening was Jarrod Lowe, who flung himself to the ground, dragging his boss down with him. A second shot from the unseen assailant whistled through his hair. Somewhat surprisingly, Alan Flannery got wind of the situation at virtually the same instant and, taking advantage of the stunned immobility of the man to his right, Demetriou, hurled himself at him and managed to knock him off his feet.

Of the group of five standing by the mine entrance only Innes and Pat were still armed. That number was reduced to one when Pat discovered that Chuckles' gun had finally run out of ammunition. The click of hammer on empty chamber was followed almost instantaneously by an outraged cry of pain as Lowe's shot from a prone position hit Pat's gun hand and sent the useless weapon spinning away. Elaine Bates, wondering why her own police sidearm was pointlessly sitting in her flat back in Shepparton, had by this time taken inadequate cover behind some sort of rusting pulley device. Lucy had bolted off towards the trees to the left with some vague idea of coming to the assistance of Flannery.

Dawson had not thought so fast and had backed his way up to the iron gate leading to the actual mine. Lowe had him in his sights and, having scrambled to his feet, pointed his gun straight at Dawson, smiled and pulled the trigger. Dawson shut his eyes and, forgetting to pray, swore instead, flinching at the same time. The next thing he knew he was toppling backwards, still apparently alive, into the mine entrance. Lowe's shot had missed him by a nanometre, shattering instead the padlock by his right shoulder. The gate was flung open by Dawson's weight.

The path, with the railway lines embedded in it, dipped steeply downwards immediately past the gate, and Dawson found himself rolling helplessly downhill into the darkness. After a few seconds, the track turned sharply to the left and Dawson's head came up hard against an unforgiving wall that knocked him into a state of unconsciousness.

Up above, the third shot from the shelter of the woods finally did it for Jarrod Lowe, who was now unthinkingly upright and something of a sitting or, more factually, standing, duck. He went down with a bullet through the head.

Crouching and taking in the scene as calmly as he could, Innes spotted Bigg, still lying on the ground seven metres or so in front of him. He didn't seem an immediate threat but there was a lot more happening over to Innes' left. The man Dawson and Lucy had recognised was still lying on top of a thug with thinning ginger hair, but he was beginning to come off worse. The other gang member was engaged in spraying a series of rounds from his semi-automatic into the approximate part of the surrounding woodland where the initial shooting had come from. Innes had no idea if any of them had found their mark, but he wasn't about to stand around wondering, so fired twice at the thug. It was fifteen years since Innes had last used a gun outside of a range, and his first attempt missed. His second shot caught Riley's man in the thigh, however, and with a screech of pain he fell to one side and dropped his weapon.

Meanwhile, Lucy had reached the struggling pair of Flannery and Demetriou and threw herself bodily on top of them. She immediately bounced straight off again, but the diversion had given Alan the opportunity to grab Demetriou's right hand, which was closing in on the gun in its underarm holster. Demetriou swung his left arm in response and connected with Alan's head. Alan was sent sprawling, but under

Newton's Third Law the exertion also saw the hoodlum fall back across the railway tracks beside them. Thinking swiftly, Lucy hurled herself towards the mine train and knocked the chocks away from the front wheels.

She wasn't quite fast enough. Demetriou managed to roll himself away from the small, murderous train just in time. Picking up speed, it hurtled away down the tracks, crashed through the half-open gate of the mine and, with a dreadful creaking and moaning, disappeared into the darkness. A couple of seconds later, there was a muffled crash from within the mine, and then silence.

Into the silence strolled a tall, broad-shouldered man in T-shirt and bush trousers, holding an automatic pistol at the ready as he took in the scene around him. Dismissing the still-prone Riley Bigg, he trained his gun at Demetriou, who was propped up on his shoulders by the rail track with Lucy by now standing over him holding his own gun, with a just-try-it expression on her face. Another thug was lying to one side clutching his bloody thigh and moaning. Jarrod Lowe and Bunny were not far away, but they were not moaning and never would again. Alan was starting to sit up, shaking his head, when he spotted the man walking towards them.

'What the hell happened to you?' he asked.

'There's gratitude,' said Laurie McGee. 'I've gone without a night's sleep on your behalf.'

Suddenly there was a piercing scream from Riley Bigg. Elaine was the first one to reach the gang leader. 'Shit!' she shouted. 'Snake!'

Innes came across at a dead run, took aim and blasted the snake's head off, but too late. It had already sunk its fangs into Bigg's leg. 'Eastern Brown,' Innes said succinctly. 'He's got no chance, not out here. Shame. I'd like to have taken this one in alive.'

'Still, there's a couple still breathing,' said Laurie. 'Better than nothing.'

'Better find something to secure them. And Elaine, can you do anything to help our big German friend here?' Pat was leaning against a tree looking very pale, holding a blood-stained jacket around his shattered hand, stoically bearing the pain.

'Wait a minute,' exclaimed Lucy, looking around wildly. 'Where's Saul?'

Laurie's fortuitous and completely unexpected arrival had turned the situation downside up in less than a couple of minutes, and I was still trying to get my head around the sudden increase in the death rate when I realised we were one short. Dawson was nowhere to be seen.

'Where's Saul?' I panicked. I was pretty sure that while the old Saul Dawson would have scarpered as quickly as his legs could carry him, the new improved version would do no such thing. So where could he have gone? I had been standing next to him in front of the mine entrance the last time I'd noticed him and I turned now to find the gate bent hard back against the wall. The train had crashed straight through it. Had it taken Saul with it?

'Christ! Saul! Saul, where are you, you daft bugger?' I yelled through the entrance, but there was no reply and I found myself brushing a small drop of what could only be perspiration away from my cheek before plunging into the darkness of the mine. Elaine joined me. The passage inside was in almost impenetrable darkness. We stopped, and Elaine turned back and called, 'Has anyone got a torch?'

The cheery tones of Laurie drifted back. 'In the car. Just a jiffy.'

'Elaine,' I said. 'Go back and wait for Laurie's torch. I'm going on.' I was far too concerned about Saul to wait for a light. I called his name again, as loudly as I could, and then 'Dawson!' for good measure in case he wasn't answering to Saul, as I started down the steeply descending tunnel, running my left hand lightly along the rough wall to keep my bearings. I realised I still had the gun I'd taken from Bigg's man in my right hand, and stuck it in the belt of my jeans.

Gradually my eyes became more accustomed to the gloom and I sensed as much as saw a darker mass in the tunnel ahead. Suddenly, my right shin came into painful contact with something hard. I reached down and felt the unmistakeable shape of a wheel. It was one of the mine trucks, and it was on its side. 'Hey, guys, where are we with that bloody torch?' I yelled back up the tunnel, and Laurie's voice came calmly back.

'Here,' and immediately the passage was bathed in a bright white light. When Laurie said he had a torch, he wasn't kidding. This one could have illuminated the Royal Albert Hall. I was momentarily blinded, but only momentarily. A scene of destruction appeared in front of me just as Laurie arrived at my side.

'Bloody hell,' he said in a low voice. 'I sure as hell hope Dawson isn't under that.'

So did I, but I couldn't see any way that he wasn't. A sharp bend in the tunnel had been too much for the runaway wagons to negotiate, and the front car had somehow shot upwards off the rails and half buried itself in the rock wall. There it had stayed, wedged in place by the bent remains of the second. The collision had dislodged what could easily be a quarter of a ton of rock and loose scree that was piled over and around the whole wreckage.

I started tearing at the loose rock with my hands, but I'd hardly started when Laurie called out, 'Wait!' I stopped.

And there it was, a faint but definite groaning coming from somewhere under the front wagon.

By this time, Inspector Innes had joined us. 'Reinforcements and an air ambulance are on their way,' he said. 'Now, let's get started.'

So we did, and a few minutes later, the groaning stopped and a woozy version of a familiar voice suddenly said, 'Fuck, that hurts.' Then it said, 'What's all this shiny stuff?' Then it said, 'I think I'm rich.' At that point, Laurie and Innes hauled away a boulder almost as big as me, and we all bent down and peered into the gap it had left. Saul was lying there on his back in a sort of cave created by the wagon buried in the wall over his head. He was filthy and virtually unrecognisable, and had blood running down his face, but he was alive and conscious. And he was covered in a cascade of diamonds. Hundreds of them, mixed in with stones and dust, but unmistakeably diamonds.

Laughing uncontrollably, I dived forward into the cave and landed on top of Saul. 'Ouch,' he said. 'Don't be so rough!'

'Sorry,' I said and, almost without thinking, kissed him on his dirty, bloody lips.

'You only want me for my diamonds,' he said as I came up for embarrassed breath.

—

We got back to Yackandandah that evening with some of the formalities completed and more to come. The diamonds had been gathered into bags and some bigwig with an overabundance of gold braid, who was apparently the Victoria State Police Commissioner, had taken them off for safekeeping. Presumably to be fought over by various representatives of the governments of Germany, Britain and Australia.

I say we, but it was only Saul, Innes and me left by the time we were back in the bar of The Sun. It was approaching midnight but none of us was particularly tired. Saul had been patched up. It turned out that by some miracle he was entirely in one piece once the dirt and blood had been washed off and three stitches inserted in his head. 'Only three?' he'd said aghast. 'I think

I deserve a lot more than that.'

Laurie had made a statement and gone off to report back to Juliet in London. Apparently, she's his cousin. Didn't see that coming. 'Where did Elaine go?' I asked.

'Back home to Shepparton,' said Innes. 'She wasn't really supposed to be here in the first place.'

'Will she get into trouble?' asked Saul. 'I owe both of you big time.'

'No, she'll be okay. I'm the one in trouble. Still, worth it, I'd say.'

Pat had gone off to hospital to have his hand fixed up. He was a bit aggrieved that the Commissioner had not taken his claim to the diamonds seriously, but I imagined it would all come out in the wash.

And Alan? He'd gone with the Commissioner too. In handcuffs. Understandably, he didn't seem too happy but I'd reminded him that by rights he should be dead, and he shut up.

'That only leaves one person,' said Innes. Saul and I looked at each other. 'Forgotten your pal, Martin Evans, have you?' We had.

'Bugger,' said Saul. 'Where's he got to? He's missed a hell of a story.'

'Not a story he'd have been allowed to tell, I'm thinking,' said Innes.

We were just debating about retiring to bed when the door opened, and four familiar faces walked in. Balaclava Lemon collected some drinks and wandered over, looking miserable.

'Why the long faces?' asked Saul.

'First gig not go too well?' I added. It seemed pretty obvious.

'It turns out that our set involves rather more use of the fiddle than we previously thought,' said Tony. 'And unfortunately, we have misplaced our fiddler, as you well know.'

'It was embarrassing,' added Alice. 'We're thinking of cancelling the other two performances.'

We had a flight booked (by Juliet) for Sunday morning, which gave us three full days to kill. We'd already decided to see if we could fill them by trying to imbue Saul with a love of folk music, but I thought I might have a better idea.

'If all you need is a fiddle player, I'm your girl,' I chipped in impulsively.

They all looked at me. 'You play the fiddle?' asked Alice in apparent disbelief. I didn't take offence; my offer had come slightly out of left field. 'Are you any good?'

'A bit rusty,' I said. 'But I did dozens of gigs for Footlights back at Cambridge Uni. Fiddle, violin, bit of cello too. If we can fix up a spot of practice before you're on next, I reckon I can do a job for you.'

'Is there actually anything you can't do?' asked Saul. 'You're already way out of my league.'

I patted him on the knee. 'The thing about leagues is you can always get promotion,' I said. To Alice I added, 'I can't sing, I'm afraid. Not a note.'

'I should hope not,' she said. 'That's my job. You're hired. I managed to, er, borrow the Russian's fiddle. Oddly, he forgot to take it with him to prison. You can have it. It's quite a good one.'

In which Lucy gets a new job, and
she and Dawson go to a pub and
talk about names

There were two people in Alan Flannery's old office. Juliet was sitting to one side of Alan's desk on an uncomfortable upright chair previously reserved for the company's non-existent visitors. Behind the desk was a suave-looking black man in his early fifties wearing what was clearly a very expensive dark grey suit and what looked to be a tie from one of the more important British Regiments. He had been gazing out of the window but swung back to face them as Dawson and Lucy entered the room.

He stood up politely and gestured towards two more chairs that had been somehow shoehorned into the cramped space in front of the desk.

'Jason Underwood,' said the man. 'Please sit.'

'Who are you?' asked Dawson.

'I'm the person you probably imagine me to be,' replied Underwood with a thin smile. 'We'll leave it at that for the time being.' Dawson and Lucy looked at each other and then at Juliet.

'So, Juliet,' said Lucy. 'I always thought you weren't quite what you were supposed to be.'

'That is because you are an exceptionally clever young lady,' said Juliet. 'Yes, I was asked by Mr Underwood to apply for the position of office manager here, and under no circumstances was I to fail in securing the post.'

'I never doubted that your application would prove successful,' murmured Underwood.

'As I recall, sir,' said Juliet, 'you had concerns that Mr Flannery might choose someone, er, younger.'

'I think you do Alan a disservice,' said Underwood. 'There are many things we can accuse him of, and indeed have accused him of, but not appointing the right person to the right position isn't one of them. Witness Mr Dawson and Miss, um, Smith?' He looked at Lucy with raised eyebrows.

'If you like,' said Lucy.

'Anyway,' continued Underwood, 'back to the matter in hand. I imagine you have some questions about your recent experiences. I dare say we can try to answer at least some of them.'

'But not all,' said Dawson.

'Of course not *all*, Mr Dawson, what on earth do you take us for?'

'As you now know,' said Juliet, 'Alan Flannery was playing all ends against the middle with the intention of acquiring at least the lion's share of the diamonds for his own use. We believe he always intended on producing a handful of them for Her Majesty's Government on the basis that nobody had any idea how much was in the cache. In that way he could retire from the service with honour intact and set himself up in luxury abroad somewhere.'

'Was he always like that?' asked Dawson. 'He was my friend after all. I'd like to think that he wasn't crooked all the time I've known him.'

'Oh, it was quite a recent epiphany, we think. He sailed through all the initial checks and didn't start causing any of us sleepless nights until after he met up with the late unlamented Séan MacGuffin a couple of years ago. Now, we already knew MacGuffin was a bad 'un, but it wasn't in our interests to share that information with Irish Intelligence.'

'Why not?' asked Lucy. 'They're our allies, after all.'

'Nobody is an ally, Miss Smith, not really. That is something you should bear in mind in your new role.'

'New role? What role would that be?'

'We were thinking Head of Aardvark, although that is a terrible name that will definitely go, and I'm afraid that the sort of autonomy that Flannery presumed to have will no longer be available to you. We may have to cut your staff numbers too.'

Lucy was stunned into silence, but Dawson wasn't. 'How is it possible to cut the staff numbers? There aren't any staff.'

'Well, natural wastage has removed the former Director from the payroll of course, similarly Arthur Jobson, for impersonating a police officer, together with a number of other misdemeanours we've discovered. Also, Juliet's talents would be wasted here with Miss Smith in charge.'

'So, just me then,' said Lucy. 'Staff one-to-ones aren't going to take up much of my time.'

'You appear to have forgotten Mr Dawson,' said Underwood. 'Assuming you are happy to continue with the agency.' This last to Dawson. 'I mean, you were previously unemployed I believe, and you have, one way or another, shown a certain aptitude for the sort of work we may be putting your way.'

Dawson nodded. 'Why not? Thanks.'

'A positive regiment of people then,' Lucy said with a grin. 'So how did everybody end up on Saul's tail? Riley Bigg, for example.'

'Most of it comes back to MacGuffin and Flannery, and our friends from Moscow, of course. As for Bigg, well, I guess Patrick Bootle might be partly to blame for his involvement. Or more likely the other German agent who he was sent to find. Bit of a Teutonic cock-up, frankly.'

'Pat definitely wasn't expecting me to show up,' said Dawson. 'Came as a hell of a surprise to him. He could have left me in Riley's clutches, but chose to blow his cover and rescue me. Nearly did for him. I don't like the guy, but I'm glad I didn't turn out to be responsible for his death. I'd never have had him down for a German though.'

'Mr Bootle is as English a German as you could find, probably the only reason he drew the short straw. German Intelligence hung him out to dry. He wasn't really qualified for the job. Involving Miss Whyte, for example, wasn't a particularly bright move.'

'In fairness, he did all right in the end, didn't he?' said Lucy. 'And I understand Rachel and he are, I think the expression is, "talking over their differences". Or shouting over them, maybe. So the diamonds are back in Cologne, are they? Seems a shame after all the trouble we went through.'

'They are, unfortunately, the legal property of the German Government,' said Underwood. 'Still, it turns out that Flannery can teach us something after all, and a finder's fee seemed reasonable in the circumstances.'

'A finder's fee of...?'

'Oh, not much, just enough to put a very small dent in the national debt.'

Lucy had been thinking. 'The Russians seemed to have been chasing their tail. Using Maurice Jeffers was a mistake. It certainly put the enthusiastic Inspector Innes on the trail, and without him and Elaine, it could have all gone pear-shaped.'

'The Russians couldn't afford to have Mr Dawson locked up in an Australian jail, so they had to do something, and Jeffers was really their only option. And it worked, of course. Saul was, after all, where he was supposed to be when Prokofiev turned up to relieve him of the information.'

'But I didn't have the information.'

'One of several flies in the ointment. Along with Innes and Bates, and of course you, Miss Smith, together with your journo friend.'

'You weren't too hard on Martin, were you?' asked Dawson. 'I seem to be rapidly losing what few friends I had.'

'Gaining some in exchange though,' smiled Lucy.

'Martin Evans, as you know, has returned to the rolling valleys of his homeland,' said Juliet. 'We could not allow him to publish anything about what happened, which unfortunately did not endear him to his employers.'

'I hope he finds another job, anyway,' said Dawson.

'Even if only to keep him in the pubs to which he is accustomed,' added Lucy. Even Underwood smiled.

Half an hour later, the two of them found themselves outside in the drizzle. 'Talking of pubs,' said Dawson, and they turned into the Golden Eagle. 'So, Lucy Smith, "if you like",' he continued when they were ensconced at a corner table. 'What's that all about? How many names does one girl need?'

'Fewer than I've had recently,' she conceded. 'I think I'll stick with Lucy Smith. I quite like it.'

'But it's not the name you were born with.'

'Most women don't have the names they were born with,' she pointed out.

'Okay, but it would be nice to know what it is.'

'I'm not that keen on it.'

'I'm not that keen on Saul, but strangely the girl I love insists on calling me that.'

'I'd rather not. It's not who I am. Not now.'

'This is me you're talking to. Remember, I'm a fully licensed intelligence agent now. I imagine I could find out.'

'You're right, you could. Okay, here goes nothing.' She took a deep breath. 'Saul Dawson, you have the absolute honour of addressing Joanna Delamere.' She paused and added quietly, 'That's Lady Joanna Leigh Delamere in full.'

'So did they name the motorway service area after you, or the other way round?' She noted that he was deliberately ignoring the "Lady" bit. So far.

'Shut the fuck up, you. I knew you'd say that. My parents have a warped sense of humour.'

Dawson thought. 'So, if you're a Lady, will that make me a Lord when we get married?'

'You're an avid reader of *Debrett's*, then.'

'I'm hardly ever without a copy. But since I seem to have momentarily misplaced it, perhaps you could clear that up for me.'

'Sorry to disappoint you, but I'm afraid you won't be a Lord.

And in any case, who said anything about marriage? Now that I'm your boss, I think that would be a terrible idea. I couldn't possibly marry beneath me, and it wouldn't do much good for staff morale.'

'I'm the staff, remember. And it would do wonders for my morale.'

'Maybe, but as your line manager, I have to consider your wellbeing at all times.'

'So, is it Joanna or Jo?'

'Neither. As I said, I'm Lucy now.'

'Not Greta?'

'Ah yes, the Scandi-Welsh Super Spy. Mustn't forget her. But no, I think not. I couldn't master the accent.'

'I noticed that you had no trouble with Russian though. All right. How about we bring in a new company policy. If you insist on being Lucy, then I can insist on staying Dawson.'

'Agreed. First decision of the new Aardvark regime.'

'Not Aardvark any more,' he reminded her. 'I wonder what they'll decide to call us.'

'Probably just a room number, if I'm any judge. Not very...' She stopped suddenly and stared at him. 'What was that you said earlier?'

'Erm, which bit?'

'You said, "the girl I love insists on calling me Saul."'

__ The End

Steve Sheppard was born in Guildford, the youngest by some distance of three brothers, and spent his formative years in the heart of the Surrey stockbroker belt, where he played a lot of sport (poorly), met a lot of people (friendly) and had a lot of jobs (of varying degrees of noteworthiness). He also appeared on stage in a number of amateur productions, whether anyone wanted him to or not. Disappointed at failing to meet any actual stockbrokers, he moved to West Oxfordshire over twenty years ago, where he now lives in a quintessentially quirky English village with his wife, son and the latest in a series of recalcitrant cats.

A Very Important Teapot is his first novel. The title came to him a quarter of a century ago but he did very little with it until early 2017 when, flying home from Australia, Steve decided that he would probably never find a better time to write the book he'd been thinking about, on and off, through all of life's normal and abnormal travails. So he did.

If you enjoyed *A Very Important Teapot* then check out other great books from **Claret Press**.

Claret Press publishes political fiction and creative non-fiction. While all our books have a political edge, we mean politics in the widest meaning of the word, from the esoteric to the commercial. We love stories that introduce readers to new ideas, unexplored places and pivotal events both here in the UK and across the globe.

Claret Press books inform, engage and entertain.

To know more about our books, like us on Facebook or subscribe to our website **www.claretpress.com**

Claret Press

CPSIA information can be obtained
at www.ICGtesting.com
Printed in the USA
LVHW041301310520
656808LV00006BA/656

9 781910 461402